IN AT THE DEATH

IN AT THE DEATH

Judith Cutler

SEVERN
HOUSE

First world edition published in Great Britain and the USA in 2025
by Severn House, an imprint of Canongate Books Ltd,
14 High Street, Edinburgh EH1 1TE.

severnhouse.com

British Library Cataloguing-in-Publication Data
A CIP catalogue record for this title is available from the British Library.

ISBN-13: 978-1-4483-1347-1 (cased)
ISBN-13: 978-1-4483-1348-8 (e-book)

All Severn House titles are printed on acid-free paper.

MIX
Paper | Supporting
responsible forestry
FSC® C013056

Typeset by Palimpsest Book Production Ltd.,
Falkirk, Stirlingshire, Scotland.
Printed and bound in Great Britain
by TJ Books, Padstow, Cornwall.

Praise for the Harriet & Matthew Rowsley Victorian mysteries

"A treat for historical mystery fans"
Booklist

"Cutler's quirky series blazes its own path"
Kirkus Reviews

"Fans of other married sleuths, such as Anne Perry's
Charlotte and Thomas Pitt, may want to check this out"
Publishers Weekly

"Twists and turns aplenty"
Booklist

"Offbeat cozy of manners"
Kirkus Reviews

"Thrilling, engaging and enjoyable from beginning to end"
Mystery People

"A gripping locked-room mystery with a suitably twisty plot"
Booklist

"Recommended for fans of Downton Abbey"
Library Journal

"Readers will look forward to seeing
more of this enterprising duo"
Publishers Weekly

"A Victorian twist on the ever
popular upstairs-downstairs storyline"
Kirkus Reviews

"Sparkling . . . [an] entertaining cast of characters"
Publishers Weekly

About the author

Judith Cutler, Birmingham's Queen of Crime, is the author of fifty novels, most of them crime series featuring strong women protagonists. Her prize-winning short stories have appeared regularly in anthologies and leading crime fiction magazines. She is married to fellow crime-writer Edward Marston.

www.judithcutler.com

To the musicians, past and present,
of the City of Birmingham Symphony Orchestra,
who have inspired and delighted me for over sixty years.

Thank you for all the joy!

ONE

October 1861

Oxford

My life in Shropshire, though always busy, was quiet, and I felt strangely out of place in this gathering of the great and good of Oxford in the Ashmolean Museum. I had forgotten how loud men could be when their company was undiluted by women, of whom there were perhaps only five or six present this evening. The only one I had eyes for was the delight and mainstay of my life, Harriet. She squeezed my arm lightly, glancing up at me with a smile that merged apprehension and pride. Montgomery Wilson, the Croft Family lawyer from Shrewsbury who accompanied us on our trip and was also a guest of our archaeologist friend, Francis Palmer, looked almost bewildered.

'Pray silence for Sir Francis Palmer!'

The hubbub slowly died down. Almost imperceptibly, a space formed, into which our old friend, who had led all the excavations on the estate and was now our host, ushered Wilson, Harriet and me. I was aware of a slight frisson – one Palmer subtly addressed.

'Mr Mayor, ladies and gentlemen, we have gathered tonight to thank three remarkable people for their part in a British, indeed a *world*, archaeological miracle. Mr Wilson' – he gestured – 'is the chairman of the Thorncroft trustees, a group of most conscientious people who have taken over the running of the Thorncroft Estate in Shropshire until the owner, Lord Croft, is well enough to resume his place in society. Here also are Mr Rowsley and Mrs Rowsley, the estate's land agent and housekeeper. Together, they represent the entire board of trustees; as a body, the board has had to make decisions that many of us would baulk at. One was to implement Lord Croft's wish to replace dilapidated cottages on his estate. He wanted a new model village, with healthy homes to be proud of. It was while work was in progress on this philanthropic project that ancient masonry was discovered. Mr and Mrs Rowsley immediately stopped further digging and sought my advice. Many of us here' – spreading his hands, he looked around the room, nodding towards his fellow experts – 'can testify how important their decision was. But the Roman buildings and artefacts uncovered there fade almost into insignificance beside the treasure we are welcoming here tonight to sit alongside our beloved Alfred Jewel. We did indeed uncover it in one of our Roman trenches – but it was largely the determination of Mrs Rowsley that enabled us to discover where it had actually come from.'

I glanced at Harriet, who had in fact been the one to stop the work on the footings of the new buildings, but had never told anyone, and indeed never reminded me that I had been furious with her for failing to consult me first. She was listening to the praise Palmer was heaping on her with just the right expression on her face – amused self-deprecation.

'Accordingly, ladies and gentlemen, I am asking Mrs Rowsley to reveal what the trustees have agreed to place on extended loan here.' Her face changed. Not her! Gasping, she clutched my hand as the man who called her his little sister continued, 'Not just the aestel henceforth to be known as the Thorncroft Jewel but the exquisite Anglo-Saxon Gospel in which the aestel has lain for a millennium. Mrs Rowsley!' He led the applause, which from a slightly faltering start grew in enthusiasm.

She might have taken a deep breath, but, relinquishing my hand, she stepped forward as if she were the Queen herself. If this was her duty, she would do it and do it well.

She drew aside the curtain. 'Mr Mayor, ladies and gentlemen, may I present to you the Thorncroft Jewel and the Thorncroft Gospel.'

This time, the applause was immediate and loud. Her smile was full of delight in the beautiful artefacts. But then she simply stepped back with a gesture that invited all who had not already seen them to make their acquaintance, at the same time contriving to direct the ovation away from herself.

In the surge forward, I was separated from her. Wanting her to take all the plaudits that were her due, I left her in what I knew would be the safe hands of Palmer. I would have had to anyway;

Wilson and I were almost mobbed. Explanations were demanded but largely ignored as we spoke. It was clear that we were not scholars, and though we had been useful tools, we might now be laid aside.

'My dear Rowsley, did she not acquit herself well!' Wilson looked at Harriet as a father might have looked on a favourite daughter. 'And yes, I think we trustees made the right decision. To your very good health.'

'And yours.' Accepting champagne from a passing waiter, we toasted each other.

Within moments, the Reverend Dr Benjamin Wells, one of the site archaeologists – though he preferred the title 'antiquarian' – was trying to catch our eyes as if he were a long-lost friend. Clearly, he had forgotten that he had not always treated others, including Harriet, as well as he should, and that he had been in open conflict with many in what should have been a team. 'Ah – excuse me, Wilson. I need to rescue someone!' Yes, there was another familiar face, that of Jeremy Turton, one of my cousin Barrington's godsons, a lad afflicted with a crippling stammer. He looked far from happy – in fact, far from well. I managed to ignore Wells as I pushed my way through the press. I would apologize to Wilson later if Wells cornered him.

'Jeremy! How good to see you!'

We shook hands vigorously and, in my case at least, with genuine affection. We had met at a cricket weekend at my military cousin's estate; the young man's artistic skill was amazing, but he was destined for the Church and was a Divinity student here. How he – or indeed, any congregation – might survive a sermon, I could not imagine. Even though he knew me well, his face worked as he forced out the words, 'And you, Matthew.' My heart bled for him; his impediment was as bad as ever.

'How are you?'

His shrug spoke for him: there was much wrong with his life, but what could not be cured must be endured, as the saying went. But he looked near to tears. Harriet would have taken him in her arms, but how could I, a man?

At last, I remembered how Harriet had made things easier for him – asking questions he could respond to with a short answer, preferably a monosyllable. 'Do you know many people here?'

He had chosen a good vantage point from which to watch both the proceedings and his fellow guests. Would there be other undergraduates there whom we knew? Graduates? I knew my other cousin, Mark, the barrister, was working in London and could not attend.

He shook his head. Then he took a deep breath, as if about to dive into a pool of sharks. 'Divinity, not History or Archaeology,' he explained. It was easier for him to speak like a telegraph. 'Fewer syllables to fluff,' he'd once explained with his anguished grin.

'Any non-University men?' It was easy to be just as terse.

Nodding across the room, he said, 'A lot. Don't know any to speak to. None of them pretty. Old man looks like a butcher. Trade, here, in this gathering? Dear me. Couple of squires. A clergyman or six. A lawyer or two. Big nose there? Medical man. Don't know that tall man there – shoulders.' He gestured. 'Harriet should teach him to bowl!' He grinned.

'She'd rather say hello to you; come over with me!' I said, already knowing the reply. In this crowd, it would surely be too much to expect of him.

'I . . . Ah! Excuse me.'

'A moment. Here's my card. Have you got a pencil? Thanks. This is Francis Palmer's address. Please call and see us at the manor. Please. And bring your sketchpad – you'll see why when you come. Palmer's assembled a wonderful eclectic collection. And remember, Harriet will never forgive either of us if she doesn't see you. She's very fond of you, Jeremy.' I pressed his shoulder.

He smiled, his face suddenly boyish with emotion. But a newcomer had stepped directly in front of us: Wells. Loathing strangers, Jeremy bowed to us both, merging with the crowd by the door and slipping away.

When I eventually detached myself from Wells, the broad shoulders that young Jeremy had noticed were already bending towards my wife. I could not see the rest of the man's body or his face, but I could see hers. Rarely had I seen such pure delight.

TWO

'Mrs Rowsley! Harry!' He seized my hands, kissing first one then the other.

'Gussie! Augustus,' I corrected myself quickly. That was still wrong, of course. 'Beg pardon. I mean, my lord.' I tried to curtsy, but since he still held my hands, it was impossible.

'I'm happy to be Gussie. Actually, these days my friends call me by one of the other first names my parents liberally bestowed on me: James. I did toy briefly with Hector and indeed Julius, but I had had enough of the classical world. So, Harry, will you call me James?'

'I would call you Attila the Hun if you asked me to. But I forget myself.' Gently, I freed my hands. 'Lord Halesowen, may I introduce to you my dear friend, Sir Francis Palmer? Francis, this is my . . .' Dare I call him friend? 'Lord Halesowen, the High Court judge.'

James shook his head. 'Ah, it was two of my young friends who told you that, Harry. Young Webbe? Forsythe? They confessed they had exaggerated somewhat to get you out of an awkward situation. Palmer, I am indeed a county court judge, but, more importantly, I am Harriet's former pupil,' James said. 'She taught me everything she knew about cricket. And a lot about social justice,' he added, kissing my hand again, but looking at Francis as he did so.

There was a tiny gap when Francis should have spoken.

I filled it. 'I was under the impression that you taught me. Francis, all the young men of the house where I was a very junior maid were struck down with measles, all except . . . James.'

'Who was bored to tears and demanded someone toss a ball for me to hit. They chose this young girl who worked with a will to learn. Soon it was she who was my instructor: batting, bowling. We strove to match each other's skills. And catching, of course – young Webbe, or possibly Roddy, said something about a miraculous catch at your cousin's home. You saved a baby's life, Harry?'

'It might have been a good catch, but socially it was the greatest faux pas imaginable. "A true lady would never make such an exhibition of herself,"' I said in mock-frigid tones, delighted when they laughed with me. 'But here is Matthew. Oh, Matthew, after all these years I have found him – or he me!' In front of everyone, I ran towards him, almost dragging him back with me. All too clearly, I was not a true lady! The men made their own amused introductions.

What happened next? I hardly know. Mysteriously – I remember hardly anything of the rest of the reception or the journey back to Francis's cold and draughty Elizabethan manor – we found ourselves, now with Mr Wilson, who was also his guest, in the drawing room, drinking more champagne, while his staff stretched the informal supper for four old friends to a more formal dinner for five. What did we talk about? Conversation whirled round. It seemed we hurtled from the Roman finds to rights for women – Francis had a friend he wished to introduce me to – to the state of the nation to who knew what.

Did we even know where we dined? The beauty of the Tudor dining room in which we sat possibly added to our joy, but no one remarked on the remarkable plasterwork, the linenfold panelling. Did we notice what we ate? All I know was that it was excellent.

It seemed there was no question of my withdrawing on my own to let the gentlemen enjoy their port and cigars. We adjourned to his much cosier drawing room as a group, as carefree as the children James and I had once been.

As Francis poured tea and James passed it round, there was a discreet knock on the drawing-room door. The butler entered, a telegraph on a silver salver, which he presented to Montgomery. Francis gestured: he must feel free to open it.

As he read it, a strange expression spread across his face. 'What I always hoped would be good news has come at a most inopportune moment. It seems that my continued efforts to locate his lordship's heir have come to fruition. A gentleman – an American gentleman, Mr Claude Baker – has presented himself at my office. He wishes to see me and, of course, to visit what he describes as his ancestral home. I fear I must return to Shrewsbury tomorrow and ask you both to prepare for his arrival.'

'Can he not wait, at least for a few days? His lordship's illness is no worse, I trust?' Francis asked.

'Thank God, no. According to his doctors – and I cannot fault Doctor Page's diligence in seeking the very best advice about his treatment – physically, he is still very well. No, I should see him because my work here is technically done. Indeed, I fear I must make preparations to depart tomorrow.'

'Indeed, Montgomery, you cannot. We have all accepted James's invitation to dine with him tomorrow,' I said. Perhaps it was the champagne talking.

'Harriet is right, my dear friend,' Francis declared. 'Make this importunate man wait one more day at least.'

'You have not, after all, been called to a death bed, have you?' Matthew said. 'And tomorrow we are all to meet the trustees of the Ashmolean, to discuss what else would be appropriate to lend them; it is essential that you are there. You know the law. You know the conditions that should be part of the loan. And then we are due to meet the head librarian at the Bodleian on Thursday; whether you like Professor Marchbanks or loathe him, he knew which books were of importance to scholars.'

'And wished the trustees to consider no other library,' I murmured. 'And even more important, Montgomery, we're meeting the British Museum librarian on Friday, aren't we? I can't imagine that encounter without you.'

'Indeed, we will have just as much need of your assistance then. More, perhaps.' Matthew turned to James. 'The trustees want the most people possible to have access to the treasures – but it is not in our power to do more than lend them.'

James assumed what must surely be his official judicial tone. He even pursed his lips and steepled his fingers. 'You all want to ensure that the most good is done to the most people. Am I right? In that case, you must keep your various appointments – and I would be delighted if you can still be my guests tomorrow.' He gave his thirteen-year-old's grin. 'You obviously have a duty to the man who claims to be the heir – but not just yet.'

'It might even be another false claimant,' I added.

'The evidence in his favour is strong,' Montgomery said. 'But, yes, we have been misled before, sadly misled by one claimant from Australia, James. Dear me, had the young man in question not saved Harriet's life, he would surely have been handed over to the police. Instead, he is working for – of all people – a bishop.' He looked at me reproachfully.

I ignored him. 'Ironically, he found the reality of being thrust into the aristocratic sphere absolutely daunting – terrifying, in fact. All the strange social nuances – dealing with servants, hobnobbing with the local landed gentry – take a long time to learn, do they not? More importantly, perhaps, such a lot of responsibility falls on a conscientious landowner's shoulders – and Thorncroft House itself must overwhelm many people by its sheer size. That's why Montgomery is trying to locate the heir now, James – so that he has time to grow into the role, as it were.'

'A long time, one trusts. If the present Lord Croft is still young, he may live for many years. He may even recover,' James said.

Matthew shook his head sadly. 'We understand that his madness is a symptom of syphilis, James. No one expects . . . the prognosis is not good.'

'Dear me! So the poor man exists – no more than that – in an asylum?'

'Indeed no! A public asylum, with all the horrors we read of? Not a single trustee, not a single Thorncroft servant would dream of agreeing to such a thing,' I said. 'His lordship – that is what he still is, after all – lives in private quarters in a wing of his own home, enjoying the gardens and the lake when he is well enough. His former valet is his devoted companion, counsellor and even friend. The local doctor has appointed full-time nurses.'

'The wing is also now effectively a small hospital, caring for present and retired servants and also people from the surrounding villages,' Montgomery added. 'I venture to boast that the trustees have been exemplary in this too.'

'So this man's putative inheritance *may* not be his for a few years yet. Furthermore,' James continued in what was now an obvious parody of a judge's delivery, his voice assuming a strange gravitas at odds with his twinkling eyes, 'Harry and Matthew are professionals doing professional work in this city and in the capital – they cannot reasonably be summoned by a click of the fingers, any more than you should be, Montgomery.'

Montgomery coughed. 'Indeed, I have to point out that Harriet is more important at the meetings with the librarians than either of us. His late lordship's will put the entire library into her exclusive care. As trustees, we can support her – there are those in this world, are there not, who feel it incumbent on them to deal exclusively with men – but we cannot overrule her. His late lordship's will made that eminently clear. No one, in fact, but she may ever be alone in what he regarded as a sacred space.'

James's eyebrows shot up. 'That is an honour indeed. But it must come with attendant disadvantages.'

'It does,' I admitted.

'Especially when our dear friend is also doubling the roles of hostess and housekeeper,' Francis added, smiling at me. He gave his impish grin. 'This is the advice you should give, James: "Wilson, bid your clerk, tell him that you have an appointment with His Honour Lord Halesowen and you would not wish to cause offence by cancelling it."'

James pulled a face. 'Heavens, my friends, if I am endowed with such a mouthful of a title, we might as well make use of it!'

Perhaps his champagne was talking too. I was sure that Montgomery's was when he agreed, with no further crisis of conscience, to stick to our original plan.

After all the jollity, Matthew was inclined to be quiet when at last we bade goodnight to James, who was returning to his official lodgings. We followed Montgomery up the magnificent manor staircase and, with a last wave, retired to our bedchamber. Perhaps Matthew was as tired and overwhelmed by the evening's events as I was, though my pulse still raced with excitement. It had, after all, been an extraordinary time, quite unlike anything I could ever have dreamed of. All that public pomp at the start, meeting all the dignitaries, though that was not nearly as terrifying as being asked to unveil the treasures. All the subsequent melee, too.

And then the arrival of James.

Surely that was not worrying Matthew? Yes, James was notably handsome and very affectionate. But I detected no hint of anything remotely sexual in his attitude to me. Would I have even thought of flirting with him? Heavens, it would have been like flirting with Francis, my self-proclaimed elder brother. We had been – what do schoolboys call their fellows? – we had been chums.

Brother and sister, if you like. But how could I say all this to the man I loved more than the whole world without implying he might be jealous?

After what seemed an hour of silence, but was probably less than a minute, I found something I could say: 'My love, was that young Jeremy Turton I saw you with? How is he?'

'As tongue-tied as usual, poor lad. And, I'd say, not at all well. Yes, I tried to persuade him to come over to you, but obviously . . .' We shook our heads as one. 'Actually, I'm not quite sure why he was there – he is, as he pointed out, Divinity, not History. Perhaps he hoped to catch us on our own. In the end, he was overwhelmed by none other than Wells.' He sat heavily on the bed. 'What an ordeal every day in the ministry will be!'

I sat too, tucking my arm into his. 'And such a talented artist – even your philistine of a cousin counselled him against wasting his gift. Do you think we might introduce him to Francis? He might – I don't know – find work for him as a site artist on one of his excavations.'

'That's an excellent idea – you need skilled draughtsmen as well as Palmer's ubiquitous camera. But would that notion suit his relatives? I got the impression when we first met him that he was under some family constraint to go into the Church. I begged him to come and see us here – bring your pencil and pad, I said – but who knows whether he'll come or not.'

'Or, of course, if we'll be here to receive him. We have a busy couple of days before us.'

'Busy? Exhausting!'

'Even more exhausting if you're trapped in this dratted corset. Let me out, I beg you!'

'Only if you promise not to wear your hair like that again. I know Her Majesty has that vicious central parting and that half the country is aping her, but you have your own style. Even with your hair like this, though,' he added with a kiss on my nose, 'you looked wonderful tonight: you did not need jewels and your new gown, chic as it is, to shine. No wonder your James has fallen in love with you all over again!' he added, definitely not looking at me.

'In love with me!' I hooted. 'Never! We were as brother and sister. With all the bickering that implies. I could never fall in love with a man whom I'd seen worrying a scab or – ugh! – picking his nose. Heavens, you are thinking of something . . . something like, like incest! In any case, my love, no one could ever free me from my corset as dextrously as you. Or,' I added, 'let down my hair.'

Even as it cascaded into his hands, I had a tiny, fearful thought, one I could not share with even Matthew just yet because it was so scandalous, so downright dangerous. If James was smitten with anyone, it was with Francis. And Francis, I was sure, with James.

THREE

Our business with the Bodleian and the British Museum Reading Room librarians was at last completed to Wilson's satisfaction. We gathered for a farewell supper for him before his return to Shrewsbury on the morrow. Palmer had invited some of his closest friends, including Lady Verney, who was using her new-found power as a widow to support a number of excellent charities, some of which she had even founded herself.

It seemed that Lord Halesowen had suddenly become an old friend too; despite myself, I was anxious. I might glance at him, surreptitiously, from time to time. But I would not be a jealous, possessive husband. I had seen all too many marriages harmed that way.

On the other hand, was Palmer worried too? He was quite assiduous in his customary role as Harriet's chaperon, introducing her to everyone but making sure she was comfortable in their company before moving on. In fact, it was only when she and Lady Verney were deep in a conversation that seemed to invite no one else that he turned his attention to supporting Halesowen, should that be necessary. I found myself engaged in a fascinating conversation with an artist who had just returned from Paris, where he had spent time in the studio of a man from the French colonies who was working on a quite different style from our Pre-Raphaelites'. He struck me as just the sort of man to assess the paintings in Thorncroft House – but before any new expert was let loose there, we would check their bona fides very carefully. We did not want a repetition of the recent debacle. I looked round for Harriet; by now, she had left Lady Verney's side and was talking to Halesowen. Palmer hovered beside them: was he anxious too?

Lady Verney smiled up at me, so I joined her. 'Mr Rowsley – Matthew – I have been hearing so much about your work to improve the lot of your local poor. Might I ask you a question or two?' Patting the sofa, she added, 'Georgiana, if you please.'

'Of course. But if you will permit me, I would like to invite Mr Montgomery Wilson to join us. Harriet and I can only do what we do with the consent and indeed the encouragement of a board of trustees. Mr Wilson is the chairman . . .'

Dinner itself was a delight. Palmer was not only a generous host, providing a feast of excellent dishes and a veritable cornucopia of first-class wine, but he also had a broad range of friends – here was a woman who had explored parts of Africa, there a distinguished doctor. Wilson was deep in discussion – across the table, an amazing piece of informality for him – with a man who had helped develop the new savings bank. Suddenly, we were raising glasses to the memory of William Cubitt. I might have been back in my student days, relishing the animated discussion of events that would never have reached the dinner table in our part of Shropshire. How would Harriet deal with it? A glance in her direction showed she was in her intelligent sparrow posture, head to one side, eyes agleam. Yes, she was, to say the least, happy. She caught my eye and beamed back, before returning to her partner again, nodding and then firing in a question. My heart swelled with pride in her and with my own happiness – what a joy was good conversation. For a moment, I thought of poor Jeremy – unless there was a miracle, he was forever barred from it. But now the discussion had turned to women's emancipation, and it was clear every guest wanted to join in. How would Palmer deal with the chaos?

By signalling to his staff to serve dessert.

'And after this, I suggest we adjourn for our free-for-all to the drawing room,' he said. 'James, will you adjudicate?'

'I wish,' I said, closing our bedchamber door and leaning on it, 'that this trip could go on for ever. As you do, don't you?'

Harriet laughed. 'Meeting people like this? Arguing with them? Sharing ideas and experiences? Being treated as an equal, never once patronized? This is my idea of heaven. And yours too, my love? I thought so! Oh, if we were as rich as Croesus, how much good we could do in the world!' She spread her arms expansively. 'But look at Lady Verney; even with far less at her disposal, she is transforming lives.'

'As are you, my love. Think of all the hours you've spent teaching the staff how to read and write. Think of the ideas you've submitted to the trustees for action.'

'Some are pretty self-serving,' she said. 'Like the running water and the water closets in the House.'

'And in the new cottages in the model village,' I pointed out gently. There was a knock on the door. 'Damn and blast!' Shrugging on my dressing gown, I opened it.

The servant bowed, offering a telegraph on a silver salver. 'Sir, madam, this came for you.' Another bow, and he closed the door gently behind him.

Harriet stared. 'My God, what on earth—? Has someone died? No, neither Dick nor Bea would send . . . they would write. The House itself? We have to open it, my love. Please, can you?' It was clear her hands were shaking too much.

I obliged. 'Dear me, it's from Constable Prichard.' Pritchard was our much-respected village bobby. 'Listen.'

STRANGE GENTLEMAN BODY ON THORNCROFT
ESTATE STOP BEHEADED STOP OTHER INTERFERENCE
TOO STOP PRITCHARD.

'Beheaded? Dear God. And this "other interference" – does he mean the body has been mutilated? It's not quite a demand for our instant return, but it might as well be,' I said, sinking beside her on the bed.

'Indeed it is. But what can *we* do?' She shook her head as if to clear it.

'I think the term "gentleman" must be the clue. Pritchard is used to country crimes, isn't he, apart from those where we've been there to guide and support him.'

'So he wants guidance and support? Surely that's what Sergeant Burrows is for! Not us! Oh, forgive me. Elias Pritchard is our friend, isn't he? Yes, of course we must go back and go tomorrow. Oh, dear.' She pressed her handkerchief to her lips, then her eyes. What a sacrifice she was making as she prepared to put others

first once again. 'Poor man . . . And the poor victim too. I wonder
who it might be?'

I took her hand. 'Pritchard would recognize anyone he'd seen
at the House, wouldn't he? But why should he think we might
know a stranger?'

'Perhaps – I don't know – perhaps he carried a letter addressed
to someone at the House?' She frowned; already her brain was
working, perhaps to shut out her emotions. 'My goodness, Matthew
– and I admit I am not being strictly logical – what if it's the
mysterious Mr Baker from America! How would Montgomery
feel? Should we – for his sake – not broach even the remote
possibility until he thinks of it himself? If we feel unease at the
thought, imagine how he would feel. He would be guilt personified.'

'I'm afraid he would. You're right. The less speculation the
better, for our sakes as well as for his.' I stood. 'Oh, my darling,
to have to leave in the middle of all this!' I gestured. She would
understand what the spread hands encompassed. 'One of the best
weeks in all your life – in my life, too – and it has to be cut
short.' I lifted her into my arms. 'We can come again soon. You
and Palmer will never stop being brother and sister. Georgiana
Verney wants us to stay with her. I can't imagine James letting
you fall out of his life again,' I ventured at last.

'Of course we will all meet again. And next time we will make
sure we see Jeremy properly.' She squared her shoulders.
'Meanwhile, we must do our duty. We should start packing now,
shouldn't we, if we're to catch the early train Montgomery is to
travel on?'

We knew that Palmer would do everything in his power to ensure
a swift and easy departure: a cab called, servants to help with
our luggage, another sent ahead to the station to buy our tickets.
What none of us expected was the farewell party at the station.
How had Palmer run Jeremy to earth so swiftly? The youngster
had bought with him magazines and periodicals for our journey.
Harriet took him on one side, taking one thin hand between both
of hers and speaking earnestly to him. At last, she did something
I'd never seen her do before: she lifted her hand to his cheek,
kissing him. He managed a pallid smile, at last kissing her hand
and waving an awkward farewell.

Finally, she had to turn to Georgiana Verney, who had brought a bouquet of autumn flowers for her. And James? An envelope that proved to contain an invitation for us to join him at his New Year's house party. Wilson had a similar invitation. There was much laughter, but sadness too. We had all hoped for longer together – I had never seen Wilson so unbuttoned. Even if our private speculations about the murder victim were groundless, he was going back to deal with what could be a very problematic situation. He might know every detail of the possible heir's lineage, but it seemed he had no sense of the man himself. His clerk had not thought it necessary to describe the man's appearance and attitude, nor his reaction to being told he had to kick his heels after going to the trouble of crossing the Atlantic. At least, being stranded amid the wonders of Shrewsbury might have consoled him somewhat.

It was time to board the train.

We had barely sat down – to our relief, there was no one else in the compartment – when Wilson sprang up. 'What if Mr Baker decided not to wait, but to make his way to Thorncroft and arrive unannounced? What if – oh, my goodness, what if he is the mysterious stranger whose body Constable Pritchard has found? I could not live with the guilt!' There was no room to pace, of course, so he sat down, clutching his head. 'I have so enjoyed these last few days, but now—'

I leaned across to him. 'My dear man, can you imagine how we would have managed at any of those vital meetings without your advice and support? Harriet and I would have been treated as mere ignorant provincials,' I said, with blithe inaccuracy, 'but you brought knowledge and, yes, gravitas to them. Had this Baker telegraphed ahead, made an appointment, he would have grounds for irritation. But to turn up and expect instant service – no, you have nothing to blame yourself for.'

'Except for enjoying yourself,' Harriet said, overriding a protest. 'Am I right? The very thought of abandoning duty for pleasure is so . . . so foreign to us! If we had been busy tending the sick or sweeping streets, we would not be feeling guilty now! Any of us,' she added with a wry smile.

'Quite,' I agreed. 'You might have missed a client, but we – well, we missed a murder. And if I am uneasy, I am sure Harriet almost blames herself.'

She shook her head. 'In truth, whoever is to blame for the stranger's death, it is not us. We did not kill him. Someone else did. And somehow we have to accept that.'

'Even,' I said with some force, 'if the corpse is your American.'

It was raining hard when we bade farewell to our friend, who promised to call on the heir the very next day, notwithstanding that it was the Sabbath, and telegraph his news. We had to change for the Wolverhampton train to take us to the little halt on the Thorncroft estate. To our surprise and relief, the village doctor, Ellis Page, was waiting for us there, with another trap behind him to take our luggage. 'A sergeant from Shrewsbury arrived early this morning,' he said, as he set his horse in motion. 'No, not Burrows; he had his arm broken when he tried to stop a robbery and can't return to duty for a while. Anyway, I took the liberty of suggesting that his replacement – Swain – might stay at the House. Bea has arranged for Sergeant Burrows' usual rooms to be prepared. Your suite is being aired; Bea knows you'd have preferred your own home, but she thought – we all did – that staying in the House would be more convenient, in the circumstances.' As always, he blushed slightly as he mentioned Bea Arden, technically Thorncroft's cook, though occasionally, as now, she took on housekeeping duties. Why the blush? We all knew that he was courting her and that she returned his feelings.

I frowned. 'This is all excellent, Page – but what about what we really want to hear? Pritchard summoned us here because he felt unable to deal with a murder. What's going on?'

He did not reply immediately. Through the fast-fading light, I exchanged a glance with Harriet: it was not like our friend to be evasive, was it?

'Do I gather that . . . that perhaps this death was not, not straightforward?' she asked.

'I'm afraid it wasn't. But I promised Sergeant Swain not to say anything.'

'Really? Heavens, man, surely—'

'Look out, hedgehog!' Page tugged on the reins. The little fellow rolled into a ball. He had to wait until it decided it might be safe to finish its errand. 'Won't be long before they hibernate, will it?' he reflected brightly. This must be how he evaded awkward medical questions; I was briefly inclined to resent it. We were, after all, not just allies and fellow trustees; we were good friends, honest and truthful.

And then we were home. There were Hannah, the new senior maid, and Dick Thatcher ready at the top of the elegant flight of steps leading to the front door. Usually, we used the servants' entrance, but it was always a treat to indulge a walk through the breathtaking circular entrance hall with its wonderful dome.

'Mr and Mrs Rowsley, Doctor Page.' Dick bowed, every inch a butler. 'Sergeant Swain and Constable Pritchard await you in the yellow drawing room.' His undue formality was no doubt to reflect the seriousness of the occasion about which he probably knew far more than we did, village and House gossip being extremely efficient. 'They appreciate that you will need to freshen up after your long journey and are drinking tea while they await your presence.'

'Tea? I'll go and join them, Mr Thatcher.' Page might have meant to go and find them himself, but Dick bowed and led the way.

Now at least smut-free, we had changed from our travelling attire into suitably sober garb. As we joined the group in the drawing room, Dick arrived with fresh tea and refreshments. He was quick to withdraw, however: a good, discreet colleague.

The men stood politely as we entered. Sergeant Swain – in his forties, perhaps – wriggled and coughed as awkwardly as a man half his age when we gestured him back to his seat. Perhaps he would have preferred the rigours of my study and its hard chairs to such opulence, or perhaps – he kept looking at Harriet and then at me, rubbing his very pronounced knuckles – he was unsure how to broach the topic. Colour washed over his face, blending awkwardly with the freckles that matched what remained of his hair.

At last, Harriet took matters into her own hands. 'I gather that what you all have to tell us about the murdered man will make unpleasant listening. Perhaps you think that as a woman I ought not to hear it? Come, gentlemen, you know you can rely on me not to faint – unless,' she added with a smile at Pritchard, 'I fear I have killed someone.'

He nodded. 'Ah, indeed so, ma'am. A rare move, that was, and it certainly saved my bacon.' He glanced sideways at Sergeant Swain, who, judging by his pinched lips and tight jaw, did not want reminiscences. 'But this is . . . not nice.'

'Violent death is rarely nice,' I said. 'Do I gather that the cause of death was particularly vicious? Or that the corpse is no longer . . . intact?'

Page said quietly. 'Indeed. As I believe Pritchard may have told you, the victim lacks his head – and has been castrated.'

FOUR

did not faint.

'Have you found the missing parts?' I asked as dryly as I could.

Poor Sergeant Swain. He was now crimson with embarrassment, his Adam's apple bobbling in a regrettably scrawny neck. 'The head, yes, ma'am.'

'Where was it found? And by whom? And . . . I don't recall you saying where the rest of him was found.' Dear me, I sounded as if I was addressing a recalcitrant tweeny.

Sergeant Swain pursed his lips so tightly they almost disappeared. 'Why should you need to know – ma'am?' he added belatedly.

The young constable winced at his sergeant's tone and replied to my question. 'Farmer Twiss's cowman found the body in the lane between the grounds here and Farmer Twiss's fields. Not hidden at all. As for the head, Mrs Rowsley, it was left on my doorstep.'

I gasped. 'Did your children see? No? Thank God for that!'

'To state the obvious, it seems that someone wanted . . . everything . . . to be found,' Matthew mused.

'Except for his – er, genitalia,' Ellis muttered.

'Does the head help you identify him? Your telegraph said he was a stranger, Pritchard.'

'He's not from round here, Mr Rowsley, that's for sure,' Pritchard responded. 'Not a working man, not at all. His fingers don't look as if they've ever touched more than a bell-pull all his life. Manicured like a lady's they were, and soft. And the quality of his clothes and shoes – no, a city man, I'd say. A rich one, I would venture. The trouble is, whoever killed him took his wallet. Nothing else, though. His watch, his spectacles were still on him.'

'Did his clothes still have a tailor's label in them?' Matthew asked.

As one, the officers shook their heads. 'Never thought to look.' The sergeant blushed again.

'If I wanted to make sure no one could trace a man,' Matthew continued, 'I would remove anything connecting him with his tailor. Most tailors keep details not only of the clothes they make but also of the men who bought them – their measurements just as much as their address. They're above my touch, but Henry Poole and Co. and Gieves, both of London, would certainly want their labels in suits.'

'So if we found that the victim's suit was made by Someone and Sons, this Someone might be able to identify him.' Pritchard nodded sagely.

'On the other hand,' Sergeant Swain said, 'that suit's in a pretty poor state, what with mud, blood . . . and what have you,' he added lamely. 'Ma'am, I wouldn't let the word pass my lips, not in company.'

I nodded. 'Perhaps you don't need to just now. Apart from the two – dear me, the word "injuries" seems inadequate! – apart from the hideous damage to the body, were there other injuries?'

'There were,' Ellis said, 'but they were . . . You see, I suspect the mutilation took place after death. Can I spare you these gory details? Thank you. But the other injuries were certainly inflicted while he was still alive. Scratch marks. Bruises on his shoulders as if someone had grabbed him very hard. Actually, a bruise and abrasion to the dead man's chin. I would venture that someone had knocked him out. There was a cut as if he had struck the side of his face as he fell.'

'You can tell all this from a corpse – even from a dismembered head?' Matthew asked, trying, I think, to elicit more information rather than express doubt.

'Indeed. And I can tell some other things from the body. Stab wounds – it must have been a very sharp knife to have penetrated his coat, the suit jacket, the waistcoat. All that material. They're all on the left side of the body, rib height. Very shallow, of course, some no more than scratches – they wouldn't have killed him.'

'The killer would have had to be mighty strong,' the sergeant observed dourly.

I stood, lifting my arm and pummelling the air as if . . . I took a deep breath. 'Matthew, might you hold me as if we were about to dance? And then let go of my right hand? Thank you.' Closing my eyes, I made the same gesture.

Suddenly, I could hardly stand. I was glad of Matthew's steadying grasp and tried to smile reassuringly. But clearly he knew there was something wrong. He could probably guess what it was.

Sergeant Swain stared. 'You think a female might have done it, ma'am? Surely not! It is not a lady's crime! Apart from anything else, it would require strength.'

'Or desperation,' I said, my voice as steady as I could make it.

'She was only demonstrating, sir,' his colleague declared, as if he had to defend me. 'A man might hold another like that in a brawl. Holds him with one arm, grabs his knife from his belt – the sort a man might take rabbiting – and . . .'

'So it could be a poacher that did it,' Sergeant Swain declared. 'Many poachers round here, Pritchard? Round them up, if you please. You take precautions against them, Mr Rowsley?'

'Of course.' He grinned ironically. 'Actually, two of our best young gamekeepers were once the bane of old Forrest's life. But – do you remember, Ellis? – he shot one and was so overwhelmed with guilt he made sure the young man's family were fed until he recovered.'

'In the Family wing here, as I recall,' Ellis said with a wry smile.

'And then he trained him up: Edwin Ash,' Matthew continued. 'And then Ash's brother-in-law signed up too. Joe Wilkins. So Forrest retired, effectively, though they still call him their gaffer. See if either of them has heard of any trespassers.'

'And why fight chest to chest with our gentleman?' Ellis asked. 'And why decapitate him? It's not as easy as one might think,' he added.

'Not to mention the other . . . injury,' Sergeant Swain muttered. No one did. In fact, no one spoke.

At last, Matthew broke the silence. 'Where exactly did all this happen? Oh, I know where the remains were found, but where did the crime take place? Not in the lane, surely. On the estate, you said, but it's a pretty wide area. Woodland? A meadow?' When Sergeant Swain looked blank, he added, 'His boots or shoes – was there mud or grass on them? Or leaf mould?'

'What's that got to do with anything?' Sergeant Swain demanded.

'Who knows? But I presume they're safe somewhere and might give someone some information.'

'We know he's dead, sir – surely that's enough.'

Constable Pritchard might have been carved from wood. No wonder he had sent for us.

Meanwhile, Matthew's voice was so calm and controlled it was clear he was furious. 'Did anyone sketch a likeness of the head? Or take a photograph, as Sir Francis would have done? No, I suppose no one round here has the skills,' he said sadly.

Sergeant Swain straightened. 'We might not have the skills, but of course we have the head. Or, rather, you do. It was your Thatcher's idea. It's in your icehouse. And the rest of him too. Barring . . .'

'The icehouse!' I suppressed an appalling desire to laugh.

'What a good idea,' Matthew said quickly, adding, 'though I don't suppose there's much ice left now. I trust it's guarded.'

'Not exactly, but we've locked the door and chained and padlocked it for good measure.' The sergeant produced keys from his breast pocket, then buttoned them safely back in. 'Would you be willing to cast your eyes over him, Mr Rowsley?'

Clearly, the idea did not appeal to him. 'Surely if Birmingham Constabulary can take a likeness of living criminals' faces, they can lend a photographer to their Shropshire colleagues to take a likeness of this man.'

Ellis said tartly, 'Surely there are police artists too.' He glanced at Sergeant Swain, who pursed his lips.

'I trust you will find one, then, Sergeant,' Matthew said. 'Because if the man was a rich Londoner, the chances of my ever having seen him, let alone been acquainted with him, are remote. You will need to share the sketch or photographs with Scotland Yard. And one of their officers might be here tomorrow if you send for help now.'

Sergeant Swain pulled a face. 'Sunday travel, Mr Rowsley? Surely not!'

'No worse than Sunday examination of corpses,' he snapped. 'We will even accommodate an officer here if a return journey would be difficult.' Matthew stood. 'Sergeant, we all know that this needs police officers to do it. Even if it involves Sunday travel for you, and possibly others. On the other hand, you are more than welcome to stay here in the House. I believe you have been shown the suite your colleague Sergeant Burrows used when he was here.'

The sergeant looked pointedly at the ormolu clock. 'The last train's in half an hour.'

'You ride, Sergeant?' Matthew was already ringing the bell. 'Dan will have you mounted within five minutes.'

The order given, I said, 'There's something we've been meaning to ask. Have you any idea how the dead man might have come to Shropshire, let alone Thorncroft? Did he alight at our halt, or did he take a cab from Shrewsbury? If it was the former, did he come from the north or the south? Was there anything in one of his coat pockets to associate him with us – an envelope with a letter from one of us? From anyone mentioning the House even?'

I had fired too many questions; Sergeant Swain merely gaped.

However, I would continue to question him. 'What,' I asked, as Matthew turned back into the room having given Dick his instructions, 'if we are all wrong to assume it is a gentleman from London – from Birmingham or anywhere in England? What if he was American, if he was his lordship's heir?' I explained.

Matthew, calm again, resumed his seat. 'That would mean he had decided not to discuss matters with Wilson, wouldn't it?' He spread his hands. 'In his position, I can imagine wanting to go to inspect my inheritance as soon as I could. Wouldn't you?' he asked rhetorically.

'But why should a stranger get himself killed?' Ellis asked. 'People don't usually go around killing complete strangers.'

'Robbery – that's my bet,' Sergeant Swain said.

But surely a thief would have taken more? Suddenly, I could bear the theorizing no longer. 'Gentlemen, I know I started it, but all this speculation will get us nowhere. We can discover nothing tonight. Montgomery has promised to call on the claimant tomorrow at his hotel or his lodgings. If he sees him in the flesh, then we have one answer. If he seems to have made a rapid exit, never to be seen again, that is quite another. And Matthew is quite right. We may not have stomachs for viewing a corpse, but others are paid to do it. Let them be summoned, and summoned soon. Ah, Thatcher!'

'The horses are at the front door, ma'am. And the stable boy has ridden ahead to tell the station master to hold the train.' He turned to Pritchard. 'Mrs Arden has put together a basket of cakes and jellies to tempt your little invalid.'

Sunday's torrential rain reflected our mood. We all arrived at church very damp, the service, with our rector's sermon punctuated by drips on to the altar. It was not one of Mr Pounceman's finest.

Was it wrong to pray that the dead man be swiftly identified – and not, for Montgomery's sake, as the heir? I apologized to the Almighty even as I addressed Him. And then it was time to turn out into the rain again, gusts of wind defeating our umbrellas and even turning a couple inside out. Had Sergeant Swain's aversion to Sabbath work stopped him sending the telegraphs we had suggested – perhaps, to be honest, demanded? Would Montgomery find the heir still in Shrewsbury?

Matthew and I were both inclined to a slightly sullen gloom: why had we been dragged away from our friends for an urgent matter that wasn't urgent on a Sunday? And although I had to admit that having all the resources of the House to deal with our now soaking clothes made life easier, I longed for the intimacy and privacy of our own home. Tomorrow I might ask Hannah to see that fires were lit there and the place aired so we could start living there again.

After the cold luncheon, Pritchard returned. All the telegraphs had been sent – by him, not the sergeant – but no answers had yet arrived.

His news delivered, he was ready to return home – and the rain came on again in earnest. Both of them donning oilskins, Matthew insisted on driving him home in the trap; I suspected he wanted to question him again.

I did what I often did on a Sunday. Samuel, the old butler who had once been the keystone of the House and who had trained me to his own rigorous standards, was now a resident in the Family wing. Unlike his lordship, he was free to come and go. But old age had not been kind to him. His sight was fading, and with it his confidence to find his way round once-familiar corridors. As a consequence, he ignored Ellis's pleas to move as much as he could to keep his rheumatism at bay, and would spend hours slumped in a chair, gazing into the parkland as if he could actually see, not just remember it. When the weather was as foul as today's, he could take to a chair by the fire he needed now he felt the cold so badly.

Sometimes Nurse Webb, who ran the hospital that the Family wing had become, persuaded him to play cribbage or dominoes with one of her elderly patients. Often, he simply waited for one of the household to come and read his favourite psalms or a cherished Bible chapter to him.

So here I was.

I began with our favourite, the Sermon on the Mount.

To my surprise, as I finished, he put his hand on mine. 'My dear Mrs Rowsley, I have always tried to live my life in accord with the Beatitudes, and I believe you have too. I was never blessed with a wife and child, of course, but I see people like young Dick and even Luke and believe they could be my sons – my grandsons, I suppose, given my age! – and I am proud of them. I trained them well, and you have carried on what I began. I always expected, you know,' he continued, 'to retire to a cottage on the estate and grow a few vegetables and pass the time of day with other old codgers like me. I thought it was my dream. But I find I am more content than I ever dreamed possible actually under the roof of the house I love so much.' He fell silent. Perhaps he slept. But finally he squeezed my hand. 'Might I ask you a favour?'

'Of course.' I turned my hand to return the pressure.

'Could you find time to read the twenty-third psalm before you go about your duties, which I know you still have, even on the Sabbath?'

'Of course.' I turned to the page. *'The Lord is my shepherd . . .'*

Although I knew Bea would not be there – Sunday was unequivocally her free day – I decided to pop down into the servants' hall to join my colleagues as they took their mid-afternoon tea and cake. Officially, I was the housekeeper again, despite the trustees' attempts to find a replacement for me. When the House was empty of visitors, as it was now, I was happy to resume my old role. But when the archaeologists returned in the spring – heavens, when, or possibly if, the heir came to stay with us – then I would find it very hard to be both hostess and acting mistress of the House and behave as the servant I had always been. It confused both guests and my colleagues, to be fair – though the latter were often more respectful than the former.

A gust of wind blew more heavy rain against the windows. 'What dreadful weather for a day off,' I observed to Dick, who, like me, could have been sequestered in his own accommodation. Both the housekeeper's room – always known simply as the Room – and the butler's sitting room had been redecorated and refurnished, so that they were very pleasant places to pass time on your own. The Room, however, was now more of an office, since Matthew and I had our own quarters, and was used for meetings. Once we had a new housekeeper, of course, she could stamp her own personality on it.

'Haven't you noticed it often is? When I was the youngest footman, I always thought her late ladyship had some control over the skies and could use it to stop us going out and enjoying ourselves and seeing our friends. Just half a day off a month and alternate Sundays.' He smiled to me as a son might. 'However did you get her to be more generous, Mrs Rowsley?' No, he would never call me Harriet, even in private.

'I'd like to tell you I threatened a hunger strike. But all I said was that happier staff worked harder. I tried to get her to permit a proper staff sitting room, but she was afraid of unspecified "goings-on" and wouldn't be budged. And somehow since she died, I've never quite got round to it. Could you talk to everyone, Dick? And see what they think? Some of the women might prefer one separate from the men? And vice versa. So maybe three sitting rooms? Heavens, we have the space here! Actually, do you see any reason why you shouldn't use the billiard room? I don't suppose anyone has been in there to do more than dust it since the archaeologists left.'

He pulled a face worthy of dear Samuel. 'What if someone was larking about and tore the baize?'

'It could always be replaced,' I said gently. 'You might ask someone to organize a simple booking system and take responsibility for everything. Think about it, anyway. I'm just talking as a friend, not giving you orders.' We exchanged a smile. 'Now, while we're alone, what do you make of Hannah? Is she fitting in?'

'She's doing well, and did you know, she sings as she works? Ah, here come the others.' He got to his feet and moved to the foot of the table. I was to take the head. 'Mrs Rowsley and I were just wondering why it always rained on Sundays. Goodness, young Evans, you look like a drowned rat! Go and change, man; we'll save you some cake!'

FIVE

When I returned from my little jaunt to the village, made all the slower by my horse Esau's sudden and skittish dislike of rain, I was in the foulest of tempers. Pritchard was clearly torn; he would never betray Harriet or me, but he had perforce to be loyal to the new sergeant, despite the man's obvious incompetence. So I was far from good company when I walked in via the servants' entrance to hang my dripping oilskins in the drying room. Luke, our senior footman, appeared as if by magic to relieve me of them and hang them up.

And then I discovered I had arrived in the middle of the afternoon break; almost everyone, Harriet and Dick included, was gathered round the long table in the servants' hall. Harriet registered my mood immediately, of course. And now it could get worse. I could not simply ignore everyone and stride on to my own office. On the other hand, I knew my presence would mute their get-together, so I would accept one cup of tea and make my excuses to leave – until I realized that they probably knew much more about the murder, or at least much more gossip, than I, and that I would do well to stay graciously and listen.

Hannah, the newcomer, was the only one who seemed disconcerted by my presence. Little Rosie, on the other hand, happily told me all about her grandmama and her new baby chickens.

How could I raise the subject of the brutal murder in front of a child of twelve? Unasked, Dan, just returning from the stable where he had been rubbing down Esau, took her off to pet the horse and feed him some windfall apples.

'How's young Daisy Pritchard?' Harriet asked me, simultaneously telling everyone where I had been and directing conversation in a more intimate direction than murder, to give me time to work out what I might and might not say.

'Asleep in her father's arms when I left. And why not?' I smiled at her and our colleagues. Yes, very gradually I was calming down. I could risk giving them information about the enquiry without swearing and striking the table in frustration. 'The police have been told to send for some experts to look into this murder, and we've been hoping to have some news when they might arrive. Telegraphs! I think Gaffer Davies on his old donkey would have been quicker!' I added with a grin.

'Experts?' Luke asked; he had returned to his place and finished a second slice of cake. 'What sort of experts, if you don't mind my asking, Mr Rowsley?'

'Oh, something to do with some of the injuries the victim sustained,' I said lightly, adding, truthfully, 'They're not the sort of thing to talk about over tea, I gather.' It was more than likely that he and some of the older servants knew at least as much as me and would understand my fears for the youngsters present. 'And they need to identify him, too. A complete stranger, I gather. Have any of you heard who he might be?'

No one did. At last, as if to encourage us, Bea's chief kitchen maid, Dora, spoke up:

'People do say that they heard a young woman screaming. Not in the dark, like you'd maybe expect,' she added. 'You know, a couple out courting, and her sweetheart tries to have his way with her. This was in broad daylight, when a decent man would be working.' She looked around, making sure of her audience and widening her eyes. 'What if she was crying rape!'

What indeed? The corpse's injuries – the vengeance taken on it – had certainly suggested that to me. But I did not feel at liberty to reveal anything that Sergeant Swain had disclosed. 'Does anyone know where the screams might have been coming from?'

'My auntie says it was from Farmer Twiss's meadows, midday, but she's deaf in one ear and thinks everything she hears comes from the other side,' a tweeny said.

'No, they were from deep in our woods,' Dora said firmly. 'His lordship's. That's what my brother says. But he thought it was later – dusk.'

Then the footmen joined in. Some of them swore they'd heard men's voices, others denied anything. Passions were running quite high when they suddenly realized that Harriet and I were still present.

Harriet spoke into the silence. 'A girl screaming – and later another scream. Are all of you quite safe and sound? And the village girls?' She dropped her voice. 'Sometimes a girl doesn't like to report . . . things . . . to the police, even such an approachable officer as Constable Pritchard. We can all understand that. But they could talk to me or to Mrs Arden. We will listen. And we'll help if we can.' She looked around the table, as if making a personal promise to everyone there.

Dora spoke again. 'As far as we know, ma'am, no one from round here has been attacked. So we're wondering – you can imagine there's been a lot of talk, ma'am – if it was some man from – well, a stranger. But then, we don't get many visitors here, do we? Unless they're ladies and gentlemen staying here or with one of the gentry families. And it'd be all over the village if a lady was hurt, wouldn't it?'

She nodded. 'I'm sure you're right, Dora. So who might it be?'

The girl seemed a little less confident for a moment. 'Well, ma'am – it's . . . Look, it was the peg-woman . . . She read my palm the other day. It was quiet, ma'am, with no visitors, and you and Mr Rowsley being away, I didn't think anyone would mind, not just for a few minutes.'

The dropped eyes around the table told me that pretty well everyone had had their fortunes told. Hannah squirmed with embarrassment, as if she thought she should have stopped it, dragooning everyone back to their tasks.

'Did your palm tell her about a stranger, Dora?'

Gulping, she nodded. 'Ma'am, a threat, ma'am!'

Even Harriet looked shocked. 'A threat?'

'Yes, ma'am. But then she laughed and said she'd found a rainbow.'

'Any other rainbows?' she asked.

'Not for me,' Hannah said. 'But she said not to worry. Except about going out alone. Any of us, especially the young ones. So I told everyone about that, didn't I?'

A murmur around the table: yes, she had.

'*Especially* the young ones,' Harriet repeated. Did I detect the tiniest tremor in her voice?

'Like young Rosie. We don't want her frightened of shadows, but one of us tries to keep an eye on her all the time. Like Dan – ever so good, he is.' Dora gave a snort of affectionate laughter. '*She*'s teaching *him* to read, would you believe?' She looked up at the big clock. 'Beg pardon, ma'am. Beg pardon, sir. But I need to be starting our supper now.' She got up, bobbing a curtsy, and headed for the kitchen, followed by the next girl in the hierarchy. They did not close the door behind them.

Their exit called for a change of tone, perhaps, but I was not sure if Harriet's was quite the right one.

'Did anyone have any good news from this gypsy? Mr Thatcher – are you going to be cricket captain next summer?' she asked.

His face was a mask. 'She said I was in danger too, ma'am – from a big change.'

'In danger? My goodness!' There was no laugh in her voice now.

'A lot of us were told about this change, ma'am. We've been ever so worried,' Hannah said.

'I'm not surprised. I would be too. Did she give any idea what sort of change?'

'We were afraid his lordship was going to . . .' Hannah began. 'And we'd all . . . have no work.'

It was time for me to speak. 'I visited his lordship this morning. I promise that though he is not well, he is not at death's door yet, thank God. Some of you have met Mr Montgomery Wilson – the Family's lawyer. You know he's a decent, honest gentleman. He assures me that he will make certain that the transition – and we hope it will be many years before it is needed – from this lord to the next will be smooth and pleasant for everyone. And that includes everyone who works here. Even little Rosie: there may be more horses to feed then!' I added with a grin. But I added more seriously, 'So the gypsies are back in the area; it's about this time of year they set up their winter camp, isn't it? In Mr Newcombe's lower meadow?'

This wasn't close to either the woods or Farmer Twiss's fields.

'They moved. All of a sudden, wasn't it?' Luke said.

Dick snorted. 'I wonder if the peg-woman had foreseen it?'

'Have you any idea where they've gone? No?'

'That's gypsies for you,' Dick said, remembering that he was supposed to be a brave leader, not as anxious as the rest of the staff.

I nodded. All the same, it was worth discussing this conversation with Constable Pritchard.

* * *

On Sundays when there were no house guests, Harriet and I ate very simple fare for dinner, serving ourselves in the breakfast room, which was closer to the kitchen and much easier to heat. It also gave our colleagues more time to themselves.

'When did anyone last use the billiard room?' Harriet asked out of the blue as we sipped the last of our wine. 'Can you remember?'

'Not since I arrived here, I'd say. Apart from a couple of archaeologists last summer.'

'Quite. So I had an idea, and I'd like your opinion. I've already mentioned it to Dick, and to be honest he didn't overwhelm me with his enthusiasm.'

'Tell me.' Harriet's ideas tended to be a little revolutionary for a young man trained by Samuel. But after her brief explanation, I said, 'What an excellent notion! And I like the idea of a sitting room for them too.' It could be like a university common room, warm, with comfortable chairs. 'Mixed or two separate ones?'

She allowed her dimples to show. 'I think we should be demo-cratic and allow a vote. Not just for the men, however – for the women as well.'

Even if I had disagreed, given the martial light in her eyes, I would probably not have said so.

Since we so often had to host guests in the House, the trustees had set aside for our private use a sitting room and a bedchamber that was ours when needed. It was there we repaired this evening. I would be as delighted as Harriet would be to return to our own house – it came with my post as agent – as soon as it had been aired. It had to be said, however, that many of our favourite books had found a space over here – and, of course, there were the immense riches of the library downstairs at our fingertips should we ever be tempted. Tonight, however, I found it hard to follow the latest adventures of Philip Pirrip. A glance at Harriet showed that she had not even opened her novel. As if aware that I was watching her, she cast it aside and got to her feet.

'Can you think of one reason, just one, why we should have been summoned here?'

'One very good one, my love. To stop Elias Pritchard killing Sergeant Swain. How did such a man ever become a sergeant?

Heavens, if the physiognomists are right, with his large jaws, low sloping forehead and high cheekbones, he looks more like a criminal than a detective.'

She snorted, as I thought she would. 'You'd have the police feeling the bumps on the heads of all their suspects next. Assuming there were any suspects. Assuming we knew who the victim might be. And if there's another victim somewhere, who screamed earlier or later than the other.'

'You're right, of course. It's basic police work to find all this. We could have been with our friends for another day at least.'

'Not all of them. I wonder how poor Montgomery got on today – and why we have had no telegraph from him. I know he would prefer to write a letter, so perhaps we will have heard by breakfast time.' She sighed deeply as she picked up her book again. '*Sir Charles Grandison* is supposed to be so improving, but to be improved I actually need to open it . . .'

SIX

It was a very gloomy Constable Pritchard who was ushered into the Room as I went through my Monday morning routine of discussing the week's tasks with Hannah. His daughter had given him her cold, and he sniffed despondently as he reported that no photographer could arrive until tomorrow at the earliest. My chief emotion was not despair but anger, especially when he added that, despite everything, Sergeant Swain had point-blank refused to summon a detective from Scotland Yard.

'It's his first case, you see, Mrs Rowsley, and he wants to prove he can do it.'

Hannah, bringing in tea, raised a disparaging eyebrow. 'Just because you're in charge of something, Constable Pritchard, doesn't mean you have to do everything yourself. Mrs Rowsley is in charge here – no one would argue with that – but she doesn't blacklead the grates or beat carpets. And Mr Rowsley doesn't have to point chimneys, does he? He brings in an expert. But he's still in charge.' She nodded, bobbed a curtsy and left.

'She may say you're in charge, but she thinks she is,' he growled.

It was the first time I had heard him so surly. 'I think you're as frustrated with the lack of progress as we are,' I said. 'Tell me truthfully: why did you send for us? Why did you think we should be involved?' I smiled. 'I think it was because you had no faith in this new sergeant and thought he would need help. We are here, ready to support you – but we are amateurs!'

'If only Mr Rowsley would take a peep at the . . . at the head!'

'You're reluctant even to say the word aloud, aren't you!' I laughed. 'Heavens, I'm less squeamish than he is, but I've absolutely no desire at all to look at the remains of someone who is probably a perfect stranger. Come, have another cup of tea, and then go home and put your feet in a mustard bath. And before you argue, remember that your sergeant has the keys to the icehouse, and even if we were both desperate to view the remains, we could not.' I did not mention Thatcher's duplicate keys.

He grinned sheepishly.

'Is Sergeant Swain planning to come over today?' I asked.

He peered over his handkerchief. 'Does that mean if he comes, you will look?'

'No, it does not! Look, no one just arrives from nowhere in order to be murdered. There must be somebody who saw him. If he didn't take a train, did he come on horseback? In a carriage? And if no one local saw him, does that mean that he arrived somewhere else, where he was killed, and his body was brought here? If so, why?'

There was a tap on the door. Hannah again. 'Beg pardon, ma'am. Dan's just back from the village with the post-bag.'

Had the poor constable been a dog, he would have been sitting up with his ears pricked, raising a paw to beg. Was there a bone I could toss him? Not until I had been through the post with Matthew – and it was the House custom that it was the butler who would sort it out and distribute it. I would not usurp his role. In the past, letters had been mainly for the Family, of course, and the agent; now, as more of our colleagues could read and write, it was a more time-consuming task.

'Would you tell Mr Thatcher too, Hannah?'

She curtsied. 'He knows and he's on his way, ma'am. So is Mr Rowsley.'

'Thank you. And well done.'

She curtsied and was gone.

Was Hannah too sure of herself? I saw her as a young woman who might well replace me. I could use the quiet days before the return of the archaeologists to train her. The annual clean – in a house this size, it was not confined to the spring – would give her an intimate knowledge of all the rooms, not just those she was currently responsible for. So in the summer, when the House was full of guests requiring me to be their hostess, I could happily step back from my domestic duties.

'Don't say I didn't warn you,' Constable Pritchard said, sounding like a gloomy donkey, his sneeze decidedly like a bray. I hoped and prayed he would keep his infection to himself.

'Would you prefer to wait here until we see if there's anything useful in our post? With another cup of tea and a cake?'

'Just in case,' he said, managing a grin as he tossed my catch-phrase back at me.

Clutching our mail, Matthew and I adjourned to his office, dropping on his desk anything concerning the estate.

Our joint post included affectionate letters from James – whom I still thought of as Gussie – and Francis. Jeremy sent what was surely meant to be a jaunty account of his life at university, illustrated with some wickedly funny sketches.

Matthew and I exchanged glances: beneath the laughter, we both suspected tears. 'The poor boy. As soon as this case is over, we must invite him to stay with us, must we not?'

'Of course – preferably with Palmer and other sympathetic souls as well,' he added. He rifled through the envelopes again. 'Nothing from Wilson, I'm afraid. No, here it is, mixed up with the estate correspondence.' He pulled a face. 'Hmph. It seems our American heir told the hotel staff to keep his room for him while he saw some of the sights – he vaguely mentioned Stratford-upon-Avon and Lichfield, apparently. But he gave no indication of when he might return. As for Wilson himself, he begs the favour – oh, he would, wouldn't he! – of accommodation for himself when eventually he can escort Mr Baker here.'

I held out my hand. 'Given that heap on your desk, shall I reply to him? Oh, look, this note is from Lady Verney, reminding us of her invitation to visit her. And this is from Doctor Wells, congratulating me on being such a fine student and on my performance last week. Performance, Matthew! Still, I hope he means well.'

'Next, you'll have that toad of a bibliographer asking for thanks for his help in identifying the Thorncroft Gospel. Professor Marchbanks!'

I knew I must tell him about Mrs Marchbanks's last words to me. I must.

But there was a sharp tap on the door. 'Sergeant Swain, sir – ma'am,' Luke announced. 'Shall I bring tea?'

'If you please,' Matthew replied. 'And perhaps you should take the sergeant's cape?'

Something about Luke's bow suggested that he had already offered but that the officer had preferred to drip his way along the corridors.

Still standing, Matthew waited. 'What a filthy day, Sergeant. Come and sit down.' He added a log to the fire before he took his place behind his desk. When Sergeant Swain remained stolidly on his feet, he added, 'I believe Constable Pritchard may still be in the House; shall I invite him to join us?'

'If you have information to share, I'd be obliged.' The clear implication was that he was not.

Soon, four of us were sipping tea, which at least obliged the officers to sit down.

Matthew opened the proceedings, summarizing what had been said in the servants' hall.

If he had hoped the sergeant would be interested, he was to be disappointed. All he got was a curt nod. He was more interested in the contents of the letter in Matthew's hand; obligingly, Matthew read it aloud.

'So the American gentleman probably did not venture here,' I said, sighing.

'But he might have changed his mind,' the sergeant sniffed; I think it was in disparagement, not as a result of a cold. 'And then where would we be?'

'Exactly where we are now,' Matthew said. 'Unless you have more information?' I would not have liked the chilly hardness creeping into his voice.

'Our enquiries are proceeding,' came the lofty reply.

But sadly not apace.

'And something you have discovered or heard brings you here?' Matthew asked, his tone clearly the one he used to recalcitrant tenants.

'Well, Pritchard?' the sergeant thundered.

It was his turn to sniff, but he quickly dabbed his nose. 'I've spoken to Wilkins and Ash – that's the gamekeepers, Sergeant – and they know nothing. But they did say that the gypsies have moved on.'

We nodded: yes, we knew that.

'And there's a rumour they've gone to somewhere near Kynnersley. The common there.'

'That's near Farmer Burton's land,' Matthew said. 'One of his lordship's tenants, Sergeant.'

And near the great house where I had lost my childhood innocence and my ability to bear children.

'So we'll go and round them up and question them,' the sergeant said.

'Just like that?' Matthew's voice rose in disbelief.

'Mob-handed if necessary.' It was a shame his was the sort of chin that could not jut belligerently.

'If I were you, I'd go and talk to the leader of the group first – Pecker O'Malley, as I recall. Yes, he's got a big nose, and he nods his head in emphasis. I've no idea what his given name might be. Farmer Twiss has always got on well with him. My advice would be to ask him or, better still, Mr Newcombe to go with you. He's a Justice of the Peace, after all.'

'I'm not afraid of any gypsy, Mr Rowsley,' the sergeant predictably declared. 'Never have been and I'm not going to start now.'

'I'm not suggesting you are. I'm suggesting that Mr Newcombe's help getting Pecker on your side will make your work a lot easier. His word carries a lot of weight. Well, Pritchard?' He glared at him, expecting confirmation.

At first, the young man avoided his eye. Then he straightened, turning to Sergeant Swain. 'It's because Pecker and Mr Newcombe respect each other that his game never gets taken. Shall I speak to him, sir? Ask him if he could spare some time – say – this afternoon?'

'Would you care, Constable, to tell me who is in charge here? Don't try to brow-beat me into decisions, *if* you please, Pritchard!'

What started with a smart salute and a respectful 'Sir!' ended with a violent sneeze.

'Good God, man, you're neither use nor ornament – take yourself off home now. And that's an order.'

To my shame, I was almost relieved when, saluting, he marched out. But I could see that Matthew was ready to lose his temper.

In a tight, controlled voice, he asked, 'So how do you intend to proceed today, Sergeant?'

'I don't think that's any concern of yours, Mr Rowsley.'

Actually, in law he was probably right, but I jumped in quickly. 'On the contrary, Sergeant, it is every concern of ours, especially

as we were summoned from a number of important meetings
to assist you. As trustees, we are honoured to be Lord Croft's
representatives. As such, we are bound to take an interest in
what happens on or near his land. Mr Newcombe is another
trustee, a highly respected landowner and, as my husband
pointed out, a JP. At the very least, you owe him the courtesy
of updating him on what is – and moreover what is not –
happening to solve this crime. In fact, I suggest I drive you
down there now to meet him.'

'Bear with me; I will write a brief note of introduction.'

Even as Matthew did so, Sergeant Swain bridled.

'That's all very well,' he said, 'but the main problem as I see
it is that you and your husband are obstructing me in my enquiries
by refusing to look at the evidence.'

Matthew stood, drawing himself to his full height, and opened
the office door. 'I suggest you avail yourself of my wife's kind
offer, Sergeant Swain, before I telegraph your superiors and make
a formal complaint. Good day to you.' It was to me that he gave
the note, the seal like a bright drop of blood.

SEVEN

Every inch the most formal of butlers, Thatcher threw open the door of the yellow drawing room. 'Mr Rowsley, sir. Mr Baker.'

'Welcome to Thorncroft, Mr Baker,' I said. What was going on? How could he simply turn up without warning? But I must remember my manners. Smiling, I put out my hand to shake his.

Our visitor, whose clothes declared they were the work of an excellent tailor, was a tall, broad man in his mid-thirties, whose skin suggested that he worked in the open air. Getting up from the Louis Quinze sofa, he bowed. 'My dear cousin! Delighted to meet you. Claude E. Baker at your service.'

Having at first ignored my outstretched hand, he now took it in a firm grip. Admirable. But a thought struck me unbidden: if this was the heir, to whom did that head belong? But for the time being, I must concentrate on the current situation, which was, to say the least, disconcerting.

'I fear you did not catch my name, sir. I am Matthew Rowsley, his lordship's agent.' I bowed. 'I am afraid his lordship is indisposed and unable to receive visitors himself.'

His smile faded a little. 'Well, sir, what about Lady Croft?'

'His lordship's mother? I fear that she is no longer with us, sir.'

'Well, where the hell is she?' He sounded bemused rather than angry.

'I apologize. I did not make myself clear. She is dead.'

He laughed, though not entirely with amusement, I suspected. 'Let's get this straight: I come all this way through godforsaken rain-soaked countryside to find – nothing. Well, then, Mr Rowsley, just who is in charge here?'

I gestured: would he be seated again? I sat opposite him.

'I am, Mr Baker,' I said.

'In charge – of all this?' He lifted an eyebrow often used, I suspect, to depress pretension, just as Harriet's was. 'My dear sir, that is a job indeed!'

'Indeed it is!' I laughed. 'I'm actually in charge of all his lordship's properties – his other houses, his estates, his tenant farms.'

'All of that?' His eyes rounded. 'On top of this?' He gestured. 'You are undoubtedly a busy man!'

I shook my head self-deprecatingly. 'As to this wonderful House, my wife, currently occupied elsewhere, is in charge of the entire contents and of all the female servants. Mr Thatcher, whom you just met, is the butler, and in charge of the male servants.' And surely someone had been sent to find Harriet and to urge her – and the dratted slug of a horse Robin – to return home. Why on earth had she never learned to ride? 'It is my wife and her team who look after rooms like this.' The furniture glowed with the care regularly lavished on it, even if it might never again be seen by its owner. 'We are all supervised by a group of trustees led by the Family's lawyer, Mr Wilson, whose acquaintance you may already have made.'

He snorted. 'Wilson? Hah! I went to see him last week. And what do I get? Turkish treatment! "Away on important business, sir,"' he said, in a finicking faux-English accent. '"Returning next week." What sort of attorney is that?'

I smiled, man to man. 'A very busy one, I assure you! Last week, he was with us in Oxford, meeting representatives of the University Library and the Ashmolean Museum. Then, our work there approved by a judge, we travelled with him to London, to negotiate with the British Museum. The trustees wish some of the greatest volumes in the Thorncroft library to be put on loan there where they will be studied by experts.'

'Can I believe my ears? You are *lending* things from here!'

'Exactly. Lending. Hence all the legal advice.'

'But why?'

'Because as you will appreciate when you see the rest of the contents, they are national treasures, sir. And after his late lordship's death, they were locked away, never touched. And they deserve to be appreciated.'

'Why not have the experts come here?'

'As you have just found to your cost, getting here isn't easy.' We exchanged a smile. 'And there are very strict controls on who even enters the library, as I am sure Mr Wilson will explain to you. Anyway, after our London meetings, Mr Wilson returned – as soon as he could, Mr Baker – to Shrewsbury, to serve you. I believe you will work well with someone as conscientious and reliable as he. Meanwhile, how may I help you?' I thought longingly of all the urgent work on my desk. And less longingly of the problem of the head.

'Get Wilson here now, for one thing.'

'I will see a telegraph is despatched at once.'

'And tell me where I may bring Mrs Baker to stay.'

'I hope you will stay here, sir, of course. A bedchamber will be prepared for you instantly. Will you excuse me for five minutes to send that telegraph? I'm afraid that with the best will in the world, Mr Wilson cannot be here till late afternoon.'

'My dear sir, I intend to leave before nightfall. These roads in this weather! No, if Mr Wilson is waiting in Shrewsbury, forget that telegraph. I'll make my way back there this afternoon.'

Furious with myself for sounding like Dick on a particularly obsequious day, I responded, 'In the meantime, may I offer you more tea?'

'You English and your goddam tea!' But he laughed as he said it, shaking his head as if indulging a child.

'Coffee, perhaps?' Laughing with him, I stood to ring the bell. 'And, before you leave, perhaps you will join Mrs Rowsley and me for luncheon?'

Before he could reply, Harriet, a veritable dea ex machina, arrived – announced very formally. She had clearly been warned in advance of our guest's presence. She had changed into one of her smartest day dresses, augmented by two or three discreetly placed jewels. She might not be an aristocrat, but she looked every inch the mistress of this House as she swept into the room. She approached with her hand outstretched. Yes, she expected him to kiss it.

Mr Baker obliged – with considerable aplomb.

How would she maintain this superb act – which owed much, I suspected, to the regular dramatized readings we so much enjoyed when the House had guests? Certainly, she poured the coffee which Thatcher now brought with grace and elegance, and asked all the disarming questions I had forgotten to put. She discovered that he was the father of two children, brought up by a nanny and educated by a governess. He owned an estate in

Virginia – a plantation, he called it – producing tobacco. Yes, it was sizeable enough – some two and a half thousand acres. And he had other interests involving oysters. He had just completed building a new home – no, of course not on the plantation itself – with thirty-five rooms. He and his wife were looking to buy appropriate English or French furniture. And paintings, of course. His wife was now headquartered in London, looking to purchase not just gowns for herself but also fabric for curtains, that sort of thing. Each new piece of information came with a more charming smile.

At last, she repeated my invitation to be our guest for lunch at very least. Of course a room was ready for him if he cared to make a longer stay; of course we could accommodate any of his staff he cared to bring.

'Staff?' he cut in sharply. 'You mean, servants?'

'Indeed. But we always refer to our colleagues as staff.' Her smile might be undiminished, but I sensed the steel in her, even if he did not.

'Colleagues? My dear Mrs Rowsley, that is the strangest term for – what? – people who empty your slops and peel your potatoes.'

'As to the slops, Mr Baker,' I said, 'I am happy to say that running water and flush sanitation have been installed in the House. But a kitchen maid has her place in the health and happiness of the household just as my wife does. So we are happy to use those terms. Now,' I added, hoping to move to safer waters, 'may I suggest half past twelve for luncheon?'

'Sure.' That charming smile again. I had seen many similar on the faces of my grandfather's friends when they wished to be particularly insulting. 'And do you sit down at table with the whole kit and caboodle of *colleagues*?'

'My dear Mr Baker, there is still a hierarchy,' Harriet said, refusing to rise to the bait. 'There are even strange House rituals for servants that you will probably encounter during your stay here. As my husband has possibly told you, when the House has guests, my husband and I are required to act as hosts. In general, we maintain the habit of lunching and dining on our own.'

He shook his head. 'So are you or are you not servants?'

What was going wrong? 'Perhaps you would prefer to see us as his lordship's representatives?' Harriet said. 'His deputies?

For that is what we and our fellow trustees are. I am sure Matthew has explained our responsibilities. We are here to maintain the status quo until his lordship's recovery or his death and all that that implies.'

Dear Harriet – the workhouse brat who could now use a Latin phrase as easily as I could.

'Is my cousin so very ill? Is he suffering badly?'

'For an answer to that, you will have to turn to Doctor Page, the physician who sees his lordship on an almost daily basis, and the distinguished experts in the field who visit him regularly.' Unasked, she rang the bell. 'Mr Thatcher, would you be kind enough to show Mr Baker to his bedchamber? And we will take sherry before lunch in about ten minutes.'

Mr Baker had got to his feet and seemed ready to follow Dick. But now he turned in a flash from charming guest to zealot. 'Sherry, Mrs Rowsley? I will have no alcohol served – no, no alcohol at all in any room where I am present!' He turned on his heel and left the room.

Watching his retreating back, she dropped an ironic curtsy. 'Well, that's told me, ain't it?' she said in the tones of a cocky village child. 'Matthew, I expected the American equivalent of a yokel; Mr Baker is a man used to power – used to wielding it, too.'

'Indeed. Take away that slight drawl and replace it with an Eton accent and you could pop him straight into the House of Lords and no one would notice the difference.'

She gave a snort of laughter. 'Except for the alcohol!'

Luncheon – without wine, as was in any case our wont when we were alone – went as smoothly as we could contrive. Bea had produced a miracle of elegance. A fine autumnal salmagundi took the centre of the table, surrounded by wafer-thin slices of cold meats. Given the state of the icehouse, Bea had improvised for dessert, replacing the iced dishes she excelled in with tiny apple turnovers with fresh cream; a hastily baked luncheon cake took pride of place in the centre of the table. Thatcher took it upon himself to serve us.

Did I misjudge him when I suspected he was blending duty with a chance to eavesdrop on our guest? And could I blame him? He and all our colleagues had a vested interest, after all. I had the shrewdest suspicion that he would report back any significant conversations and also remark on our guest's ease at dealing with the array of fine silver cutlery either side of his plate.

We kept our side of the conversation as bland as possible. Mr Baker learned about the Roman remains, in which he evinced round-eyed interest, and the model village, which brought a puzzled and slightly supercilious frown to his face. I was about to ask him how he accommodated his estate workers, but I had a sudden recollection that, as a Southern gentleman with a large plantation, he might still have slaves – who might not have the benefit of modern plumbing in their houses.

In any case, he had a question of his own: 'And how much did this village cost?'

'I am sure Mr Wilson as the chairman of trustees has all this at his fingertips,' I responded smoothly. 'And indeed, I imagine that should you choose to remain in this country, you will be co-opted on to the board very shortly.'

'Do you and your wife mean to stay in England long?' Harriet asked more tactfully, perhaps. 'And stay here? If so, I am sure that Mr Wilson will convene a meeting here so that you can make everyone's acquaintance. Furthermore, we could make arrangements for you to meet the gentry in the vicinity.'

'That would be Lord Croft's old friends?' Neither of us felt it necessary at this point to explain that the poor young man had had some very undesirable companions, none of whom had thought it necessary to visit him since he had been taken ill. 'Your local nobility?'

Harriet laughed. 'I fear that the only aristocrat with whom we are on visiting terms is Matthew's grandfather. And he has become decidedly eccentric, alas.'

'The grandson of an earl? But why—? My dear Rowsley, busying yourself with bathrooms and workers . . . When you could have—'

I raised my hands slightly as if in surrender. But I did not, nor would not, explain my decisions and choices to a stranger.

With a smile, Harriet changed the subject. 'In the shorter term, how long may we expect the pleasure of your company? I only ask because I understand you have not brought overnight luggage and we will try to supply anything needful.'

He raised an eyebrow. 'You should know the answer, ma'am. No portmanteau, no stay.'

She accepted the obvious snub with another charming smile. 'Of course. And naturally we will arrange for your carriage to be ready for when you require it.'

'Thank you, ma'am. Let's say three, shall we?'

'Three it is. But before your departure, would you care to see more of the House? The long gallery in particular is worth seeing for its own sake, not to mention that of the many Old Masters hanging there. We would be honoured to show you round.'

'And I would be honoured by your company.' He turned to me. 'Surely you have some expert? Some curator?'

'Not on the premises. But the trustees insist on regular inspections by visiting experts. Everything is conserved appropriately.' I smiled. 'I think I mentioned earlier that my wife knows more about the House and its contents than anyone living.'

'Heavens, most pretty women wouldn't know a . . . what shall I say . . .?'

'A Botticelli from a Bellini?' I supplied. 'As it happens, my wife could probably tell you the dates they flourished, not to mention the dates of their rivals.'

'Oh. Well, ma'am, I would be honoured, if you can spare the time.' He treated her to his smile, which contrived to be both respectful and appreciative.

'Of course! I will ensure the lamps are lit. It gets dark so early, does it not?' She reached for the bell but stepped into the corridor to give her instructions. If I knew anything about her, she would ensure that at least one footman was on duty wherever she planned to take him. Should I go with them? I must, mustn't I? And had a moment's unexpected pleasure as I did so: in one of the rooms near the gallery, a young woman was singing. I could have listened all day. But neither Harriet nor Baker seemed to have noticed it and, shrugging, I caught up with them.

EIGHT

Mr Baker said all that was proper as I led him from masterpiece to masterpiece. Occasionally, Matthew would hold a lamp at a different height or angle so that he might look more closely. But I set quite a brisk pace, taking him downstairs within half an hour by way of the staircase dominated by the Van Dyke. I hoped that he would not register the guard constantly on duty outside the main door to the Family wing and ask awkward questions.

He declined more tea or coffee, announcing that he would set off immediately the coach was ready. Luke melted away to fetch his coat and hat, and have the landau brought round to the front entrance; with the rain lashing down, it was a poor afternoon to be a coachman or footman. It was not a good one for the senior servants standing alongside Matthew and me to wave our guest goodbye. But it was a Family tradition, and I wished to be no less courteous than if he were Prince Albert himself.

At last, Dick, very much on his butler's dignity, could close, with his usual ceremony, the great doors. But then he broke his self-imposed rule of treating us in front of other servants as if we were indeed his employers. He heaved a great sigh, asking rhetorically, 'Could he be the danger that threatens us all?'

It was the first question I would have asked Matthew in private.

It was Hannah who responded. 'We must hope for that rainbow, then.'

What I needed to do was kick off my boots and loosen my corset. What I did do was adjourn with Matthew to his office. We needed a brief conversation; even just a week away meant he had a great deal to do urgently, including providing evidence for a court case and arbitrating between two warring neighbours.

There was a tap on the door: Luke carrying a tea tray. 'I thought you might need this.' He put a tray on his desk, smiling at us in turn.

Matthew's face relaxed in a smile. 'You read my mind, Luke.'

'Actually, I read your face, sir, as you went off with that American gentleman. Very pleasant, he seemed.' If ever a young man was fishing for information, it was he.

Matthew spoke first. 'Now, Luke, yesterday it seemed to me that the women – oh, please sit down: we need a sounding board – that *everyone* felt that they were in danger of losing their posts.'

He pulled a face. 'These gypsy women are often right, aren't they?' He snorted. 'Actually, what they say is so vague something's bound to be right, I suppose.'

'Precisely,' I said. 'I'd like to tell people not to worry, but they will, whatever I say.'

'They – we – all think this American gentleman is the danger she spoke about.'

Matthew nodded. 'We understand. But what I promise you now, and everyone else, is that I know of no immediate threat to you and your livelihoods. And if and when I ever do, with Harriet beside me, I will fight it with every fibre in my body. To the highest court in the land if needs be.'

'Thank you. I appreciate that. And everyone else will too.'

'We've suggested that Mr Wilson – as straight a man as ever breathed, who will have investigated all Mr Baker's credentials – comes down to discuss everything with all the trustees. All of them. So everyone here in the House and in the village will know what happens next.'

'You think something will happen soon?' His eyes widened in panic.

'Absolutely not. There's been very little change in his lordship's condition, poor man. Remember, as long as he lives, the trustees are legally bound to keep things as they are, and if one of us wants to change anything, then every single one has to agree.'

'We know some of us are only kept on because they couldn't get work anywhere else round here.'

I got up and took his hands. 'And almost all of you are "kept on" because as soon as the scholars and archaeologists return, we will need trained staff, just as the Family always did for house parties. Imagine trying to recruit footmen and maids just for the summer! No, the trustees couldn't justify keeping every last one of you on, but we're more than just a skeleton staff, aren't we?

Luke, we are all part of this team. All of us! I know you understand, but make sure everyone else knows!'

'Yes, ma'am. Thank you, ma'am.' He backed out.

Matthew took me in his arms. 'Thank you. And thank you for
handling Mr Baker so wonderfully.'

A sudden gust brought rain lashing across the window.

'Sergeant Swain won't enjoy being out in this, will he?'

Matthew grimaced. 'I suppose I should have taken him myself.
Only I was afraid I'd tip him in a ditch deliberately.'

Over the tea, we chewed over our visitor. He seemed pleasant
enough, willing to be pleased. Or was there an edge? Could it
possibly be he who posed the danger that the fortune-teller had
predicted? It was a possibility Matthew would not rule out.

We tossed ideas to and fro; I wondered if he was simply out
of his depth in a foreign society which had far more unwritten
rules than written ones.

'*Perhaps!*' Matthew tossed back at me. 'Oh, he was charming
enough, especially to you. But a man doesn't get to be as rich
and powerful so young without an element of ruthlessness.
Remember: we are just servants. And there's his attitude to
alcohol. That's hardly going to endear him to his neighbours and
members of the Lords.'

'Poor man.'

'Reserve your pity! We may need that rainbow,' he concluded.

I meant to ask lightly how and where we might find one, but
suddenly I knew I must tell him what Mrs Marchbanks had
said to me. It might have been in her dying breath as she left
the House—

'Heavens, Harriet, look at the time! Confound him, I dare say
Sergeant Swain will be here any moment now. Important though
he is, can we leave the heir on one side? How did you get on
with Sergeant Swain this morning after you'd dragooned the poor
man into paying a morning visit to Mr Newcombe?'

Was I frustrated by the interruption or grateful? The latter, I
suspected. Whenever I awoke in the night, it was to worry how
to broach the subject.

'The poor Sergeant! He had to sit in the Newcombes' servants'
hall kicking his heels until Mr Newcombe was free. Meanwhile,
I had a good long talk with Mrs Newcombe, who bade me call

her Adelaide – yes, we have progressed to first-name terms!' I said. 'Of course. I gave her your note. She would make sure her husband – whom she does not refer to as Tertius, but as Mr Newcombe – got it – and read it – before he took the sergeant to Kynnersley. She also promised she would talk to her servants, especially the women and girls, about the murder and tell them not to go about alone.'

'What about the attack on the body? Did you risk mentioning that?'

Did he mean in terms of social class or conversational appropriateness? 'Indeed, Matthew, even you sometimes forget that women are capable of discussing quite serious matters – and so you may tell the sergeant!' I might have sounded playful, but my point was serious. 'We wondered, actually, if the man had made a nuisance of himself to a number of women – exposing himself or far worse – and someone decided that enough was enough. No, no evidence at all, of course, but remember the castration—'

'Of course. And someone was angry enough to remove the head too.'

'Do not for one minute imagine that we are walking out in the dark and this rain to see if you can break into the icehouse. I am more than happy, my love, to look at gruesome photographs, or a realistic sketch, but no, not . . . And the smell,' I added with a shudder, replacing my cup in its saucer with a decided rap.

'I will not dare to argue!'

'I should hope not! Oh, if only the sergeant would cooperate with us – just a very little. To speed things up, I had not dear old Robin but Paragon pull the trap. Paragon, who's had no exercise for a week. A very lively Paragon. And it seems our poor sergeant does not like a frisky pony, especially when a woman is holding the reins. Apart from his gasps and words of advice on how to hold a whip, we had a silent journey. Actually, that was a shame: I would have liked to have a gentle conversation with him, not another confrontation. What can we do, Matthew?'

'As with the heir, watch and wait. My note to Mr Newcombe suggested that, as a JP, he might demand Scotland Yard take control of the case.'

'Ah! So that's why you were kind enough to give the sergeant a letter of introduction! What a devious man you are to be sure.' I blew him a kiss. 'Now, how are you getting on with that battle between Mr Gates and Mr Letts?'

'Well enough. Tell me, this morning, did you hear—?' Cursing under his breath, he broke off as Dick tapped at the door: 'Sergeant Swain, sir. Ma'am.'

'This man of yours wasn't sure if you were at home,' the sergeant said without preamble, taking the seat he had used before. 'But I'm on my way to that little station on the estate here,' he continued, 'so I thought I could tell you about my meeting with that gypsy of yours.'

Silently, I rang: yes, Dan would be ready to make sure he didn't miss the train.

'Mr O'Malley?' Matthew asked, somewhat repressively.

'Him. Yes. He knows something, all right. Clammed up as soon as I told him I was looking for a murderer amongst his men.'

'Really?' Matthew was impeccably neutral.

'Yes. If it hadn't been for that Mr Newcombe, I doubt if I'd have got a word out of him.'

'But you did? Ah, do you have time for a glass of sherry before you have to catch your train?'

He sat to attention. 'Sir, I am on duty!'

'Of course. My apologies. So between you, did you and Mr Newcombe obtain any useful information?'

'Nothing. Except that this O'Malley would ask everyone if they knew anything. Fine chance!'

'Did he give any reason for leaving their usual winter campsite?'

'That's what gypsies do, sir, isn't it? They move around.' He shrugged. In other words, he had not asked.

Matthew's nod was at best noncommittal. 'And what time do you expect the photographer from Birmingham to arrive tomorrow? I can arrange for him to be met at the halt and brought here, if you like. After all,' he said dryly, 'we are hosting the object of interest.'

'Not exactly here, in this building, sir.' He got to his feet. 'Now, it's time I was on my way. But before I go, Mr Newcombe told me to give you this.' He handed Matthew a letter. 'Good evening to you.' He nodded at Matthew.

'Just one moment, Sergeant,' I said.

He stared as if the desk had spoken, then squirmed a little. 'Ma'am?'

'Could you tell us what time to expect the photographer, please? I will arrange for Dan to meet him. I presume you would wish to accompany him to the icehouse, so you might wish to be taken there too?'

The poor man. When had I last mimicked the chilling tones of her late ladyship? 'Yes, ma'am. If you please, ma'am.' He was backing out.

'And the time?'

'The twenty-past-ten train if you please, ma'am.'

'Thank you.' I rang. 'Perhaps you would be at the stables by ten.'

Dick must have been very close indeed to the door to respond so quickly. And his face was so impassive he must have heard every word. 'The trap is waiting for you at the back door, Sergeant.' He ushered him out with remarkable speed.

I counted to thirty. No, he was not about to pop back in. 'That was very naughty of me,' I said, putting my finger in my mouth like a guilty child.

Matthew's eyes gleamed. 'Her ladyship would have been very proud of you. I am. Now, this here letter.' He opened it with a flourish.

> *My dear Rowsley,*
>
> *What a dunce the man is! We have come to expect better with our excellent Pritchard and the usual sergeant.*
>
> *If the experts Sergeant Swain has promised do not materialize tomorrow, I shall go over his head and ask the Chief Constable to contact Scotland Yard.*
>
> *My wife tells me that she and dear Harriet had a very interesting conversation this morning. It would be delightful if they could continue it – or a less unpleasant one! – at a dinner party. We would like to invite you one evening next week. Adelaide will be sending out formal invitations in due course.*
>
> *Very sincerely yours,*
> *T. Newcombe*

'Mr Baker will be impressed,' I said, straight-faced.

'He will, won't he? Or he would be if plain Mr Newcombe had had the sense to be knighted or born a lord! My love, I have never had the least need or desire to hobnob with neighbours who were once inclined to be snobbish, but I am truly delighted that the Newcombes have invited us into their circle. I doubt if the conversation will match that in Oxford, but—'

The knock on the door sounded urgent. Barely waiting for a response, Luke appeared. 'Beg pardon. But there's another body!'

NINE

'Where? Who?'

'Don't know, ma'am. Young Edwin Ash found him. He's run to tell us!' Luke caught his breath.

And Sergeant Swain had left only minutes ago! 'Get someone to saddle Esau. I'll ride to the station to let the sergeant know!'

My speed, Esau's speed – all in vain. Whistling, the train puffed off. By the time I'd settled Esau, who had objected strongly to the sudden noise, it had disappeared, its irritating passenger unaware of the drama in which he could have played a useful part. Drat and drat and drat, to use Harriet's words – though under my breath I used much stronger ones.

I took the more direct route back to the House: did I hope there would still be some activity I could report back to Harriet? Or to find something the sergeant would miss the following morning? Some act of minor heroism, perhaps? But the darkness now was almost absolute, so though I slowed to a dawdle, telling myself it was safer to let Esau pick his way, no matter how much I peered this way and that, I saw nothing except puddles and dead leaves.

And then the rain came down again.

Bea was the first to see me as I trudged in via the servants' entrance. 'Heavens, stop right there! They're just laying the table for supper and don't want to be stepping in your puddles. Evans! Where are you when you're wanted? Come on, bustle about, lad. That's better,' she added, as the harassed youth relieved me of my boots and my sodden coat and hat.

Even as I thanked him, he scampered off. And Bea produced a cup of tea. 'There's time for you to drink this while you tell me what's going on.' She sat down pointedly.

'I'll bet you know more than I do,' I countered, sitting nonetheless. 'All I know is that young Ash found a body and that I was too late to stop Sergeant Swain going back to Shrewsbury.'

'Well, as it happens, I do know a bit more than that, because they found that the lad they thought was dead was actually alive, and they sent for Ellis. He's still up there examining him, deciding what to do next. And Harriet has already invited him to dine with us. So I'd best get on and make sure that we won't all starve.' She got to her feet. 'Dinner at seven or half past, depending on Ellis and young Lazarus at the hospital. Ah – more news, by the look of it!'

A bedraggled Joe Wilkins, Edwin Ash's brother-in-law, knew better than to step into the hall without an invitation, so, seeing he was carrying something, I went and helped him off with his boots and cape myself – an embarrassed Evans seizing them and spiriting them away to join my gear.

He wiped the rain from his face. 'It seemed to me the young man that was brought here wouldn't come all the way here by that train, gaffer, without a bag. And he was so wet, poor lad, if he lived, he'd want a change of clothes. So I went off with the dogs, gaffer, and found this.' He patted what I now realized was a sizeable portmanteau.

'You did well, Joe. Thanks.' I shook his hand, slipping a coin into his that would show my appreciation. 'Family all right?'

'Oh, ah.' He smiled slowly. 'Can't wait for that school to open, Mr Rowsley, sir. That young wench of mine is only trying to read the family Bible – bigger than her it is!'

'And what about young Johnny?'

He shook his head. 'Takes more after me, gaffer. Likes nothing better than walking the woods with me. No, I lie: he likes taking Scamp and walking the woods himself, for all he's only seven.'

'I don't suppose either of you heard any screaming the other day?'

'Ah, that real body everyone's talking about. Not me, that's for sure, or I'd have told young Pritchard.' He sucked his teeth. 'Tell you what, though, Johnny's had a couple of bad dreams – woken us up shouting, he has. So I'll have a quiet word with him. Just me and him, if it's all right by you, gaffer? Don't want no policeman putting words in his mouth!'

'Quite,' I said dryly. 'But I might not be able to keep them away altogether if he has seen or heard anything.'

'And I wouldn't want to. Got to do right by the dead man, haven't we? What I'll do is I'll tell Pritchard. Not that town bastard, begging your pardon. Now, best be on my way, if it's all the same to you, gaffer.'

I was actually delighted, glad to have the chance to look at the new guest's luggage. Might there be a label attached, with his name and destination? No. On the outside, it was quite anonymous. It was good quality – possibly its contents would still be dry.

I thought briefly of the drawer in the luggage room: Dick maintained Samuel's tradition of keeping a variety of keys to avert crises when guests had left theirs at home. But I would suggest that only in an emergency; I would much prefer Lazarus – trust Bea to come up with an apt name – to wake and rise and produce his keyring for his luggage. A valise suggested clearly that he meant to stay – could it mean that the police artist had arrived early? At least if it was a young man, it was not one of our intimate friends: no one could describe Palmer, Halesowen or Wilson in those terms. Youthful despite their middle years, perhaps – as Harriet and I saw ourselves.

I shook myself. This was a mystery easily solved.

But I reckoned without Nurse Webb.

'My dear Mr Rowsley! Visit the patient!' At the door of the Family wing, Nurse Webb looked me up and down as I might shame a youthful scrumper. 'I must say I'm surprised at you. The poor gentleman is in no fit state for any visitor. Doctor Page is still with him, and I must return with no more ado.'

'If this gentleman was visiting the House,' I persisted, 'it is possible that either Harriet or I would recognize him and be able to summon his family.'

'Or you might not, and our patient would be disturbed for nothing.' She turned towards the ward, offering me, over her shoulder, a tiny sop. 'You may return in – let us say half an hour? – and I will see what Doctor Page thinks. But I am not optimistic.'

It did not take me long to run Harriet to earth: she was in the library. The air was thick with the dust of old books. She looked unusually distraught.

'We need to work our magic on Nurse Webb,' I explained.

She shook her head slowly. 'She is not just any nurse, Matthew; she was trained by Miss Nightingale herself. Let us give her the half hour she asked for, and maybe a few minutes more. You've probably guessed that Ellis will be dining with us – he will tell us everything he knows, I should imagine. If not, ask him.'

I shook my head. 'That would be to ask him to do what I did once – overrule the woman in charge!'

'Touché! You are quite right. But he might give reasons that she feels she should not reveal why the young patient must not be disturbed.' She held up her dusty hands. 'Meanwhile, I should change for dinner. And you, my love, still have mud spatters all over your face from your dash to the station.'

Perhaps impressed by my clean face, or more likely reassured by the presence of Harriet, Nurse Webb nodded slowly. 'You may have thirty seconds, Mr Rowsley. And during those thirty seconds you stand at the door, out of sight. In silence.'

I obeyed to the letter. But it was hard to hold back an exclamation when I saw the pale, thin figure in the hospital bed. What on earth was he doing here?

Harriet, her face all anxiety – yes, for me – took my hands as I returned. 'You know him, my love, don't you?' She pushed me down on to a chair.

I nodded. 'I can hardly believe it – Harriet, it's young Jeremy Turton!'

'Jeremy! I knew he was unwell on Saturday – but what has brought him here?'

Nurse Webb coughed. 'So you can furnish me with his name – Jeremy Turton, I deduce – and his address?'

'Yes. That's his name. But as to his address . . .' I hesitated. What crisis had precipitated such a journey? Had he thought of the House as a place of refuge? 'We met him at my cousin's house, and again at a function in Oxford. So we have no idea where he lives.' And if we did, should we reveal it?

'We will have a room aired for him when you have nursed him back to health,' Harriet said firmly. 'You should know he has a very severe stammer; he hates questions requiring a long answer. At times, even a simple *yes* or a *no* can be a trial.'

'Thank you, Mrs Rowsley. That is helpful. I gather you were not expecting him?'

She shook her head. 'But that does not mean he is not welcome.'

'Yet you don't know where he lives? I need his address so that I can write to his parents to tell him where he is.'

'As Matthew told you, we have no idea where he lives, except when he is in college. I suspect – no, I know we should wait until he can respond to you and then do exactly as he asks.'

'Indeed? That is . . . unusual.'

'The circumstances are indeed unusual.'

'Mr Rowsley?'

'My wife is absolutely right, Nurse,' I said formally. 'Let us wait and hear his wishes.'

TEN

When Ellis came down to join us for sherry before dinner, he brought good news. The patient would live. 'Young Mr Turton seems to have fallen as he made his way from the station. He has a badly sprained ankle – it might even be broken. I have strapped it tightly – the pain was so great I have given him enough laudanum for him to sleep till morning.'

'So how did he get here? With a broken ankle?' Bea asked.

'Needs must. The alternative would be to spend the night in the open. So my guess is he left the halt – someone must have pointed him in right direction – but tripped. Unable to walk, he literally crawled the rest of the way. His trousers are beyond repair, and his knees as bloodied as a schoolboy's. His hands, too. But all those injuries will heal in time – and more quickly given his youth.'

'Let us drink to his speedy recovery,' Matthew said, raising his glass.

Our toast over, Ellis continued, 'He is so thin I feared consumption. My first examination has failed to find it, thank goodness.'

'When we met him earlier in the year, I would have called him whippy,' Matthew said. 'But he looked gaunt when we saw him last week.'

I said quietly, 'Those are physical problems, Ellis. But I fear – how can I put this? – that there is something wrong here.' I touched my temple. 'Why else should he come here, to comparative strangers, rather than go home?'

'An argument? Young people sometimes have difficulty accepting their parents' wishes,' Bea said.

'Their wishes, we gathered when we met him, were that he take holy orders. In fact, he's currently studying Divinity at Oxford. But he has the devil of a stammer,' Matthew said, rather inappropriately but accurately. 'Cripplingly bad. Actually, he was bullied and mocked for it when we first met him. His godfather is my cousin. He's a military man, not specially perceptive or indeed tactful, who told him he was unsuited to a career in the Church and that it would be sinful to ignore his God-given artistic talent. I couldn't argue with that.'

'But perhaps his family did,' Bea mused.

'Knowing that with an impediment such as this, a career involving preaching, let alone carrying out parish duties, would be unending torture? Words escape me!' Ellis shook his head in furious disbelief. He emptied his glass in one draught. 'Why on earth— No, forgive me.'

'My dear Ellis, if you can't rage amongst friends, where can you?' I asked, as Matthew topped up his glass. 'But would you be happy to answer a very mundane question? I don't suppose Nurse Webb found keys on him?' Ellis shook his head. 'You see, what is probably his portmanteau is in the laundry. If we could open it, all his clothes could be aired.'

He spread his hands.

I rang for Luke: yes, he would go and ask Nurse Webb. 'And if she didn't find any, ma'am, there's always Mr Thatcher's key drawer, isn't there!'

'There is indeed, Luke. Thank you.'

With a bow, he was on his way.

I turned back to Ellis. 'I was so worried about Jeremy last Saturday that I told him he could come and stay with us whenever he wanted. At the time, he shook his head and muttered something about a task that he had to finish. It was his duty, he said.'

Ellis nodded. 'Duty or our *conception* of duty can be a terrible master, can it not?'

Bea and I exchanged a rueful smile.

'Harriet is one of the few people he seems comfortable talking to, so she may be able to get to the bottom of this,' Matthew said. 'He was at the Ashmolean when we handed over the aestel and the Gospel. I'm not entirely sure why. Perhaps he simply wanted to see us – but in the event, he was too terrified by the press of people even to say hello to her. I made sure he knew where we were staying and begged him to visit us while we were with Palmer. But then when Pritchard summoned us home, that was impossible, of course. But he made a special effort to see us off on the train, didn't he?'

'He did. He had an armful of periodicals for us. It was then that I issued that open invitation to come here. I never thought he would simply turn up. But thank God he did, provided he did himself no lasting harm.'

'He's young,' Ellis observed bracingly. 'I fancy when he wakes, he will sit up and demand a decent breakfast.'

'And if he does?' I asked.

He laughed. 'Nurse Webb and I ought to prescribe thin gruel and weak tea.' He pulled a face. 'And then the invalid diet served to everyone in the Family wing.'

I frowned. 'For how long, Ellis?'

He snorted. 'Till tomorrow morning! Actually, the sooner he can resume normal life the better. But the ankle is the problem – when he's getting dressed, of course. Pulling his trousers over his injured foot and all the strapping. And, even if that can be overcome, getting around.'

Bea said, 'Don't I recall a chair with wheels so that Samuel could be pushed around? We should be able to find it somewhere. And there'll be crutches aplenty in the Family wing itself, surely to goodness. As for getting trousers over the bad ankle, if young Luke can't undo a seam in a trouser leg and pin it together again, I'm sure I can. Not that I'm any needlewoman.'

'In that case, once you think he's fit enough, need he remain with the invalids?' Matthew asked. 'Heavens, he can have nothing in common with anyone there, and he would have to speak to strangers. To *attempt* to.'

'A fire is already burning in the room we thought Jeremy would be happy in,' Harriet said. 'It's got a lovely view over the Roman excavations. It's near our quarters. And he could simply be what he wanted to be: a guest. In fact, as soon as his clothes are aired and pressed to Luke's satisfaction, they could be hung in the wardrobe ready for him. He could move there the moment you gave permission.'

'Excellent!'.

'And it's close to one of the grand new bathrooms,' I added, exchanging a smile with Bea.

'You know that you are setting a fashion in the village?' Ellis asked. 'Tertius Newcombe and I are both having running water installed too. A water closet, of course, and a bath. In fact,

I consider a hot bath to be very therapeutic. I know that many physicians favour plunging into cold water, but everything has a time and a place, in my view. Yes, cosset the lad a little.'

'We will indeed,' Matthew said. 'Now, between ourselves, we have had to disagree with Nurse Webb.'

'Ah! So I have heard. In normal circumstances, I would support her to the hilt. But from what you have told me, I can't this time. What we can do, when the young man is better, is suggest he writes to his family himself.'

To my surprise, Matthew asked tentatively, 'Perhaps I could write – in confidence, of course – to my cousin and just say that Jeremy is safe with friends?'

Bea pulled a face. 'That military man, Matthew? A soldier might feel honour-bound to say where he suspects the lad is lurking.'

'*Lurking?* You make him sound like Shakespeare's Edgar,' Ellis guffawed. 'Dear me, I so enjoy our evenings of play-reading. But I fear they must be suspended if you think our patient would find them intimidating.'

'Only if he were required to read. But he might enjoy sketching us, or even providing sound effects if such things are called for. But *Macbeth* and *King Lear*: is it time we chose something a little less . . . tragic?' Matthew pulled a face. 'My apologies for the pun.'

Jeremy was still asleep when I slipped into the Family wing the following morning.

Nurse Webb clearly disapproved. 'I like to have all my patients washed and tidied up before breakfast, Mrs Rowsley, but Doctor Page has given very clear instructions. The young man is to sleep his sleep out.'

'And then?'

'I would prefer to keep him here under my eye until Doctor Page has seen him. But he has a difficult labour to attend to, so I would not anticipate his arrival before patients' dinner or even beyond.'

Like our colleagues, the patients had their main meal at midday.

I nodded. 'Is there any reason why he should not read? I can send up whatever he might fancy. Periodicals, some amusing novels?'

'If he is an undergraduate, might he not want more serious reading?' She sounded genuinely affronted.

'Between ourselves, I think he might have had enough of that for a few days at least.' I smiled. 'A pencil and some paper might be welcome.' She would think, perhaps, he would be writing home; I suspected he might sketch his fellow patients.

Much as I loved my little excursions to the halt in the grounds, today I thought it might be more appropriate – or, in truth, more intimidating – to despatch Dan, in his formal livery, to meet the police photographer and Sergeant Swain.

It was a very hangdog policeman who presented himself in Matthew's office just before ten. He had had a telegraph announcing that the photographer was unavailable till the following day.

'So how will you be occupying yourself?' Matthew asked Sergeant Swain as if he had a right to. 'I understand that you have not yet interviewed any of the indoor staff here, nor most of the outdoor men.'

He stared. 'You don't suspect them, surely.'

'Indeed, no. But they hear and see things, they pick up gossip. I am sure Constable Pritchard did his utmost to be thorough, but you saw how ill he was.' In other words, he was making sure the sergeant did not disappear back to his office having made no attempt to make progress. As I saw it, he was risking yet another invitation to inspect the head, but I kept my counsel.

It was Ellis's professional opinion, given in the middle of the afternoon, that Jeremy could leave the hospital area and become the guest he had always hoped to be.

I suggested the three of us might dine very informally in our private sitting room, which was on the same floor as Jeremy's. He arrived, splendidly swathed in what was probably one of his lordship's dressing gowns, on the chair on wheels. Luke and Matthew transferred him to a dining chair, adjusting his footstool. If the dining table was really a picnic trestle table, none of us cared.

He did not want to talk; that was clear. So neither of us asked him to explain what had happened in the last sixty hours. Instead, we brought him up to date on what had made us cut short our longed-for adventure and forsake friends old and new.

'A head? Your icehouse?' he gasped at last.

'Exactly. The head of a complete stranger, whom the good sergeant wanted me to identify,' Matthew said dourly. 'When I declined, he finally agreed to get help from the police photographer in Birmingham.'

Jeremy nodded appreciatively. 'Very modern town. So many discoveries. So much innovation. Police using cameras! Amazing!'

Matthew told him about Francis' enthusiasm for photography, especially for his archaeological work. 'If the weather improves, we will take you to see what they have done. Mind you, I should imagine that for a few days the whole site will be under water, despite the tarpaulins covering everything.'

'Please!'

'And if it rains, we'll show you the House. Do you know, you can actually play skittles in the long gallery?'

At last, as with a satisfied sigh Jeremy patted his lips with his napkin and set it beside his empty plate, I felt able to ask, 'Did you bring your sketch pad? No? I am sure our friend Mr Wilson will be able to procure one, and whatever paints and pencils you want, in Shrewsbury. He can send them or bring them when he comes. Could you write down a list of everything you need? You'll find paper on the desk of your room.' Dared I mention writing home? On the whole, I thought it was better not to disturb his equilibrium. 'Can you manage dessert? Mrs Arden, the wonderful cook, will be very disappointed if you don't try her perfect apple pie . . .'

He tried it and clearly thought of asking for more. But by now his head was nodding.

I accompanied him as Matthew manoeuvred him to his bedchamber, where Luke was waiting to act as his valet. Our young colleague had transformed the polite, bland room into a place of refuge. We had chosen a pile of books to stack on the desk. The lamps were trimmed so that if Jeremy had the energy, reading would be a tempting option. There was indeed plenty of writing paper. A nightshirt was warming in front of the fire. There was even a pair of slippers beside the bed.

As we bade him goodnight, I prayed his mind might soon be as comfortable as his body should be.

ELEVEN

To do him justice, Sergeant Swain was as disconcerted as I was, though perhaps less furious, when no one got off the eleven-fifteen train from Birmingham at Thorncroft halt.

'Perhaps the silly bugger got off at the village station,' he suggested.

'Let's go and see, shall we?' I clicked Paragon into action. He responded willingly, almost seeming to regret being brought to a halt a couple of miles later.

Sergeant Swain clearly did not. I let him go in search of his colleague; he might as well enquire for telegraphs while he was there.

He returned puce with rage, waving a piece of paper. 'The idiots need him in Birmingham today. He will try to come tomorrow! Dear Lord, give me patience!'

'And me too,' I added. 'Well, Sergeant, what do you propose?'

'Won't you just *look*, Mr Rowsley? Not touch. Just look?'

'Would you rather I were sick on my boots or on yours?'

'Ah. What about that missus of yours – she's tough, goodness knows.'

'Would you ask *your* wife?' I asked rhetorically. A friend would have been worried by the coldness of my voice.

He shuffled. 'No, but . . . the two are quite different.'

Now my voice was arctic. 'Indeed? In what way?' That was cruel; who could compare with Harriet? 'Listen, Sergeant, telegraph them again and warn them that the Thorncroft estate, representing Lord Croft, will lodge a complaint with the chief constable unless a photographer – or an artist – arrives by three this afternoon. Any later and there won't be enough light, will there?' I summoned a lad strolling along the street. 'Take Paragon's head for me, will you, Tom? Walk him if necessary but make sure you're never out eyeshot of the station; I shall need you immediately I come out.'

'Very good, gaffer.'

'A bright lad,' I told Sergeant Swain as we walked into the station again. Unsurprisingly, he bolted off to send his telegraph.

I buttonholed the porter – Tom's brother, Arthur, a rising star in our cricket team. 'This murder, Arthur; what have you heard about it? You and the other lads? You see, I can't believe a stranger turns up here out of thin air, so I'm betting that he came on the train?'

'Ah. That man you came in with was asking me, and I did say I'd talk to folk – which I did – but he never came back.'

I grinned. 'Well, I'm here now and I'm asking you.'

Arthur gave the sort of smile I was used to seeing as I bowled and he knew he could take a catch in the slips with those soup-plate hands of his. 'Well, there was a gentleman travelling that no one knew. But this is a railway, sir, and a railway transports all sorts of people who've never been here before and we've never seen before. I managed to find out one way or another he'd got on the train at Birmingham, sir. But then, so many trains come and go from a town that big, and I've no idea where he started out from.'

'Did anyone here speak to him?'

'Well, he spoke to another porter, like.'

'Is he on duty today?'

'Ah. That's him over there. Bob. Bob Timms.' He put two fingers to his mouth and whistled.

Timms lumbered over, a man big enough to carry a trunk on his shoulder if necessary. Yes, he remembered the man well enough, he admitted without enthusiasm. 'His voice was one you could hear from t'other end of the platform. Not shouting – didn't have to shout. Like those gentlemen who came to dig up those old Romans. But not one of them as I recognized.'

Could he have been an actor, used to projecting his voice to the back of an auditorium? 'Did he tip well?' I asked with a grin.

'Not badly enough to make you accidentally drop his case, that's all.'

His colleague smothered a laugh.

'Do you think you might describe his face if someone drew what you told him to?'

Timms grimaced. 'I don't forget faces, gaffer. They just stick here. But as for the words to make someone else see them – no.' He shook his head. 'And before you say it, I'm not keen on seeing him again now he's been hacked about. A tickle stomach, that's what I've got.' A whistle announced the arrival of a local train. ''Scuse me, gaffer. Ah, thank you kindly, gaffer.' He pocketed the coin I gave him unobtrusively.

I shook Arthur's hand too, with a slightly larger coin, as he went off to join Timms.

'I hope I didn't see money changing hands there, Mr Rowsley,' Sergeant Swain declared.

'I hope you did! He's a good man and needs encouragement. He's bright enough to pick up more information quite unobtrusively when he hears it – and to get his mate to pass it on to me. And thus you, Sergeant. Our man caught the train at Birmingham; he had a carrying voice like an actor's.'

Sergeant Swain brightened. 'And would this porter—?'

'He gets queasy easily, so I'd wager the answer is no. I wouldn't be the one to ask him anyway,' I said pointedly.

Sergeant Swain pulled a face and headed off to speak to him. He did not choose the best moment. Arthur was carrying a case in each hand, with one under each arm. He swung them easily and gently into Newcombe's trap. Arthur did not wish to be interrupted and lose his tip; Newcombe did not, it seemed, wish to interrupt his conversation with his guest and talk further with the officer. At last, Newcombe set his trap in motion, and Arthur chose to notice the sergeant. Looking ostentatiously around to see if anyone else needed assistance, he at last listened to his questions. Even from where I stood, I could see a firm shake of the head. He repeated it as Sergeant Swain jabbed his chest. And then help came in the form of another passenger and he was able to escape. The sergeant watched, arms akimbo, while he pointed and retreated through a door marked 'Private'.

He was clearly not in a good mood when he returned to me. 'Might I trouble you to drive me to the police house?' It sounded a good deal more like an order than a request. 'It's time Pritchard was back on duty, not lying around in bed.'

It was a walk of some hundred and fifty yards, but I acquiesced, asking ironically, as I brought Paragon to a halt, if I should wait. He gaped, as if it was obvious I should be at his beck and call.

For poor Pritchard's sake, I did wait, though the sergeant lingered so long I regretted it. And then out slipped Aggie, his wife, who had once been nurse to the Newcombes' children.

'It's a sin, Mr Rowsley, it is, truly. Poor Elias has got such a fever, and he can't speak, no, not a word, and that wretched man is making him force the sound out. Even if he was well enough to go out, what good would a silent constable be?'

'Mrs Arden has a wonderful remedy for bad throats; I'll get some sent down for the lad.'

'Thank you kindly, Mr Rowsley. Heavens, the man's making enough noise for two,' she added, as Sergeant Swain's stentorian voice rang out.

'Louder, man! Make some effort! Well, I shall put you on charge for dumb insolence and dereliction of duty!'

I smiled at her. 'Let him but try, Aggie. And he'll have me to answer to. Would you hold Paragon for just a minute?'

My presence made the constable's bedchamber very full. 'Just get back into bed, Pritchard. Lie down before you fall down,' I said, adding a straight-faced lie: 'Doctor Page is very worried that you may have the putrid throat that's going round the village. His message is to do nothing, nothing at all, till he has seen you. Don't even try to argue. You know the estate will settle his bill. Very well, Sergeant, now that you have wished our invalid well, I think for your own safety you should leave. This is an infection you cannot risk catching. I'll drop you at the inn, where you may get some bread and cheese while you wait for the reply to your telegraph.'

His eyes popped. 'But what if—?'

'If necessary, the landlord will find someone to bring you up to the House. If there is no progress and you have to return to Shrewsbury, send him up with a note. I can't dawdle here any longer – I have my own duties to attend to. I hope to see you later, Sergeant. Actually, shall we meet at the icehouse? It would save you having to make your way to the House, after all.'

His eyes gleamed. 'So you will—?'

'Absolutely not! I hope you'll be better soon, Elias.'

An hour or so later, my correspondence at least in some sort of order, over lunch I regaled Harriet and young Jeremy with my morning's adventures – adding, shamefaced, how I had stranded the sergeant.

'Sometimes people with a little power like the sergeant get above themselves,' she said.

'Which is what I fear happened to me,' I confessed. 'I bullied the bully. And should not have done.' But could I bring myself to apologize? I feared not. But I must be less icily courteous and more helpful. If he managed to organize any colleagues to help, of course.

'You know, I doubt if he realized what you were doing. The man has the hide of a pachyderm, Jeremy. Not at all like the sergeant who has solved crimes here before. Now, the sun is shining – it's pretty watery, but it is sunshine – what would you like to do? I am sure that Doctor Page would recommend some fresh air, and I am happy to drive round the grounds with you, provided Robin can be persuaded to leave his stable.'

The young man looked from one of us to the other with a seraphic smile. 'Go with Matthew to meet this sergeant. If he turns up. Take some paper – anything will do – please.'

Even I was disconcerted. Then I recalled the sangfroid with which he had dealt with a corpse on my cousin's estate and the amazing quality of his work. 'If you're sure, I'd love your company,' I said sincerely. 'But I trust you will understand if I don't share your enthusiasm for the sight.'

He laughed. 'Go now? Sun's shining.'

'The sergeant has the key,' I warned him, 'so I'll need to get the spare one from the butler's key cupboard.'

Jeremy saw me weakening. 'Be ready like this!' He clicked his fingers. 'Need paper. Pencils. A lot. Damp bread. Excuse me!' Dabbing his mouth with his napkin, he rose to his feet and, as fast as he could on his crutches, he bolted. He darted back in. 'A piece of board to support the paper. Some clothes-pegs.' And he was gone again.

'The young, God bless them!' I said. 'And there we thought we would have to mollycoddle him as an invalid! But why would he want bread?'

'No idea. But I'll get some. Do you think that ordinary writing paper will do?'

'Anything that doesn't have lines, I'd say. Ah! The larger sheets you used when you were planning the new village. I'll find some little lavender bags. We can tie them under our noses with scarves. That should help . . .'

If anything, it was Jeremy who mollycoddled me at the icehouse, not I him. Once I had unlocked the padlock and the two heavy doors, one a yard or so inside the building, he simply took over, easing me to one side with his crutches as if I were an aged uncle. I did not protest. I indulged in a long one-way conversation with the pony. I suspect he was more interested in the apples I carried than in my anxiety at leaving the lad alone in there.

Was he taking an unconscionable time? It felt like it. Then a halloo told me that I had company. Striding along the path towards me was Sergeant Swain. Alone.

'And what might you be doing?' he demanded. 'That's evidence in there, that is!'

'Good afternoon, Sergeant,' I said as if we had just met at a church fête. I added more coolly, 'I take it that no expert photographer is forthcoming?'

'Who's that and what does he think he's doing? All masked as if he's going to rob a bank. You too,' he added accusingly.

'He is Mr Jeremy Turton, a gentleman from Oxford who has previously worked with the Herefordshire Constabulary.' Heavens, if only we had the intelligent young sergeant we had worked with there! 'His drawings and keen eyesight helped solve two terrible murders at Clunston Park. As for masks, if you wish to go any closer, you are welcome to mine. No?'

Perhaps he did not hear.

But his eyes opened wide when Jeremy emerged with half a dozen sketches. As did mine. Surely I had once seen the owner of that head. But for the life of me I could not remember where.

TWELVE

Why should I be just pacing up and down the library, always my refuge in any emotional storm? Why stride purposelessly, when I could either seek inspiration in one of the great tomes or – more prosaically – look for the will which might or might not be concealed there? Why had Mrs Marchbanks declared that her husband had deliberately hidden something that would change our lives? Why, without telling me where it might be hidden? Though I would deny it, I knew she had taken away my peace – not least because should the will ever be found, the contents could change what mattered most in my life, my relationship with Matthew. It had already done harm: never before had I deliberately kept a secret from him.

My feet kept walking.

I must think of something else, though the icehouse brought no relief. I was torn. I was sure I could have dealt with the sight of the head better than Matthew and should in truth have offered to spare him the horror. But to do so might have made him question his . . . his worth . . . as a man. As for young Jeremy, why on earth had I helped, even encouraged, the young invalid to deal with so vile a task? In vain did I tell myself he positively relished the idea, that he was using a God-given skill. What if it gave him a memory he could never erase? The sort that would wake him, shaking and crying out in the night?

By now, not just my feet but my hands were moving of their own accord – they wrung invisible cloths as if I were Lady Macbeth.

No, I had done no one any physical harm; yes, I had exposed a vulnerable friend to mental strife. He had sought us out as a refuge, not to have his talent exploited.

At last, it dawned on me that someone was knocking on the library door – with some urgency.

'Come in. Ah, Dick!' I said stupidly.

He stepped forward, looking at me anxiously. 'Are you all right?'

'You know where Jeremy has gone? To look at the head, for goodness' sake! And I let him!'

His laugh was like a dose of medicine. 'And if you'd tried to stop him? Oh, Mrs Rowsley, would he have taken a jot of notice? Luke says he's got something worrying him – something deep, he reckons – but even that and that bad ankle of his don't mean he's not a lad with a lad's life to lead. And from the look on his face as he set out, he thinks he's involved in one big adventure.'

'Thank you, Dick. It's just that I can't stop worrying—'

'With respect, Mrs Rowsley, something arrived that might take your mind off young Mr Turton. It's a letter for you and Mr Rowsley. I know you like to deal with such things together, but with him . . . otherwise engaged, you might say . . . I wondered if you wanted to open it, and if so, where? It's very chilly in here, with no fire lit, isn't it?'

It seemed as though I was being taken care of. The very notion made me feel better.

We walked as one to the state drawing room which had so intimidated Sergeant Swain; the fire burned brightly and a tray of tea lay enticingly on a table beside the letter on its salver.

'Mr Wilson's writing,' I said.

'I will ask Hannah to ensure that his usual rooms are aired – just in case,' he added with a grin, tossing my motto back at me as he bowed his way out.

Were good servants born with such powers of anticipation or did we learn them from our predecessors? My dear young colleague had been absolutely right. Montgomery did indeed propose a visit. He anticipated being accompanied by Mr Baker, with whom he understood we were already acquainted, and perhaps Mrs Baker, travelling direct from London. Would Friday be a convenient day for them to arrive? If he did not hear from us, he and Mr Baker would arrive on the ten-past-four train at the halt. He would telegraph us once he had ascertained if and when Mrs Baker would arrive.

Finishing my tea, I carried the tray down to the servants' hall. My arrival coincided with servants' tea, so I sat down with them at the long table. If everyone was anxious about their future, the least I could do was share hard facts with them. Yes, the familiar figure of Montgomery, always polite and unassuming, would soon be amongst them, as would the heir who had caused them all so much alarm. Yes, and possibly his wife too. Yes, we must expect company: the trustees must meet him, of course. Yes, neighbouring gentry might dine too, but surely not until the Bakers had been their guests.

'It's going to be busy, then,' Hannah observed. Then she smiled a correction. 'Busier, ma'am. It'll be a bit sad – no, that's the wrong word – if he doesn't like the place and goes back home, won't it?'

'Yes,' I agreed. 'A bit of an anticlimax.'

She snapped her fingers. 'That's the word, ma'am. Thank you, ma'am.' Some might have found her grin familiar rather than respectful, but I smiled back. Then I turned to the youngest at the table. 'And it's a good word for you to learn, Rosie. How is your list of new hard words getting on?'

Rosie had got as far as *benevolent* when we heard the sound of the trap in the yard. Rosie hot on his heels, Dan immediately disappeared to deal with Robin. The sergeant, very much on duty again, hovered, clearly longing for a hot cup of tea, but too superior to ask for it. Bea, bustling in to take her place at the table, solved the problem: 'You're in the way there, Sergeant. Join the gentlemen round the fire, if you wish, or sit down at the table. Oh, take that cape off, do, and hang it in the passage with the others. Thank you. Now, you two: will you take a pew? Anywhere!'

Matthew, clutching what looked like Jeremy's sketches, sat beside me. The only space left for the artist himself was next to Hannah, who was in charge of the teapot. Her behaviour was modest and entirely respectful, but I could see that she did not object to having the young man sit beside her. It was easy, when he was ill or thwarted in mid-sentence, to forget his good looks, but, bright-eyed and slightly windswept after his afternoon's activities, he was handsome. On the other hand, her beauty might render him completely tongue-tied. For the time being, however, he was not required to speak but to just make sure his crutches did not slide sideways and hit her.

Bea caught my eye and winked. 'Tell us, Sergeant, are we safe to sleep in our beds yet?'

'I am in possession of certain information which I shall impart to my superiors,' he conceded.

'And perhaps to some of his lordship's trustees,' I said. 'I'm sure by now you know the way things are run here.'

He mumbled something.

'Perhaps we should adjourn to my office,' Matthew said, 'as soon as we have finished our tea,' he added as I kicked his ankle. 'Mr Turton has been more than helpful. Will you join us too, Jeremy?' He saved him from having to reply by gathering up the sketches and getting to his feet.

'But these are scarcely suitable for a delicate female eye!' the sergeant objected, before realizing that he had another problem as Bea stood too.

'Are they not?' she asked cheerfully. 'The trouble is, Sergeant, that I too have the honour of being a trustee and need to be kept abreast of anything that affects the House and the Family. But I warn you all in advance: it will have to be a short meeting, or I can't guarantee that everyone's dinner will be ready tonight!' Another wink at me: Bea would produce a feast whatever the circumstances.

Matthew's office was undoubtedly crowded, our skirts and their voluminous petticoats not helping. But he clearly wanted to make the whole thing as swift and businesslike as possible. He drew a chair up so that Jeremy might join him behind the desk, on which lay the sketches, face down. Then he added one at the side for the sergeant. When we were all settled, he simply tapped Jeremy on the arm. It was time. He lifted the first sketch.

The face might have been a sketch of one of the Roman statues unearthed during the summer. It was that of a man in his later years, his face fleshy enough to suggest high living. He was balding. Mercifully, Jeremy had allowed his pencil to stop short of where . . . No, I could not quite frame the words. Did he look in any way familiar? I tried to shut down the very notion. And yet . . . No. I would not swoon. Would not. Would clenching my fists help? If only I could breathe!

'You wouldn't want to meet him on a dark night, would you?' Bea observed matter-of-factly. 'Looks a nasty piece of knitting, if you ask me. A thug.'

I nodded slowly. Yes, talking might help. 'But they say his clothes were those of a gentleman—'

'Aye, a rich one too,' Sergeant Swain said. 'According to your husband.' A glance from Matthew prompted him to add, 'I have removed the tailor's label from the deceased's garments – Messrs Gieves – and asked my Scotland Yard colleagues to enquire about possible clients.'

'Not the clothes themselves?' I asked, surprised I could sound so calm. 'Ah, perhaps not. But perhaps some of the cleaner fabric? And certainly they might have one of Mr Turton's excellent sketches.'

Silently, Jeremy removed one from his collection and passed it, face down, along the table. Sergeant Swain shifted uneasily.

Matthew reached for an envelope. 'You could pin some fabric to it,' he said pointedly.

Jeremy flushed to his ears. The poor boy. Yet he was more coherent than I feared. 'Sure I've seen him before.' He covered his face with his hands. 'No. Sorry.' And then smiled. 'Ah. Oxford. But no idea where. Don't go to prize fights!' He tailed off in desperation.

Matthew clicked his fingers in irritation. 'Heavens, I've just remembered what one of the village station porters said. Apparently, he had a very carrying voice. Not loud. Didn't need to shout. He just – what do actors call it? – he just *projected*, in the way some of our archaeologist guests do.' He glanced at Jeremy, whose mouth was working furiously. 'Ex-public school, ex-university, would you think?'

Jeremy nodded vigorously. 'Phwaah, phwaah, phwaah!' he said, projecting well himself. Then he blushed scarlet.

Bea jumped in. 'Sergeant, could you send one of those sketches to the Oxford Police?'

Matthew shook his head. 'Sadly, it's not as simple as that, is it, Sergeant? There are two sets of Oxford police: the Bulldogs, who are employed by the University itself – yes, I promise you I am telling the truth! – and the others, who are employed by the city. One lot works in the day, the other at night.'

'Quite right, sir. Now, I'm thinking that if you gentlemen know Oxford, you must know some of the people there. So perhaps you should ask your friends—'

Before Matthew could explode, Jeremy said, 'Might have seen him recently. Not around my college. No.' He peeled off two sketches. 'There, one for Town, one for Gown.'

Silently, Matthew produced envelopes. 'You might just catch the last post, Sergeant. Shall I summon a trap for you?'

The sergeant heaved a sigh of relief. 'Would you, sir? I'd take that very kindly.' He looked at his watch. 'I must be on my way if I'm to collect that coat from Pritchard and catch my train home.'

'And arrange,' Matthew said pointedly, 'for the undertaker to visit the icehouse tomorrow and remove our uninvited guest.' He reached for the bell.

The sergeant leaving the building and Bea leaving us to return to her kitchen, there was a moment of calm in Matthew's office. I broke the silence.

'Jeremy, forgive me but I need to talk seriously, if I may? You came here for peace and quiet, and you know we want you to stay as long as you like. Till Christmas and beyond. But now I'm afraid you won't be here on your own. On Friday, the House is to receive unexpected guests: Mr Wilson, whom you've met, of course, Mr Baker, whom Mr Wilson believes is his lordship's heir, and possibly Mrs Baker.' Before he could respond, I would take a risk. 'Your family and friends – do they know you're safe here?'

He tapped his nose. 'Tutor thinks I'm at home. Family think I'm still up in Oxford. Friends think I'm on a walking tour with other friends.'

'So you don't want any of them to know any different?'

He shook his head emphatically. 'If I'm in the way, I could go on that walk.'

'In the way!' Matthew repeated, tactfully refraining from pointing out that he would be walking nowhere for a matter of weeks at least. 'My dear fellow, do you know how many rooms there are in this place? Over sixty. There's plenty of room for everyone. There always will be as long as we trustees are in charge. Whether you want to meet Wilson and the Americans, mixing with them at meals and so on, or whether you want to keep to rooms where they will not go, and eat on your own – that decision is yours. Yours alone. We will not press you. And it can change from day to day.'

He nodded, as if weighing up his options. Then he asked, pulling a face. 'This new heir? Changes afoot?'

'Who knows? But I should imagine he can't do much as long as his lordship is alive.'

'Big temptation!' He spread his hands to encompass the House and all its treasures. And then he yawned, hugely, uninhibitedly, like a child.

The office clock struck half past six, and we were ready to go and change for dinner when Luke knocked on the door. 'Is it too late for you to see a visitor? Bob Timms – yes, the porter – has just arrived and is asking for you, Mr Rowsley.'

THIRTEEN

'Give us five minutes, please, and then show him in. And, Luke, perhaps Mrs Arden might be able to hold dinner back by ten minutes? Maybe fifteen? We both need to hear him.'

'If Mrs Arden can't, no one can,' he responded, bowing as he left.

Harriet looked at Jeremy. 'I know you could get to your bedchamber unaided, but you've had a long day, and I think you could do with an arm to lean on. Might I suggest that when he returns, you ask Luke to assist you? He'll want to help you if you decide to change for dinner – no, nothing formal! He'll advise. And, Jeremy, if you want to rest for a few minutes, just tell him.'

Having delivered Bob, Luke helped Jeremy out – not like an orderly, more like a friend helping an injured team-mate from a field of play.

Bob gaped, open-eyed as well as open-mouthed, in something like terror. Thank goodness we were in my office, plain and businesslike. As he bowed, fumbling with his cap, I pushed a chair forward as Harriet smiled a welcome. She might well have known him since he was a boy.

Writhing with embarrassment, he sat, perching on the edge and still worrying his cap.

'You've got more news for me, eh, Bob?' I sat myself, hoping it would make him feel more comfortable.

He managed a grin. ''Deed I have, gaffer. I just had this thought, see. That none of us can recall carrying the gentleman's bag for him – and that sort of gentleman would never carry his own, mind. So I got to thinking, what if it was in left luggage? And there it was, sitting there, proud as punch. At least, it might be his,' he added doubtfully. 'It's the only one there, see, and Sam Higgs, who's in charge of the office, says it's been there since the day a smart gentleman came.'

'Any luggage labels?' I asked urgently.

He shook his head, as if he had known I would ask and he had known he would disappoint me. 'So I'm wondering, gaffer, what I should do. I was going to bring it to show you, only Sam said no.'

'I think Sam was right. But I tell you who you should take it to: Constable Pritchard. He's laid up with a bad cold but he's surely well enough to lock it up safely.'

'Ah, it's safe enough where it is for now, gaffer. He might be feeling better tomorrow, mightn't he? – well enough to open it, like, and maybe he'd want a witness, such as yourself, gaffer.' We exchanged a grin. 'I might just take it to the police house at – what, nine o'clock? – sir.'

'That would be a very good time,' I said. 'I might just be passing the police house myself then. In which case, I'd see you.' I stood.

He took the hint and stood too.

'Are you happy to walk or would you like Dan to take you back home?' I asked, only to kick myself for being tactless.

He flushed to his ears. 'I got my old dog tied up outside, thank 'ee. He might just see a rabbit for the pot.'

'Of course. Happy rabbiting, Bob. Here, just in case you work up a thirst.' The coin probably represented a week's wages. He'd feel its size but not demean himself by checking in front of me.

He bobbed low to both of us, with a special tug of the forelock for Harriet, who gave him the warmest of smiles. Heavens, she was going to escort him out!

'Tell me, Bob, how's young Jessie these days . . .?'

Thursday morning dawned unexpectedly fine, and Esau and I could step out into sunshine, feeble though it was at this time of the year. Though I suspected that Pritchard would have his own unofficial collection of useful keys, I took Dick's – 'just in case', as Harriet said as she pressed them on me.

Pritchard, already dressed but not in his uniform, was looking much better.

'Doctor Page says he still mustn't talk,' his wife said, adding cheerfully, 'It means he has to listen to me for a change. Can I make you a cup of tea, Mr Rowsley? Oh, that's very kind of you,' she added, taking the bag Harriet and Bea had filled for them.

Bob arrived before I could explain the reason for my visit. I had expected Pritchard's eyes to light up, but his face was full of doubt. He shook his head vigorously when I suggested he might open it.

'Shouldn't I wait till Sergeant Swain is here?' he whispered.

'Are you expecting him today? Just nod or shake your head, man!'

He shook it.

I could have said any number of things, but it seemed unfair in the circumstances to say any of them. 'I suggest that we open it, so you can send for him urgently if there's anything of interest. A name, for instance.' I grinned. 'Look, if I use our keys, you can say it was already open! In fact, leave Bob and me to it and come back surprised and shocked!'

It took several attempts to open it, but at last a key slid in sweetly and turned without protest.

With a laugh, Bob fetched our host. The young policeman unpacked deftly, taking care to crease nothing. Soon there was a small pile on his desk and a puzzled expression on his face. Looking at me, he spread his hands.

'There are no names, no initials, on anything, Pritchard!' I said, trying to spare his throat. 'All such good-quality items – look at that brush. You'd expect to find initials on that cartouche – the little shield-shaped plate.'

Bob shook his head. 'No letters. No diary. No name in that book there. I know Sam sometimes has to open cases in front of people who say they've lost their receipt, and there's usually something with their name on. Actually,' he continued slowly, 'there's not much in there at all. Nightshirt. Change of socks and underwear. He didn't mean to stay very long, did he?'

Pritchard shrugged sadly and started repacking, checking and rechecking every item. 'No further forward,' he rasped. 'And nothing left in his pockets, either! But you didn't hear me say that, Bob Timms!'

'No I didn't, not hardly. Lemon and honey, that's what you need, man, with a drop of rum to help it down.'

'That's what Mrs Arden has sent you,' I said. 'No rum, as far

as I know. But I know that cordial of hers warms the cockles of
your heart.' Possibly because it involved a large quantity of
whisky. 'Now, I am going to visit Mr Newcombe and ask him
to send for a Scotland Yard detective, whatever Sergeant Swain
thinks of the idea. With luck, the sergeant has caught your cold
and won't be able to tell us.' I paused. 'And, you know, I think
you put your finger on something, Bob. He didn't mean to stay
very long, you said. He came with something in mind, I'd say
– and was going to leave as soon as he'd done it.'

'So where would a gentleman like him have stayed – assuming
he'd got the chance?' Pritchard asked. 'At the Royal Oak?' Then
he shook his head. 'Not really. Not unless he had the private
parlour and all.'

'I could ask the innkeeper, Marty Baines, if he had heard of him
on the way home.' I said. 'Now, lad, you've used that voice of
yours more than enough. Go and try some of Mrs Arden's special
mixture, and you'll be ordering Sergeant Swain around tomorrow!'

Marty Baines, one of the trustees, was to my mind one of the
most interesting men in the village. Though he was a stalwart of
the Methodist church, he not only drank himself but also sold
ale to others – just not enough to let them get drunk or to eat
very deeply into their meagre labourers' wages. I had never heard
anyone, man or woman, say a bad word about him. Many used
him as a sort of father confessor, pouring out their woes and
getting sound advice back – safe in the knowledge that he never
gossiped about their private affairs. If, on the other hand, a topic
was generally known in the village, he was more than happy to
join in the conversation and have a good chinwag.

He greeted me in his yard, where he was apparently rebuking
his latest stable lad – who slunk away and was soon sweeping
and shovelling as if he were cleaning the Augean stables.

'Is it about the interviews for the headmaster next week?
Actually I hear it might actually be a head *mistress*,' he added
with a quizzical grin. 'Or about the murder?' he greeted me,
ushering me into his own quarters.

'The latter – though we must find some time to discuss the
questions we want to put. Personally, I wonder if five of us on
the interview panel is too many – a bit intimidating, even . . .'

At last, we turned to what I really needed to know: what, if anything, had he heard about the murdered man and the dismemberment of his body?

He shook his head. 'Not a lot. My drayman thinks he saw him – at any rate, a "gentleman" veering off the lane to Thorncroft House into Farmer Twiss's woods. But he might have been answering a call of nature. Or,' and he paused for some effect, 'or he might have been going in search of a girl the drayman thinks he heard singing. Hmm.' Another pause. Then a smile. 'And yes, I did tell young Pritchard, and he'll have told that sergeant of his. Trouble is, Matthew, it gets us no further forrader, does it?'

I thought of the voice I had heard as we escorted Mr Baker round the House, but for the time being kept my own counsel.

Tertius Newcombe, receiving me in his study, frowned. 'Coffee?' He rang, gesturing me to a seat. Study it might be, but it was a most elegant room, with wonderful views across his well-maintained fields to tempt him from his daily work – much of which, rumour had it, was done by a most accomplished secretary. Yes, I told myself, it was time I renewed my efforts to find a suitable candidate for the role at Thorncroft.

Until the footman had taken his orders and returned to serve us, we exchanged village gossip. Was Mr Pounceman, our rector, tending to Methodism? How did we find the new blacksmith? And was it not gratifying to see that families were already moving into the first of the model village cottages.

At last, he turned to the topic that interested me most. 'So the esteemed Sergeant Swain has made no progress! He assured me that he expected to solve the case within a week. He further assured me he had evidence that the victim is not his lordship's heir. I hardly had the heart to tell him the whole village knew. Please thank Harriet for her note informing us – but our Boots got in first! I do believe there's a sort of osmosis that lets rural news permeate the village so quickly.'

'It certainly seems that way. Sometimes I make deliberate use of it, I must confess. And I would like to feel sorry for Sergeant Swain as he has to deal with the matching system of keeping mum about inconvenient truths – or information they would prefer outsiders did not know.'

'I don't know how Sergeant Swain can know anything if he's not here. Surely he isn't trying to solve cases in Shrewsbury as well as dealing with this murder.'

I snorted. 'I wouldn't be surprised. At the very least, he seems to have no support from anyone, and certainly not the neighbouring constabularies that ought to be helping him. I am furious, Newcombe, furious. As far as I know, the head still lies in our icehouse, though at least the body has been removed. I rather forced a very talented artist on Sergeant Swain yesterday, and I trust he will despatch the portraits of the victim to Scotland Yard for them to assist – even arm's-length support would be helpful. In fact, this morning I did something highly irregular, which has set me thinking. You will recall that the victim was robbed of anything and everything that might identify him.'

'Yes, by one of Pecker O'Malley's less respectable men, I suspect. O'Malley's going to speak to some of them – but I suspect that the killer and his accomplices have long since found it prudent to head to Ireland to sit out the winter there. Look, Rowsley, Adelaide and Harriet believe the dead man was punished for something he did to young women. They used the polite word "interfering" – I suspect that he raped one of the gypsy women and paid the appropriate price. Yes?' He shot the sort of searching glance I suspect he favoured when on duty as a JP.

I did not need to be an intimidated witness to agree. 'Yes, indeed. I think it's very likely, and it might explain why Sergeant Swain doesn't voice the theory "when ladies are present",' I intoned pompously. 'But why should the man be here in the first place – and so anonymously? I suppose you couldn't prevail on Pecker to give us a name if they found one in his wallet and anything else they stole?' I struck my thigh in frustration. 'Damn! I'm assuming he can read, of course. And that the murderers kept their booty, which I should imagine is long since sold or melted down.'

'I tried. Don't think I didn't. But he seemed genuinely not to know. I'll ride out for another chat with him if that would help. I'd suggest you come along, but he really doesn't care for unauthorized visitors, you know.' He threw his head back and laughed. 'Not that I'm suggesting for one minute that you would treat him as that oaf did. Heavens, man, I thought you'd said he was a good enough chap.'

'That was his predecessor, Sergeant Burrows. Sergeant Swain – I suppose he's showing his inexperience. He throws his weight around with the lower ranks but won't tackle the people with the power to get results. When we were at my cousin's place in Herefordshire, we came across a truly excellent young officer – I wish we could magically transport him over here.' I sighed. 'I believe he's now an inspector in Worcester.'

'Do you know him well enough to invite him up for the weekend? Just as a guest, nothing more? Ah, no! You will have the heir staying with you, will you not?'

'We will indeed – and hope to provide some entertainment for him, just not the sort provided by a visiting police officer. One problem is that Mr Baker not only eschews alcohol himself but will not countenance the demon drink in the same room.'

Mr Newcombe rolled his eyes, then leaned forward, confidentially. 'You know some of Adelaide's family are guests here? Two of them have turned teetotal. No, they don't forbid the rest of us to imbibe – they just sigh and tut and shake their heads. It's quite enough to put a man off his claret. How are his lordship's cellars holding up, by the way?'

I laughed. 'Our archaeology guests certainly had a taste for champagne, but Thatcher has restocked. Yes, when we have to live in the House, Harriet and I still drink a little – but as you'll recall from the accounts we submitted to the trustees last quarter, we pay for all our subsistence.'

His face was suddenly serious. 'What does this heir – Baker – think of your living in the House?'

'I have a terrible fear that despite his polite exterior, he considered that while he came to see the organ-grinder, he only got the monkey – and he rather thought that the animal in question had no place in the building that will be his one day. No matter how well educated, how well read, we might be, we are still servants. And as servants, yes, I suspect we are a lower form of life.'

'Which is how many servants are treated. But I would say there is indeed a proper social hierarchy, Rowsley, and we make radical changes at our peril. A word to the wise, my friend.' He touched his nose. 'Rumour has it you sit down to dinner with your cook. You and I know she is a fellow trustee and likely soon enough to be Mrs Ellis Page, but you can go too far – for some of our neighbours, at least,' he added hastily.

I swallowed my furious response, hoping my confession would be an oblique reply: 'Dear me, Newcombe, we long to be back in the home that came with my post. It is small, intimate. Above all, it is ours. Furniture we chose. Pictures we chose. Books we have time to read.'

He nodded as if he understood. 'There's little point in heating two houses, though. And those art and furniture experts we consulted last spring made it clear that the House and its contents must never be allowed to get damp. Imagine if that Botticelli suffered.' He grinned. 'If there were any risk to it, I could always offer to hang it here. Yes, on that wall . . .'

And such was my day, the better part of it wasted. All I had learned was that some of our neighbours disapproved of our friendship with Bea – and that she was about to be married! That there were clear suspicions, too, that we were living as parasites in the House, when it was the last place we wanted to live out our lives. As for the murder – no, I suppose I had gathered some new information, not least that a woman heard singing in Twiss's woods seemed to have attracted the attention of the man who was probably the victim. I must try to keep that at the front of my mind lest I take out my increasingly foul temper on an innocent person.

FOURTEEN

If Matthew took a cold shower after a day's work, it meant that something had seriously upset or angered him. As we expected Jeremy to join us in our private sitting room at any moment, I would have to wait to question him until we could speak without fear of interruption, and I knew that even then he might not dare to explain lest he lose his temper. Catching me glance anxiously at him, he managed a smile and kissed my hand, retaining it in his until a knock at the door announced the arrival of our guest, supported by Luke. He was very pale, admitting, reluctantly, to being in pain; I suspected he had declined any further laudanum.

Out of the blue, as if to save Jeremy from any questions about his health, Matthew asked something entirely unexpected.

'Have I heard a girl singing?' I repeated. 'Here, in the House?'

'Yes. I heard one the other day, and I need to talk to her.'

'Heard her this morning. Lovely voice.' Jeremy looked anxious. 'Not allowed?'

'Of course it is, especially when there are no guests. But how would that tie in with this murder?'

'Probably not at all,' Matthew said. 'But it's possible she had a lucky escape. If the man – oh, I'm sick of all this speculation! My day has been taken up with talk about it, when in actual fact we can do nothing!' He got to his feet, pacing our sitting room, at imminent risk to the sherry glasses and indeed the decanter itself on the side table. He sat down with some vehemence. 'I'm sorry. Marty tells me his drayman saw a gentleman veer from our lane on to Twiss's property when he heard a young woman singing. And if it's a maid from here, she might just have seen something. Heard something. *Might.*'

Matthew distraught? I put my hand on his. 'I will speak to Hannah tomorrow – no, if you will excuse me, Jeremy, I will go and speak to her now.' And what might I say that did not sound like an accusation that someone had slipped away from the House, someone she was in charge of?

'Singing?' she repeated with a smile as we sat down in the Room. 'A lot of us do, ma'am. I love a good tune myself – but none of us should sing where it might disturb other people, ma'am. Shall I speak to the maids, or would you prefer to?'

'I think you should. Because I— There is a story behind my questions, Hannah.' I repeated what Matthew had said, watching her frown deepen. 'If it was one of our girls, we need her to talk to Constable Pritchard, because she might have witnessed something in the woods.'

She looked genuinely puzzled. 'But we're all at work in the House during the day. Or the laundry. And if there's an errand to do in the village, it's always a footman that goes. You always ran a tight ship, ma'am, and I wouldn't want to let you down by allowing people to slack.'

'None of you slacked today, that's for sure! The place looks as if the Queen herself is coming – you should all be proud of yourselves. Thank you.'

'And we all wear our best uniforms from tomorrow until the guests have gone. Yes, they're all pressed and ready.' She pulled a face. 'Last time you had visitors, I wasn't head housemaid. I nearly forgot that Mrs Baker might need a maid – I've asked Jane, since she's always so smart herself. Oh dear, I'm afraid something will go wrong.'

'It won't. And if it does, Mr Thatcher will always help. And I will. Because I always worry I have forgotten something too – like requesting the piano tuner to come to deal with the instrument in the drawing room as soon as maybe.'

'I sent a message as soon as Mr Turton arrived, ma'am – just in case.' She may have lowered her eyes demurely, but she was teasing me just as the others did.

I had sent a message too, but I would not tell her for anything. 'Well done! Come, Hannah, all this talking! I'm making you late for supper.' I stood. 'You've done very well.'

'Thank you, ma'am – and I'll see to it no one sings tomorrow!' With a curtsy, she held the door open for me.

'Actually, both my husband and Mr Turton say what a good voice someone has. So perhaps you should all sing.'

She laughed. 'Like birds, all shouting each other down. Or – oh, ma'am – altogether, like in a choir? Imagine if we could!'

I clapped my hands. 'And why not? It's a wonderful thought! Funnily enough, Mr Thatcher and I were talking only the other day about things you could all do in your time off – especially, come to think of it, in winter, when you can't get out. Yes, Hannah – that is a truly excellent idea. Please see what everyone else thinks! Oh,' I added, belatedly, 'could you find me a piece of paper and a pen? I'll write a quick note to Mrs Twiss to ask if any of her household might have been the singer the drayman heard. Could you ask Dan to see it's delivered first thing tomorrow? Thank you.'

Dinner was pleasant, but Jeremy was clearly in so much pain that Matthew and Luke bore him off to bed as soon as we had finished dessert. He even consented to my visiting the Family wing to solicit a tiny dose of laudanum for him.

Nurse Webb was no longer on duty, but a senior orderly obliged. 'We did warn him, Mrs Rowsley, but you know what young men are. Anyway, this should get him through the night.'

I asked after Samuel, thinking he might like me to read a psalm to him, but he was already fast asleep. So it was back to our quarters to see if Matthew, after being an unfailingly kind and thoughtful host, was really in a better mood or if he was simply acting.

It was clear he was still distressed by something: his summary of his dealings with Mr Newcombe explained it.

'So our kind neighbours believe we are sponging off the estate!' I exclaimed. No wonder he was so upset. 'Parasites! Dear Lord, have they no idea of the hours that you work? No, how could they, since not one of them does anything but live a life of pleasure – oh, yes, Mr Newcombe may be a Justice, but in a village like this, it is scarcely an onerous role. Your journeys to London and Yorkshire, and yes, to Gloucestershire – all those houses and farms to supervise. I know you have some trusted deputies, but if anything went wrong it would be seen as your fault.'

'The sooner we can move back into our own home the better! What have I said? Harriet?'

This was not the moment to tell him about Mrs Marchbanks's last words to me. 'Let's talk about it when we've seen out this weekend. We have to be here every minute of the day while Mr Baker is here, especially if he wants to see the library . . . and especially if Mrs Baker joins him and needs a female companion in the midst of all you men.' I smiled. 'Young Hannah has already summoned Mr Leigh to tune the piano and organized a maid for Mrs Baker if she doesn't bring her own. And – guess what – she would love to start a staff choir! And, before you ask, she is sure it wasn't one of our maids singing that day, so I've dashed off a note to Mrs Twiss to ask if it might have been one of her girls.'

'You've been very efficient,' he said ruefully, 'after my wasted day.'

'My love, whatever happens, we are a team, are we not?'

Team or not, everyone was jittery the next morning. I sought out Hannah and Dick.

'Remember, both of you, and tell everyone else, that you have dealt with far more visitors than are coming this time. Think back to the summer: all those academics and their students. You coped wonderfully. You will with the three extra guests – just three! – this weekend.'

'But one of them is the future Lord Croft, ma'am. And we've not forgotten the gypsy's warnings,' Dick said. 'Danger. Change.'

'I think with the headless man's death, the danger might be considered over, don't you? And we have coped with change here before and will again, whatever it is. Remember, you are now employed by the trustees, and can't be dismissed on the whim of one man – no, nor one woman, either.' Some irritating part of my brain pinged: hadn't I just misquoted Shakespeare? But there were more important things to worry about, one of which came as a complete surprise.

Billy, the smallest of our footmen, limped towards us. 'Forgive my interruption,' he said, bowing, 'but the presence of Mrs Rowsley is requested in the servants' hall.'

'Thank you, Billy. If you will both excuse me?' I turned and followed him. He was technically still Boots, but as soon as the school opened, he would be one of the first pupils – and be top of the class, if my judgement was right. Some people around the village were inclined to fear or mock him for his disability, but the Thorncroft men and women had come to respect him and love him for his willingness to tackle anything one way or another. No, he could never be the strong tall young man that was an ideal manservant. But he could actually aspire higher than that. Occasionally, when he disappeared under his pile of filing, Matthew would enlist his help – and never regret it.

Now he led me not to the servants' hall but to the Room, where Mrs Twiss sat at the table, a tray of tea at her elbow.

After an exchange of pleasantries, she said, 'You're a busy woman and so am I, Mrs Rowsley. So I'll come straight to the point if I may. My youngest – little May – she came home the other day, and something had scared her. Try as I might, I couldn't get anything out of her. But this morning, with your note in my hand, I tackled her again. And it turns out . . . it turns out this gentleman grabbed her. Now, I've always taught my wenches to stand up for themselves, and you know what some men are. So he grabs her, and she does what I've dinned into her and her sister. Use your head and use your knee. So she did, and scarpered back to the farmhouse as if the devil himself was after her.'

'My goodness – what an escape!' I hoped she didn't see my hands shaking on the table.

'So I asked her, why hadn't she told me this at the time. Turns out, of course, she should have been heading straight to the village, not idling her time away. And then, of course, she's afraid the gentleman will report her for attacking him. And then when she hears what happened to him, she's afraid Constable Pritchard will come arresting her.'

'Does May ever carry a sharp knife? I thought not. Oh, Mrs Twiss, thank God he didn't . . . it's a horrible word, but I must say it . . . thank God he didn't rape her.'

To my amazement, she leaned over and took my hands. 'I know I shouldn't say it, but I'm going to: thank God that gypsy killed him. My only wish is he'd castrated the bastard before he'd killed him, not after, as they do say he did.'

'God forgive us both, then, Mrs Twiss – because I wish so too.' I made such a mess of pouring us fresh tea that she took the pot from me. 'Poor May.' I swallowed. 'Horrible though it is, I truly think Constable Pritchard should know.'

'No! Not my wench, losing her reputation! I'm not having that, and that's flat.' She bit her lip. 'If he asks point-blank if you know of someone he attacked, you shouldn't lie, of course, but in no circumstances, none at all, will you give her name. Or say anything that could help him guess.' She looked at me with such compassion I nearly wept. 'If you want my advice, you'll say nowt unless you have to, my love, because all this is bringing something back to you, isn't it? Sheet-white you went, and trembling like a leaf, for all you tried to be brave. Something you'd rather forget, fast as you can.' Getting up, she patted my shoulder. 'Now, I've got work to do, and I'm sure you have, so I'll be on my way. You know what's best, Mrs Rowsley – and I mean what's best for you too.'

FIFTEEN

I found Harriet emerging from the Room, trying to look her poised and efficient self but failing lamentably to convince me, at least. But the servants' hall was full of eyes and ears, and for nothing would I draw attention to her palpable distress.

Stepping between her and the staff, I said quickly, 'May I have a word in private, please? In the Room or in my office?'

'Your office, please.' I held the door for her. 'Yes?' Tetchy, she turned to Dick.

'Beg pardon, ma'am, Dan brought up the post early today, and I've just sorted it out. I did bring yours to the Room, ma'am, but . . . I could see you weren't yourself, ma'am, and thought it best to let you be. Oh dear, ma'am.' He thrust his handkerchief into her hand.

'Thank you. Oh, Dick, it's people like you being kind to me that always turns me into a watering can!' She managed the faintest of smiles. 'I don't suppose you could bring a pot of very strong coffee to Matthew's office? Bless you!'

'Make sure there's enough for two of us, please.' My arm round her shoulders, I propelled her along the corridors. I could feel the effort she was making to straighten her back. As I closed the door behind us, she leaned against me. 'I've just . . . Mrs Twiss came. The note I sent her. Young May. A man in Twiss's woods.'

'Dear God – did he—?'

She managed a watery giggle. 'The good girl kneed him – exactly!' Harriet paused as I grimaced. 'I think she headbutted him as he came down. And then she ran.'

'Thank God!'

'Amen. But then, piously, I said to her mother that Elias Pritchard ought to know. And she said – and she was right, Matthew, she was right! – that if it became known, May would lose her reputation. And . . . yes, somehow Mrs Twiss knew I must have had . . . been . . . And she advised me to say nothing, because . . .' She tried to hold back the sob, but it burst from her.

'She said that talking to anyone would bring up what had upset
me. And we both knew it was a euphemism.' This time, a snort
of what sounded almost like angry laughter. 'His late lordship
would have been proud of me for remembering that word. He
made me learn long words, you know, just like little Rosie.'

'I can think of no time when he would not have been proud
of you, my precious one.' I dried her eyes. 'I think Dick Thatcher
is waiting outside, you know. And I think it was his kindness
that dented your self-control a moment ago.'

The coffee came with sweet biscuits. 'Mrs Arden's special
ones, ma'am.'

'Thank you. Dick, will you tell everyone that I am now well?
And, Dick, thank you.' Again, she spoke as an aunt might have
addressed a favourite nephew. They exchanged a smile as he left.

'And now to the post,' she said, determinedly businesslike,
donning her spectacles. To my frustration, she peered at the
writing on the first envelope and then on the second before
opening either. She looked up at me. 'From Francis. But I don't
recognize the hand on the other. It's got an Oxford postmark
too . . .'

'There's a simple way to find out.'

'I know – but half the pleasure in a letter is working out who
your correspondent might be. No, not in your case, when they
are all about business.'

'Please! Put us both out of our misery. The one you don't
know first?'

She managed a grin. And then her expression turned to
astonishment. 'Heavens! This is from Gussie – from James,'
she corrected herself quickly. 'My God, he thinks he may
recognize the head! The former owner, as it were. But he won't
speculate. He will make some enquiries to add substance to his
theory and contact us in due course. Look.' She thrust the sheets
of paper at me and opened her letter from Palmer, skimming
it quickly. 'Oh, and a postscript: he would love to accompany
Francis next time he comes to visit us, which he hopes will be
very soon. As soon as Francis is over a severe cold. Whom else
should we expect?' she demanded between chuckles. 'The
Reverend Dr Benjamin Wells? Professor Fielding? Those lads
– Hurley and Burley?'

'Any of them! All of them! Provided the Marchbankses do not join them. What a shame they will not be here actually to greet Mr Baker.'

'But how will Jeremy cope with the new arrivals? Three will challenge him, but two more, especially if the visits overlap . . .' She drank the last of her coffee and set down the cup. Yes, she was tempted by another biscuit.

'Come, we hoped Palmer might encourage his drawing skills – even offer him employment. They dealt well with each other at Oxford station. Heavens, you have only to offer to teach them all cricket – yes, even Mr Baker! – and they will be in very heaven!'

She gestured ironically at the window, almost buckling, it seemed, under the combined forces of wind and rain. 'Skittles in the long gallery if the roof stays on?'

Dan had worked a miracle on the barouche, which had not been used since her late ladyship's days: it gleamed as much as the horses did. Since it would seat only four, it was agreed, after some discussion, that I should greet the two – or perhaps three – guests, and Harriet, who was after all in charge of the House, should remain there to greet them as they arrived. Would she encourage Jeremy to join us? Or would he keep firmly away? There would be no last-minute preparations to supervise. She, Hannah and Dick would have seen to every last detail, just as she and Samuel had done in her late ladyship's time. She might even take five minutes to sit with Samuel and tell him what was going on.

There: Dan in full livery set the horses in motion. It was a matter of moments before we arrived at the station. The train was on time; the porters (Arthur and Bob, on loan from the village station) were ready to open doors and seize luggage. I was ready to stretch out a hand in greeting. Even as we heard the noise of the engine, I had a bizarre fantasy that it was all in vain and no one would come. But there were the two gentlemen. And Mrs Baker?

'She'll be along tomorrow, I dare say,' Mr Baker said casually.

It was too dark to see clearly, but I could have sworn that Wilson, standing a pace behind him, rolled his eyes.

*   *   *

Wilson was far quicker to enter the yellow drawing room than Baker, and, Dick, very much Mr Thatcher, the butler, having served tea, was quick to remind us why we regarded him so highly. 'Having dined with him last night, I have explained to my fellow guest that while it is possible for a visitor's personal preferences to be accommodated, there are some areas where tradition makes this impossible. Should you have other guests for dinner, for example, they may express a preference for alcoholic drink, some even for medicinal purposes – did not Saint Paul himself recommend a glass of wine for one's stomach's sake? Your admirable rector, Mr Pounceman, might confirm that,' he added with his dry smile. 'Perhaps he might make it a text for his next Sunday sermon and do us all a favour.'

'Or he might refer to Christ's first miracle,' Harriet said. 'I am very tempted to invite him to luncheon tomorrow – Mr Pounceman, I mean. And the rest of the trustees too. But Matthew tells me that we can't be sure when Mrs Baker will arrive, which makes life difficult. As for Sunday, you know that traditionally in this household Sunday is a day when the kitchen staff do the minimum. So should I suggest a dinner party for the trustees on Monday? It's very short notice, of course, for both Bea and the guests – I know the Newcombes, for instance, have house guests. A working night for Marty, of course.' She added, 'Perhaps you gentlemen might forego your port tonight and for as long as the Bakers stay.'

'Of course. Actually, we don't know how long the Bakers wish to remain. Unless Mr Baker has given you any indication, Wilson?'

'Not yet. I have an idea that he believes that, for aristocrats, life is one long house party, and it's acceptable for guests to treat their homes as a particularly pleasant hotel. Which I suspect is not entirely inaccurate, since they do not have houses and farms to run.'

A tap on the door. We sat to attention, as it were – only to hear Dick announcing the arrival of Mr Newcombe. Harriet mouthed something to the young man as I greeted our guest. He and Wilson knew each other well from the trustees' meetings, though they had never mixed much socially.

'Good to see you, Wilson,' Newcombe said, shaking his hand vigorously before taking a seat beside him. 'What's the news from Shrewsbury?'

They exchanged small talk for a few minutes, until Luke arrived with tea. The moment he had left, Newcombe changed tone and addressed us generally. 'The head, the body and – er – so on. I know you and my wife have spoken about this business, Harriet, so I make no apology for raising it now. You know I requested assistance from Scotland Yard; I have at last had a response. At last. Their letter says – very graciously! – that they will despatch an officer to Shrewsbury, to aid Sergeant Swain, should he need it. Dammit – I beg your pardon – how can he not need help if he is never here to investigate the crime? And they point out, with the maximum of tact,' he said, irony dripping from the words, 'that the person who has the authority to make the request is not me or any other JP but the chief constable alone! Thank you, Harriet, my dear.'

I hoped the tea would calm him down a little – a vein was already bulging in his forehead.

In fact, he could not have timed his thanks, his smile and his affectionate use of her name better. Mr Baker, announced by a very sonorous Thatcher, looked impressed. We stood to greet him and shake his hand, Newcombe somehow becoming even more of an English gentleman than usual. While the introductions were made, Luke reappeared with a pot of coffee.

What prompted our neighbour to embark on a positive eulogy as he spoke of Harriet and me? He commended our hard work, our commitment to the Family, our sense of duty, our deference to our fellow trustees. Then he moved on to the other trustees. Bea? She was a pattern-card of an employee. Dr Ellis Page was exemplary in his medical work, treating all who needed him regardless of their ability to pay. Theophilus Pounceman was everything one could ask of a rector – he hoped Mr Baker would join us in worship on Sunday. Even Marty Baines received his meed of praise – a publican whose main aim was to keep his clients sober and with pay left to take back home to their families.

Mr Baker took advantage of his pause for breath. 'You are telling me that one of you trustees is a man who runs a bar? A saloon?' He radiated disbelief.

Wilson smiled gently. 'He runs the village inn. The Royal Oak has been serving travellers for some two hundred years, possibly three. Mr Baines knows as much about the villagers and their

needs as the doctor and the rector. He is a good man, Baker –
apparently, a pillar of the Methodist church here. You will make
his acquaintance should the board invite you to one of their
meetings – and I cannot imagine that they would not.' His smile
encompassed all of us.

'Excellent idea!' Newcombe said. 'How soon can you convene
a meeting, Wilson?'

'I suspect Monday might be the first day that we can expect
a quorum – but that might not be convenient for you, since you
have guests. When might they depart?'

The plans rolled on. It reminded me of a verbal tide, washing
over any observations Baker might have wanted to make. In fact,
the two men almost parodied my behaviour on the morning I
had met him, when it had taken Harriet but two minutes to unearth
his background.

'I would like to suggest that Mrs Baker be invited to the
meeting, if that is possible,' she said as if on cue.

'Oh, I doubt she will want to bother her pretty little head with
business,' Mr Baker said. 'Why don't you two ladies go find
some stores instead?'

Harriet smiled. 'Do you know when she might be joining us?'

'When she has exhausted all the stores in London, ma'am.'

Harriet laughed. 'That might take till Christmas! I was just
wondering what orders to give to the maids and to Mrs Arden
in the kitchen.'

'Why, sometime tomorrow, I guess. I told her to use the
railroad. It'd take, I guess' – he smiled at Harriet – 'till
Christmas to get here by coach. And you've already got one
here – I guess that will be at my and Mrs Baker's disposal
while we're staying here.'

She bowed. 'I must arrange for the barouche to be at the station
– at what time?'

'Oh, sometime in the afternoon.' He waved an airy hand.

Wilson coughed gently. 'Much as I am sure she will enjoy
Mrs Baker's company, I fear that Mrs Rowsley's presence would
be required at any meetings we have, sir. She has so many
responsibilities that we cannot make any decisions without her.'

Wilson's quiet authority precluded any objections. At last,
Newcombe stood to take his leave, explaining that he and his

wife had a houseful of guests and that he was required to join them for dinner. However, he hoped that both the Bakers would be his guests next week.

'Sure, we'd be delighted.' Baker shook hands vigorously. 'The Rowsleys assure me there's so much to see here. I've still to see most of the House, after all. And the grounds, and the Roman ruins. And this new village that you're all so full of. I need to inspect that. I want to know all that this inheritance involves. I'm a busy man. I want to get started!'

Wilson coughed; any moment now, he must surely point out that nothing would be his until his lordship's death. But Thatcher made a timely entrance. 'Dinner will be served in half an hour.'

In other words, our very correct young butler wished to give us time to change.

With great dignity, he escorted Newcombe from our midst. Was I relieved or would I miss his presence at dinner?

SIXTEEN

Unsure of what clothing Mr Baker might have at his disposal, Matthew suggested all the gentlemen might eschew full evening dress, appearing instead in smoking jackets. Luke took a message to that effect to Jeremy. He sent an immediate apology, on the grounds that he was in too much pain to leave his room. A polite lie, I suspected. Nonetheless, I promised I would visit him later.

Perhaps Bea's wonderful cooking would keep the conversation calm. I was dreadfully afraid that sooner or later someone would mention America, and the horrors of slavery and the dreadful Civil War, and I feared it would fall to me to make sure they did not. Each time there was a pause, I diverted our guest with questions about what he had so far seen in London and elsewhere on his travels. Did he plan to see our other great cities or admire what our poets acclaimed as truly wonderful scenery – the Lake District, for instance, or the Welsh mountains? Or, since he had gone to the trouble of an Atlantic crossing, would he and Mrs Baker be touring Europe? Montgomery extolled the delights of Paris; Matthew enthused about Rome; I waxed lyrical about Florence.

At last, it was time to bring the meal to an end. I told our guest as much as I thought he needed to know about Jeremy, which was very little – just that a friend staying here had taken a bad tumble in the grounds and hurt his ankle very badly. Since he had taken a turn for the worse, it was incumbent on me to visit him while the gentlemen took their coffee in the yellow drawing room.

I had barely updated Jeremy, who was sitting by the fire still fully dressed and looking remarkably well, about our other guest, when a tap on the door announced the arrival of Luke, with a cribbage board, a set of cards and two mugs of ale. They did not need me; that much was clear. Smiling benignly, I left them, wishing quite strongly that I could spend the evening equally calmly without worrying how to keep the peace. Dismissing a variety of patently hopeless ideas, at last I came up with just one, which I broached as I entered the drawing room.

'Pardon me? Billiards, ma'am?'

'Perhaps you call it pool, Mr Baker. If you and the other gentlemen are interested, I can have the fire lit in the billiard room immediately. Incidentally, it is the only room in the House where gentlemen are permitted to smoke,' I added with a smile. I could leave Matthew to explain why, following a cigar-fuelled fire that destroyed a nearby great house, the trustees had banned smoking indoors. Then, eschewing the bell, I left them to their discussion about how many balls to use and sought out a footman.

To my amazement, the sound of singing greeted me as I approached the servants' hall. Hannah had obviously put her dream into action. It was a shame to interrupt. I found a non-singer, however, and despatched him. And then, as much to my surprise as to theirs, I joined in: some hymns, some folksongs. We all sang 'Richard of Taunton Dean', then listened spellbound as Hannah sang 'Barbara Allen'. 'Sing Your Way Home' came next – which was a reminder, perhaps, that I must go on my way and do my duty.

The billiard room was as quiet as a church before a funeral. By some happy chance, I had suggested a game that required silent concentration. Whispering to Matthew that I would sit with Samuel, I left them to it.

Next morning, I was more than happy to let the three men ride off to inspect the estate while the sun still shone – the sky promised rain by lunchtime. Having spoken to Hannah and the other staff, I retired to the library, yet again to fret over its future once Mr Baker was no longer just the heir but actually Lord Croft. When he owned and ruled the House, how would his late lordship's wishes be carried out? I might be in sole charge of the room and its contents, but if I no longer lived in the House – and it was clearly a real possibility that he would dismiss both Matthew and me – I could supervise nothing. All those books, some precious beyond my imagination, in someone else's hands: I shuddered, quite literally, to think about it. No. I would steel my resolve. I must – I would! – find the will that Marchbanks had hidden.

Assuming he had, of course.

It was as if I stood in a kaleidoscope of thoughts and emotions. If only I could shake my head and form a beautiful pattern.

Of course I must talk to Matthew; of course I must institute the most thorough of searches; of course I would find it. Of course. I made time to search another shelf – books on travel, this time – but there was nothing in, under, between or behind the volumes. And it was more than time to visit Jeremy to assure myself that his pain last night was a convenient aberration.

He was just leaving his bedchamber as I arrived, manoeuvring with some skill on his crutches.

'Not well?'

But it was he who asked the question, not I.

'I'm worried about something,' I confessed. 'But I can't explain what within anyone's hearing. Would you care to visit the library? Then I will explain.'

'*Lay on, Macduff!* Good with secrets,' he added with an ironic grin.

Our progress was slow, not just because of his injury but because he kept stopping to admire the next great painting. Some he skipped – some Lely portraits of singularly unattractive Croft women had him pressing on with a theatrical shudder. But he gazed on those he did appreciate with a lover's fervour, pointing out details in an El Greco that even his late lordship had never remarked on.

Finally, we reached the library. I gestured to the chaise longue her ladyship had used on the rare occasions she joined her husband in the room. It was too austere for her taste, but on an autumn day, like today, the sun lit it kindly, and it would support his leg. I started the fire anyway, ensuring that the spark guard was tightly in place, and sat down, not quite facing him. Nineteen, perhaps twenty, he listened to my story with the gravity of a father confessor.

'If the will exists,' he declared, grinding out each syllable, 'I will find it.'

Neither of us knew how, of course – but I believed him.

*   *   *

Jeremy was working steadily through the folios of art engravings while I examined endless volumes of political writing. Our work was interrupted by the arrival of Constable Pritchard, obviously back on duty. His voice still gravelly, he said that he had come to give me the latest news of the case. He obviously expected to speak to me alone.

'Mr Turton knows all about it,' I assured him with a smile, gesturing him to a seat. 'Mr Turton, Constable Pritchard – our village bobby.' Pritchard saluted smartly. 'After all, Mr Turton was the artist who drew the head for Sergeant Swain.' I added, as he looked blank, 'Have you seen the sketch?'

'No, Mrs Rowsley – and it's not likely I will, either. Seems it's out of our hands now, Scotland Yard being in charge.' He sighed. He must have been hoping that his good work would bring him some sort of recognition.

'Get a sketch?' Jeremy said, reaching for his crutches. 'One on the desk upstairs.'

He hobbled off at tremendous speed.

'Poor young man. Living his life like that. I can't make out one word in five, ma'am. All those stops and starts, then rushing his fences and cramming himself over them . . . Can nothing be done for him?'

'All his friends must wish there could. But it would take a miracle, wouldn't it?'

'Ah. And they don't come dropping off trees.'

I raised a finger – he was returning. 'I gather Mrs Arden's special linctus worked its magic on your throat?'

'Ah. A rare talent she's got, that lady.'

So we were talking about something quite naturally when Jeremy returned.

'Here we are. Put it on your desk, shall I?'

My desk! I had always thought of it as his lordship's! Could it be an omen? And if so, of what?

I did not care to look at the portrait again, but Constable Pritchard studied it carefully. 'Aye, you've got a good likeness there, sir. It should be a big help to those clever men down in London,' he added wistfully. 'I've got to get back to my normal duties, it seems.'

I stared.

'No, no more poking my nose in. So I don't even think I should take this, sir. Sergeant Swain's got one, hasn't he? And Mr Rowsley sent copies to the Oxford forces. And, of course, he sent one to Scotland Yard.'

'I think you could talk to Pecker O'Malley and get more results than your sergeant ever could,' I observed truthfully.

'That's all well and good – but if I'm not allowed to . . .' Disconsolate, he reached for his helmet and got to his feet. 'Funny being in this room again, Mrs Rowsley. A bit different to last time. You know she saved my life, Mr Turton – threw that little mouse thing at a man planning to kill me. We could do with her in our cricket team, I can tell you. Except she's a lady, of course.'

'And – forgive me, gentlemen – it's hard to execute a decent cover drive in a skirt like this.'

I persuaded Jeremy to take a turn on the terrace; out of the wind, the sun was quite warm, and he decided to, as he put it, try his hand at a landscape. 'And please, feel free to leave me here.'

I didn't argue. 'If you're sure? I'll be back within half an hour.'

Donning walking boots and a shawl was the work of minutes, and I strode off across the stable yard, not going in any particular direction. I loved the trees on a day like this, their silhouettes stark against the sky. Rooks' nests in that copse; plenty of mistletoe over there – decorating the House was always such a treat for us all. A buzzard circled the far side of the lake.

What was that by the lake itself? A wheelbarrow on its side. And a figure kneeling by the lake. A footman. Young Tim – yes, vomiting into the water. I hurried closer.

As I reached him, he staggered to his feet. 'Beg pardon, ma'am. It's just–it's just—' He pointed up the hill but retched again.

I held his forehead, pushing back his hair. 'It's all right, Tim, it's all right.' I found my smelling salts. 'There. Better now. Let's get you back to the House.'

'But ma'am, I didn't get the ice for Mrs Arden. And – oh, ma'am – I daren't go in there again. Daren't. A ghost. Horrible! And, oh, ma'am, I've been and left the keys and the lantern there. I'm sorry.' He was in tears.

A ghost? More likely the head. And I thought the police had moved it! How dare they leave it, how dare they?

'Tim, just sit on that tree trunk there. I'll go and get the keys. Yes, I will.' I used the voice meant to quell argument.

'But ma'am! The ghost!'

I took his hands. 'I shall simply lock it inside. And bring the keys back. And the lantern. And then we can walk back together.'

I did not need the lantern to tell me that the head was still in there. Did I dare look? No, I had no fear of the dead. But while I had managed to tell myself that Jeremy's sketches left me a tiny thread of hope that I was mistaken, I had the greatest terror of actually seeing the head. The head of the man who had raped me. There. I had admitted it at last. Dear God, he was in my dreams often enough. I did not want to see him in reality.

But, my rational mind insisted, *if you know he is dead, know beyond all contradiction, then perhaps the dreams will cease.*

When I returned to Tim, he had righted the wheelbarrow but still looked as green as I felt, and I could see how he shook. Did he need the barrow to support him? How could I get him safely back to the House? At last, I realized I was not as steady as I would have liked. I held my hand where we could both see it quivering.

'Tim, my legs don't want to work. I wonder if you would be kind enough to give me your arm?'

'What about the wheelbarrow, ma'am?'

With Luke or Dick, I might have risked suggesting that they put me into it and push, but Tim was too young, too junior, for me to joke like that. Instead, I said, 'I could send a gardener to collect it. Oh, of course, it's the ice-barrow, isn't it? I'm not thinking very clearly. I'll ask one of your colleagues.' Taking his arm, I set us in motion. 'I'm afraid Mrs Arden will have to manage without ice today, won't she?'

'Maybe Dan could go and get some from Mrs Tomkins, over at the Newcombes',' he said. 'Though they do say she's not a very givish sort of lady. Not like Mrs Arden. Always got a spare slice of cake, she has. And a kettle on the boil, ready for a cup of tea.' We walked a few more yards. 'Are you feeling better, ma'am?'

'Still a bit wobbly,' I lied, aware that I was supporting him, not the other way round. 'And you?'

He stopped. 'Just thinking about it, ma'am. Sorry.'

I dragged him to the nearest bush. All he managed was a lot of dry retching; tears rolled down his cheeks. My arm still round his shoulders, I said, 'When you've seen something horrible, you can't just unsee it, can you? But perhaps it would help if you told me about things you like to see.' For a lad from a family as poor as his, that might be a challenge, of course.

He sniffed. I passed him my handkerchief.

'What's your favourite dinner?' I asked.

'Oh, ma'am, I do like Mrs Arden's roast spuds. Something like, they are. A bit of all right. And her puddings. A bit of jam roly-poly goes down a fair treat. Custard.'

'I'm partial to her biscuits myself. Those with bits of chocolate inside.'

'I wonder why the chocolate stays hard? You'd think it would melt, ma'am.'

'One of her secrets, Tim. I wonder if she's got any biscuits left?' I took his arm again and we started walking.

'You could smell them in her kitchen this morning, first thing. And I know she was making special cakes too. Ma'am, she let us all stir her Christmas puddings. She let me scrub the sixpences before we put them in. And we all made wishes.'

'Are you allowed to say what you wished for?'

'Ma'am!' He sounded outraged. 'If you tell, they don't come true!'

'Of course. So what sort of wish would you make if you could tell someone and it would still come true?' What sort of reply did I expect? Something purely selfish? Something altruistic? Hardly, from a boy who, until he had found work in the House, never knew if there would be enough food for the whole growing family – especially from a boy who clearly loved his meals.

'I wish I hadn't seen that there ghost!' he wailed.

I should have expected that. 'When your grandpa died, were you afraid of seeing him?'

'In his coffin, ma'am? During the sin-eating? No, ma'am. 'Cos he was still my grandpa, wasn't he? Just not alive any more. And they let me kiss his cheek, all whiskery like it always was, to say goodbye. And he didn't leave no ghost behind. He was a good man, ma'am.'

'I know he was. A good, kind man. And he loved you, Tim. He took you fishing in the stream that feeds the lake, didn't he?' I took a deep breath. 'You're not afraid of seeing dead people, Tim – just ghosts? Is that right?'

'You know where you are with dead people,' he said, reasonably.

'So you do. But isn't a ghost what some people leave behind when they die?'

'But, ma'am – leaving behind just his head . . . Like one of King Henry's wives!'

'You can't go haunting with just a head, can you? Now, Tim – that wish. You can tell me. A secret wish you'd like to come true. And not the one you made when you stirred Mrs Arden's puddings.'

He scratched his head. 'I might wish to work for Mr Pounceman. Because Mary-Ann works there, and I'd see her.'

At the age of thirteen, his twin sister was second housemaid.

'And Mr Pounceman says he'll put her wages up to a full twelve pounds a year if she carries on so well. And when Effie leaves to get married at Easter, ma'am, he says she may take her place, and her wages too! But he's got enough footmen, and I wouldn't want to be an outdoors man. So . . .' He tailed off, wrinkling his nose.

'While you think about it – and this is just our game, remember, Tim – while you think about it, I would like a nice cup of Mrs Arden's tea – lots of sugar, and one of those biscuits.'

'Me too, ma'am.'

'And your being sick can be our secret if you like?'

'If you please, ma'am.'

'I'd like us to have another secret,' I added. What if, for a dare, other footmen decided to see the ghost? Or a village lad? I would not even put it past those with the greatest bravado stealing it. 'Let the ghost be our secret. Ours alone.' I played a terrible, treacherous card: 'We don't want any of the maids hearing about it and getting upset, do we? Promise?'

'Finger wet, finger dry, cross my heart and hope to die!'

We were nearly there, but I suspected being seen to support me in my time of need might earn him kudos. So we continued with a gentle gossipy chat about his family until he could steer me through the servants' entrance and sit me down. Strong, sweet tea it was, and he ate my biscuits as well as his own.

Putting my hand on his, I said quietly, 'If you ever think of that wish, come and tell me. I shall listen wherever I am, whatever I am doing. Do you understand?'

His mouth was still full of biscuit, so all he could do was nod, solemnly.

I had a lot to do before I went back upstairs.

First, I spoke to Dick: were the gentlemen back from their ride yet?

'Not yet, Mrs Rowsley. Mrs Arden is aware of the situation and will delay luncheon.'

'Thank you. Hannah, I need to use the Room for a while. I know the table is laid, but I will re-lay it when I have finished. I don't want to be disturbed unless Mr Rowsley returns.'

The first thing was to write a telegraph for Dan to take down to the station. Sergeant Swain should know of my extreme displeasure at the lingering presence of the head on his lordship's property. It must be moved by the evening. And I demanded at the House the immediate presence of both him and any Scotland Yard detectives who might be in Shrewsbury. Unable, obviously, to underline the word 'immediate', I repeated it. And then I thought again. During my life of service, I had learned that tact and deviousness were often a better combination than simple indignation, righteous though it might be. So I redrafted it: now I humbly requested that certain evidence that Sergeant Swain had thought best to leave on the Croft estate might be removed so that the site might be used again for its original purpose. I made two copies, one of which I would put in Matthew's office safe. The other, once Dan had sent the telegraph to Sergeant Swain, must go to Elias.

Then, as soon as he had eaten his dinner with the other servants, Dan must take the notes I was even then writing to Newcombe House – one begging Mrs Tomkins to send us some ice, the other for Mr Newcombe to apprise him of this morning's discovery.

The sound of hooves clattering across the yard told me the men had returned. I dashed out. 'Matthew, may Dan ride Esau so he can send a telegraph?'

It was the work of moments to explain what was in it.

'I'll take it myself! And speak to Pritchard.' He wheeled the horse round like a hero of old and was off on his errand before I could tell him that poor Elias was no longer on the case.

Dan gaped.

So, still on their horses, did Montgomery and Mr Baker. At last, Dan remembered his duties and went to the horses' heads so that they could dismount. Poor Montgomery valued correctness very highly, and it was clear that he was disconcerted by Matthew's unconventional behaviour almost as much as he was by mine.

'Forgive me, Mr Baker – Mr Wilson. As you may have gathered, there is a slight domestic crisis, and my husband is the best fitted to deal with it urgently. A footman will attend you in your bedchambers immediately to assist you to change for luncheon – in fact, should you wish to take a shower after your exertions, there is time for that.'

Duly relieved of their boots, they made their way upstairs.

'Luke, can you find Mr Turton and ask him where he wishes to lunch – on his own or with us? And make the appropriate arrangements? Thank you.'

Then I turned to Dick, asking him to keep an eye on Tim. 'He – I – we both had a very unpleasant experience this morning.' I swallowed hard. 'Please don't mention it to him. Just come and tell me if he appears unhappy or unwell. Bless him, he had to help me back home.'

Dick had developed a skill with his eyebrows similar to my own. They now expressed extreme cynicism.

I countered with my right brow: the one I used to suppress pretension. 'I will say more later, Dick. Here's Mr Rowsley now.'

'Thank goodness he was on Esau, not old Robin!'

SEVENTEEN

For Harriet to ask for such help while I was supposed to be entertaining guests was unheard of. Clearly, she had disposed of them for the time being: on her own, she was seated in the Room rubbing the fatigue from her face. Fatigue? Or anxiety? Or another emotion.

'You've been having exciting times,' I said, kneeling beside her and taking her hand.

'You don't know the half of it,' she said.

I listened in horror – no, far more than horror! – to her terse narrative. 'You recognized the man who violated you all those years ago. The judge! My God, my poor love. My dear one.' I took her in my arms and rocked her.

'I thought – when I saw Jeremy's sketches. I told myself I was imagining it. I could pretend . . . and then – up there – I knew. Oh dear.' She fumbled for a handkerchief, then pressed her face into the one I offered. I felt her straighten her shoulders. 'I can't not get through this, can I? Not with Montgomery and Mr Baker here, and Mrs Baker due . . . I wonder if another cup of tea would help.'

'My love, you need something stronger. In the privacy of our room. Come, let me help you upstairs.' I eased her to her feet; we clung to each other as if bracing ourselves for a terrible storm.

She snorted. 'With Mr Baker here? I would rather that my breath did not smell of alcohol. My dear, we are going to be late for lunch and we are not changed.'

'I can tell them that you are indisposed.'

'Funnily enough, I believe it is having to work that will help me deal with . . . all these feelings. And it is my duty . . .'

Before I guided her up the back stairs, I spoke to Luke: wine to our room, please, and Mr Thatcher should serve wine with lunch.

* * *

I suspect I might have seen even more implications than she did if she had actually identified the judge in her angry telegraph. But she was wrestling with such distress I dared say nothing. Should I beg her to rest? Or was she right – that duty had always been the frame of her life, supporting her through the best and worst of times?

Perhaps not to my surprise, it was Dick Thatcher who knocked. 'I have to warn you, sir, that Mr Baker is getting restive. Might I tell him that Mrs Rowsley witnessed – say – a horrible accident on her walk this morning and needs a little more time to recover?'

'Perhaps the word "incident"? And you have known her longer than I have – what would you wager against her being downstairs within ten minutes?'

He nodded. 'I will just drop the word you suggest in Mr Wilson's ear. And ask him not to speculate? Aloud, at least.'

'Thank you.' I took the tray inside. 'Here, my love – Dick thinks you need this.' I poured a glass of the Chablis he had chosen for her.

'I had better drink a little then. I worry more for Tim than for me, Matthew. He is thirteen, no more, and to see . . . that.'

'Country boys see a lot and toughen up fast, my love. I wonder what wish he will share with you.' I finished buttoning her dress and tucked an errant lock of hair into her chignon. 'One more sip, now, to please Dick. There. Remember, whatever happens, I will always be beside you.' I clasped her hand, as if she were a frightened child, before tucking it under my arm as, apparently serenely, we walked downstairs.

Wilson did more than rise politely to his feet as we entered: he walked towards her, kissing her hand and leading her to a chair near the fire. He whispered something in her ear as she sat, returning to join Baker, whose handsome features were sharpened by irritation as he looked at his watch.

'Are you sure that someone will be at the train station to meet my wife?'

Harriet said, 'The barouche is already there, accompanied by a stable lad who will gallop ahead to let us know the moment she arrives. Mrs Baker, her dresser and a courier, I believe you said? We have prepared accommodation for the dresser in a room adjacent to your wife's. But I cannot recall if you said the courier would be staying here too.'

'Do couriers usually stay over?'

She gave him her most disarming smile. 'You know, Mr Baker, in all my years in service, I can't recall a courier ever having been to the House before. Valets, maids, secretaries, coiffeurs, tutors, archaeologists, even police officers. But never a courier. So I truly do not know the protocol involved. Should he be in a state bedchamber like yours, or in the attics with the servants?'

I suspected he had been allocated a guest bedchamber near a bathroom, but I said nothing.

'Ma'am, I defer to your judgement!' He bowed graciously.

Luncheon was served.

With wine. And with some of Bea's fruit cordials. And with water.

Everyone's plate and glass full, Thatcher bowed and withdrew.

As if to support Harriet, at whom he was still looking with great concern, Wilson accepted wine. He immediately turned the conversation, asking her about the state of our other guest's health.

'He is improving, thank you. He's been moved from the Family wing – the hospital area, you will recall, Baker – to a guest room, since Doctor Page considers that he no longer needs nursing care. But he is far from being able to walk.'

'Might he welcome a visit from an old friend?' Wilson asked, stretching the truth more than a little. What was he up to?

'I'm sure he would – but would you forgive me if I asked him first?'

'I would expect nothing less, dear lady. Pray, how is dear Mrs Arden? I need not ask about her culinary abilities: this galantine is delicious.'

He had once proposed to Bea – that she should be his house-keeper, not his wife, however.

'She is well, thank you, and looking forward to showing off her skills this weekend. Heavens, Montgomery, do you recall those feasts she served the archaeologists this summer? Sadly, her talent is wasted most of the time.'

'But she remains here in spite of that?' Mr Baker asked sharply. 'Cooking for just you two?'

'For us and for the rest of the household, and, of course, for our guests.' I laughed. 'And training young women from the village and beyond so that they themselves can go into service. She's bound by the sense of duty that ties Harriet to the House – like many such women, she denies herself the life she would really love.'

'But you would lose your cook!' Wilson exclaimed.

'Come, sir, one can always find another cook, surely,' Mr Baker observed. 'A cook is . . . just a cook.'

'I consider her truly exceptional, sir,' Wilson bridled.

'Indeed she is,' Harriet said. 'Should she ever wish to leave the House, I hope she may reach an arrangement and simply come in on the rare occasions that we need an expert like her. What do you think, Mr Wilson?'

'I take it we are talking about a possible marriage?' He carefully omitted details, of course. I was relieved that I had not blabbed them out. 'It is, of course, very unusual for a married lady to continue to work – but you are living proof, my dear, that it is possible. Certainly, I would not object.'

Baker was looking genuinely puzzled. 'Pardon me, Mr Wilson – but how can a servant be "a lady"? Where I come from, a lady is a lady. She does not toil, does not get her hands dirty. She takes pride in her home, in her children, in her husband, above all.'

Wilson acknowledged the objection with a bow. 'Indeed, that is what many people believe a lady is – or should be. I used to myself. But I now suspect the term should be extended to women – that word itself is derogatory, is it not, in social terms? – who, regardless of their birth or rank, behave with grace, in the widest sense, and dignity. We all accept, do we not, that marriage to a gentleman raises his life partner to his status?'

'But not the other way round, surely!' Baker objected. 'If a duchess married her groom, surely that would lower her to his level in society.'

'There are many people, very many, who would absolutely agree with you,' I said. 'But a new class is rising, somewhere between the aristocracy and the workers, which is beginning, just possibly, to blur these distinctions. I fear it will not happen in my lifetime, or even before the end of this century. But I will aver very strongly that in every respect my dear wife is my equal. Indeed, my superior!'

'But you are a gentleman born, sir, as a descendant of an earl.' He looked genuinely puzzled.

'In service, we have a saying: *Gentleman is as gentleman does*,' Harriet said. She added with a rueful smile, 'As one who has met many descendants of earls and dukes, I quote, after all, William of Wykeham, a man of some authority. He was both a bishop, you will recall, and indeed the Chancellor of England. I fear I must tell you that the behaviour of many members of the aristocracy would shock you to the core. Dear me, Mr Baker, you Americans have wisely rid yourselves of the pesky nobility. Rejoice in your wonderfully equal society.'

With a discreet knock, Thatcher returned to refresh our glasses and clear away the main course.

'And now are we ready to try some of Mrs Arden's wonderful luncheon cakes?' Harriet asked.

We were soon served, and Thatcher withdrew.

I sought desperately to find a less contentious topic for conversation: heavens, my schooling as a *gentleman* should have prepared me for awkward silences like this.

It was Wilson, technically not a gentleman since, like me, he had to work for his living, who spoke. 'I was wondering, Rowsley, if you could suggest some places round here that Mr and Mrs Baker might care to visit. The great industrial activity around Ironbridge might not be to everyone's taste but it is the way of the future . . .'

At least three of us heaved a sigh of relief when Dick announced that Mrs Baker, having arrived on the three-fifteen train, would be with us within ten minutes. We trooped through the wonderful entrance hall, the great dome of which still left me slack-jawed in wonder, to stand ready to receive her. Yes, our colleagues were already in place outside, maids one side of the great rake of steps, footmen the other. All the well-rehearsed procedures were in place.

Even without her courier, who was apparently returning to London, Mrs Baker would be greeted like a queen.

EIGHTEEN

With her delicate pink-and-white complexion and golden hair, Mrs Baker might have been an exquisitely dressed doll. Everything about her was delicate – even her voice piped like a child's. Perhaps a critic might say her head was large for her tiny body, just as some might think a snowdrop's flower too much for its stem. But I felt like an elephant as I escorted her slowly to her bedchamber, giving the footmen time to deliver the mountain of luggage that implied she was expecting to make a long stay. From time to time, eyes round with wonder, she would pause to admire something pretty or to wonder at the view from a window. She was delighted with her bedchamber, admired the wonders of the bathroom, was charmed to learn that when she rang, a butler would escort her to the drawing room. Radiating an innocent delight in everything she had so far seen in the House, she surely epitomized what Mr Baker considered a perfect lady. The only flaw in her perfection was the state of her teeth, very far from white and shining. I left her to the attentions of her dresser, Mademoiselle Dubois, a Frenchwoman she had hired, she confided, in London, to make her look more English. In fact, she looked about as English as a fuchsia in a patch of daisies. As for her accent, it was much less defined than her spouse's – sometimes hardly noticeable and sometimes very strong.

She was polite too, keeping us waiting but a very few minutes despite the dozens of buttons and a very complicated coiffure.

Seated near the fire, with the screen carefully adjusted, she sipped tea ('I do so love your quaint English ways!') and nibbled one of Bea's delicate cakes. Her husband drank coffee.

'Mr Baker and I are so delighted to visit with you,' she cooed in her quiet little voice, 'aren't we, Mr Baker?'

Yes, I was nearly as enchanted by her as Montgomery and Matthew clearly were. She reminded me in many ways of her late ladyship when I had first entered her service, charming everyone into doing exactly as she wanted no matter how much effort it took them. It was only later that she had revealed her steely determination.

Mrs Baker chatted artlessly about the London stores, provoking occasional gruff but indulgent comments from her spouse, whom she consistently referred to with his title and surname, as, to be fair, many people of our acquaintance still did in public. I should imagine that if it were widely known amongst the surrounding gentry, our free use of first names for ourselves and our friends would occasion some consternation, if not displeasure. Then she turned the conversation to her children: how had someone so young and tiny produced boys who Mr Baker declared were going to be men's men?

'I declare, I am just so afraid that they will be called on to fight in the war,' she said, dabbing a blue eye with the laciest of handkerchiefs.

It was only then that it dawned on me that she was not Mr Baker's first wife. Briefly, I wondered what had happened to the first – but it was none of my business.

'It's an honour to serve your country,' her husband declared, straightening so that he might be said to sit to attention, 'to fight for the right cause. The just cause. Were you ever a military man, Rowsley?'

'Never. The English have a peculiar habit of sending their sons into careers according to their birth order. The oldest would learn to run the estate he would inherit, the second would join the army, the third study law and the fourth become a clergyman. Since my father is a senior clergyman, there is no estate to inherit, so my elder brother went into the army – but then he changed his mind and became a clergyman. I was destined for the law but ended up, as you know, managing other people's estates. My cousin was attracted to the drama of the law. What brought you into the legal profession, Wilson?'

He smiled. 'Ever since I was bullied at school by a boy who regularly cheated, I have wanted to be on the side of fairness. Justice. Alas, I was never destined to mount a white charger and slay dragons. In reality, my life has been a great deal more prosaic. Damsels chained to rocks are in perilously short supply in Shrewsbury, you understand.'

Would the Bakers be similarly forthcoming about their lives? *She* might – she had that bright eagerness that wants to share. What would *I* say? The truth? That I was a workhouse orphan who had no choice: I had to do whatever work I was put to? That, aged eleven, I was raped in my first year of service by a man whose head even now lay in our icehouse? That a good man married me despite knowing this? No, it was not a life to be dwelt on and certainly not discussed over afternoon tea.

Lest I betray any of my suddenly overwhelming emotions, I feigned surprise at the time shown on the lovely clock and claimed I had to check something.

Where might I go?

'Oi! Stop right there!' a male voice shouted. 'Yes, you!'

I turned. A strange man stood at the far end of the corridor. Tall. Thickset. Imposing in a threatening way.

'Inspector – that is Mrs Rowsley, his lordship's housekeeper, sir,' Dick said, putting out a restraining hand, only to have it dusted aside as if it were a fly.

'Touch me again and I'll charge you with assault, young fellow-me-lad. Understand? Now – you!' He pointed at me. 'Take me to your master.'

'Might I ask who you are, marching in here and insulting Mr Thatcher?' I demanded in my best imitation of her late ladyship's voice and manner, approaching him with a swish of my skirts.

'It's none of your business. I want to speak to the master of the House.'

'His lordship lies sick upstairs and not for anything should he be disturbed. Mr Thatcher is his butler. I have the honour of being his housekeeper. Together, we run this entire establishment. Do you understand?' I tried to speak with authority – and, apparently, I succeeded, the man removing his hat and looking abashed – but inside I was shaking.

'Very well. I shall expect your full cooperation, then. Ah, Swain!' he added as, somewhat hangdog, the sergeant appeared.

I waited. I prompted him. 'And whom am I addressing?'

'Inspector Willis. Scotland Yard.' At last, he showed me what I presumed was a warrant card. 'The Shrewsbury police received a telegraph from these premises and passed it on to me to deal with whoever sent it.'

'*Deal with*, Inspector? Perhaps you mean *respond to*?'

Behind the inspector's back, Dick gestured towards the drawing room. He mouthed, 'Mr Wilson.' I nodded.

'Someone was trying to tell the constabulary how to do their duty. And lying, to boot.' Disconcertingly, his eyes travelled from me to the portrait of her ladyship behind me. She was holding his lordship's hand, his late lordship beside her. Now he stared at me again,

'*Lying*? About what, Inspector?'

'Alleging that . . . that something remained on the premises. I can assure you that this is not the case, and the suggestion is a gross libel. A criminal libel.'

I schooled myself to say as little as possible – certainly, I must not protest that it had been seen there this morning by two very reliable witnesses. No doubt it was removed – by fortunate chance – after they saw it. 'Ah, Mr Wilson. May I introduce to you Inspector Willis from Scotland Yard? Inspector, Mr Wilson is his lordship's lawyer. Apparently, Mr Wilson, the inspector and Sergeant Swain wish to charge me with criminal libel,' I added with her ladyship's dismissive laugh.

Dear Montgomery grew two inches as he too laughed. 'Dear me! How absurd!'

On the back foot, the inspector pointed. 'If that's the woman who made the allegations—'

'Personally, I would not refer to Mrs Rowsley in such derogatory terms, Inspector. She was the personal appointment of her late ladyship and, lest you underestimate her importance, she is responsible for the entire fabric of this building and all those living and working within it.' He turned to me. 'Mrs Rowsley, might you find a room where the officers and I can discuss this ludicrous matter in private?'

'With pleasure. Please follow me.'

Leaving them safely stowed in a chilly, ill-lit, unheated anteroom, I retired to one of the fine new WCs. I had kept my dignity, I hoped – but now I lost my lunch.

Montgomery was waiting in the corridor near but not immediately outside the yellow drawing room when, having cleaned my teeth and washed my face, I made my way downstairs again.

'My dear Harriet, what an unpleasant few minutes for you. I am pleased to report that the inspector and the unfortunate Sergeant Swain have left the building. I can't claim, however, that their tails are between their legs. May we find somewhere to talk for a very few minutes before we rejoin the others?'

Nodding, I led the way to the library.

'You will forgive me if I remark that you are still shaking. Might I ask the redoubtable Mr Thatcher to procure a glass of brandy for you? Or – since I know you are aware of Mr Baker's beliefs – perhaps some of that quite delightful Chablis that would not linger on the breath? Excellent.' He rang.

Dick appeared on the instant, and returned more quickly than I could have imagined. But he did not leave the room, leaning anxiously towards me. 'Are you all right, Mrs Rowsley? Truly?'

'I am now.' Obediently, I sipped the wine he poured. 'Dick, if Mr Wilson permits, I would be happy for you to join us. Please help yourself and him to wine. Thank you. Now, the household must be bubbling with rumours: the three of us need to work out a plausible account for them.'

'And, of course, for our guests,' Montgomery added, as without arguing Dick took a seat.

'Firstly, you should know what provoked the officers' behaviour. Earlier this week, we asked Sergeant Swain to deal with the head while it was still in good condition. When it was established that the victim of the crime was not local, the idea was formed of photographing or sketching it, so that the images might be sent to other police forces. Nothing happened. No one came. Eventually, Jeremy volunteered to sketch it. His work was accordingly sent to the Oxford police and to Scotland Yard. We then requested the immediate removal of the corpse's head from the icehouse. Assuming it had gone, Bea sent Tim – he's the youngest of the footmen – to get ice. I chanced upon him as he ran away, terrified by what he assumed was a ghost. Suspecting the truth, I left him where he was, casting up his accounts into the lake, and checked for myself. The "ghost" was the already decaying head. So I sent a telegraph to Sergeant Swain, whose duties seem now to have been taken over by Scotland Yard, asking him to remove the evidence that he had deemed necessary to leave on the property. You saw most of what happened next.'

Dick said, 'I tried to intervene – well, you saw, didn't you?'

'I did. You nearly got yourself arrested too.' We exchanged a smile. 'Mr Wilson, what is going on? I might well have exceeded my remit by sending that telegraph, and trodden on some corns in the process. But threats of arrest?'

Montgomery shook his head slowly. 'I have never known police officers of any force to behave like this. Are you the only people to experience such hostility?'

'Mr Newcombe's request for Scotland Yard support – you recall he is a JP? – brought a very tetchy letter, putting him in what the writer obviously thought was his place.'

'Ah.'

Dick raised a finger, as if asking permission to speak. 'Sir, is it possible – I know this sounds ridiculous – is it possible that . . . No, I'm talking nonsense.'

'Kindly let me be the judge of that, Mr Thatcher,' Montgomery said, his authority tempered with a slight smile. 'Pray continue.'

Dick spread his hands. 'Mrs Rowsley and I both know that if we tell someone to do a job they hate, they either get on with it quickly to get it out of the way or they find excuses and put it off and put it off. Do you think . . .? No, I'm sorry . . .'

'Deliberate procrastination? My dear man, I have been wondering more or less the same thing. But it is the job of the police to investigate crime without fear or favour – and the fact that the villainy has taken place in rural Shropshire makes it no less their job. I wonder if it's not the crime but the identity of the victim that they do not want to investigate. And the sketches have added to their reluctance. As to the problem of what we say, I think the policy should be the less the better. I would tell your colleagues that we seem to have attracted the attention of a bullying officer keen to throw his weight around, that's all.'

I nodded. 'We have our guests to consider.'

Montgomery astonished me. 'To be honest, much as I wished to find the heir, I wish him and his wife to the devil at the moment – they are going to take up a great deal of your time and energy. Yes, caring for guests is your function, and a job done well brings its own pleasures. But – let me just ask you both to keep your eyes and ears open.'

Surely he did not mean that as far as our guests were concerned? But perhaps he did. He got to his feet. 'Mrs Rowsley, if you would leave explaining our long absence to me?'

'Gladly.'

With an immaculate bow, Dick returned to his role as butler, holding the door open for us. But the concern in his eyes as he looked at me had not disappeared.

NINETEEN

Earnest and plausible Wilson might have been in his explanation to the Bakers that an incident in the village had attracted the attention of the police and that Thatcher and Harriet, as the two senior members of staff, had been asked to help question their underlings. But I was by no means convinced. I was sure that their arrival had more to do with their recognizing the face in the sketches they had received and a desire to make sure that no one here would speculate on it. In other words, their visit here was to intimidate us. As yet, I could say nothing, and we continued our bland and meaningless chatter till it was time to change for dinner.

Once in the privacy of our room, however, as Harriet spilled out the whole distressing story, I panicked. I could think of only one thing. If they ever discovered that she could identify the head – I would no longer think of the man to whom it had been attached as a victim! – she might be in great peril. Having a strong motive, either revenge or a desire to silence him, she could be accused of the crime. Mrs Twiss had been absolutely right to refuse her permission to tell Pritchard of the man's assault on her daughter. And the story of what he had done to Harriet herself must never come out, even if she had to perjure herself. And she might have to lie to her friend Halesowen, if he had indeed recognized the subject of Jeremy's sketch and asked why he should have made his way here.

So why had he come here? I could not imagine it was to apologize. Had he meant to threaten her? Or to silence her? And how did he even know of her existence? The Oxford reception, of course!

And then Harriet, sitting down beside me on our bed and sliding her hand into mine, as if for comfort, said, 'Thank God we have the best witnesses to prove that we could not have been here when he was killed. A whole week of the most reputable witnesses Oxford could supply!'

In my panic, I had completely forgotten! With enormous relief, I took up her dry tone. 'So long as they don't ask Marchbanks, who would have lied through his teeth to prove you guilty.'

She took a deep breath, as if to say something.

There was a tap on the door – Wilson, of all people. 'My friends, I have endeavoured to – how shall I put it? – to leaven the lump. I happened to espy Ellis Page as I strolled through these wonderful corridors. Apparently, he had just set a labourer's badly broken leg up in the Family wing and was about to visit Bea. So – and I apologize for not consulting you – I asked if they might both dine with us, Bea's duties permitting.'

'That's a wonderful idea. The pleasure of their company apart, it will be highly educational for the Bakers. Should we ask young Jeremy to come down too, Harriet?'

'Forgive me, I have already thought of that,' Wilson said. 'I asked young Luke to enquire if I might visit him – and received a positive invitation. But he admitted that an evening of conversation with strangers was still beyond him. Should we do one of our play-readings, however, he would love to be our audience.'

'That is progress indeed! Thank you, Montgomery.' She grinned. 'To think I was once afraid of you.'

These days, a bedchamber was set aside for Page, with several changes of clothes, including full evening dress. Thatcher had tactfully established that Mr Baker had brought his formal wear, so tonight we all dressed up. Harriet even asked Hannah to help her with her coiffure.

'This reminds me of when I was your age, Hannah, and we had a houseful of guests all dressed up to the nines. I don't think any were more glamorous than Mrs Baker, though – and don't tell me Mr Thatcher isn't fighting off pleas from all the footmen to let them wait on her tonight!'

'What a shame Mr B isn't as handsome.' Hannah fixed another tress. 'He's not ugly, not like that sergeant – imagine having him as your *swain*! – but he can't hold a candle to you, Mr Rowsley,' she said with an impish grin at me. 'Or,' she added more reflectively, 'to Jeremy. Mr Turton, I *should* say. Wouldn't he have made a wonderful clergyman? He's so handsome, all the girls in the congregation would have listened open-mouthed.' She laid down the brush and clips. 'Sir, ma'am, I know I'm speaking out

of turn, but . . . The thing is, my cousin stammers like that. Did.
But one day he started to sing along with me. And though the
affliction was never cured, the singing helped – and he never,
ever stammered when he was singing. Isn't that strange? And I
was wondering if we dared ask Mr Turton to come and join our
little choir.'

'Now, how could you go about that?' I asked, intrigued.

Of course, she had given it some thought. 'If I could find out
where he's doing one of his drawings, I could be the one to go
and dust – and sing while I'm doing it. And see if he does what
my cousin did. But,' she added quickly, 'not if you don't think
it's right. Him being a gentleman and—'

'I think it's a wonderful idea. But make haste slowly,' Harriet
said.

'I will, ma'am.' She beamed. 'Heavens, is that the time? I
promised I'd help Mrs Arden with her hair, too . . .'

I had no idea why, but there seemed to be a general sense that
everyone needed to put on a show for the exotic creatures from
across the Atlantic – me included. Harriet affixed my best studs,
and I enjoyed clasping one of my honeymoon gifts round her
lovely neck.

And now for an evening not of comradely discussion between
close friends but of polite nothingnesses accompanied by
vacuous smiles.

'We always adjourn after dinner together, ladies and gentlemen
together, do we not? We have made it our custom. And what you
men would gain from half an hour's conversation with a man
who would not touch port, I don't know,' Harriet declared as we
descended to the drawing room. 'What would we three ladies
find to talk about? And the mind boggles at the thought of you
four skirting round the topic of the Civil War, not to mention
who works his plantations.'

'It does indeed. I have a constant sense that we are teetering
on the edge of a conversational precipice!' There were certain
subjects that would reveal opinions far too far apart to be
discussed calmly. Chief amongst them was slavery, of course.
My great-grandfather had had many slaves on his plantations,
and I was aware that it was income that these unpaid workers

generated that enabled him to build up our considerable family
wealth. When slavery was abolished in the West Indies, my
grandfather in turn received a small fortune in compensation
– he, not the slaves who had been forced into intolerable toil.
The saving grace was that my grandmother, a Quaker, insisted
that from this money he recompense as best he could the slaves
themselves, building decent houses, schools, churches and even
hospitals for the men and women who rightly became paid
workers. Grandmama further insisted that they received decent
wages. I wish she had lived longer: she would have loved
Harriet, and appreciated her all the more for the struggles she
had endured.

'Neither Ellis nor Montgomery would expect it,' she reminded
me. 'Mr Baker would be able to drink his coffee in comfort. And
our colleagues would be able to clear the table and wash up at
a reasonable hour.'

'Motion carried nem. con., as Wilson would say.' I kissed her.
'So, my darling, how on earth shall we pass the hours after dinner?'

'I wonder how they feel about charades or a drama reading
or – heavens, there must be something! No – pray do not suggest
skittles, not with us women encased in our best corsets.'

More pressing was how the Bakers would cope with the idea
of dining with the one who produced the wonderful dishes.
Perhaps our pre-dinner gathering for sherry would give us an
opportunity to judge. Baker's patent disapproval of our use of
first names for all did not augur well. We knew that such informality was not a general practice: 'Mr' or 'Mrs' So-and-So was
the normal usage of many of our city friends and acquaintances.
In fact, I knew of at least one bishop's wife who always
addressed her husband as 'My Lord', in public at least. It always
sparked a wicked question that I only ever dared share with
Harriet – did he wear his mitre in bed? Or merely his shovel
hat and his gaiters?

Thatcher announced our guests all formally, whether they were
visitors or whether they lived in the House. 'Mrs Arden, Doctor
Page,' he intoned at last – yes, Bea would have been in charge
in her kitchen till the last possible moment.

But without knowing her occupation, no one would have

guessed it. Certainly, from her appearance no one could tell she was not a duchess, at the very least. If I thought her enunciation owed something to the plays we read together, I would not for anything remark on it. In fact, she spoke comparatively little, content, it seemed, to gauge the ebb and flow of conversation before venturing in herself. Like Harriet, she was sometimes more aware of her lack of ladylike accomplishments than proud of her amazing achievements. Neither played the pianoforte or the harp; neither sang sentimental ballads. One might, of course, wish that many young women who could and did might desist. But both had a truly important quality – authority in their own sphere.

Meanwhile, the conversation was heading into a sensitive area. Hardly had Page sat down than Baker was asking him pointed questions about the patients, permanent and temporary, in the Family wing. His smile might be as charming as usual, but there was a slight edge to his voice.

'Do I hear that you take all-comers and charge them nothing?' he asked.

'It depends what you mean by "all-comers". The rule of thumb is that if an estate worker or his family is in need of care, then the estate pays for it, usually indirectly by paying the wages of the orderlies and the nurses.'

'So you can bring your own patients here and get them treated?'

Page shook his head. 'If one of my own patients needs nursing, I pay for his or her other treatment, and the patient then pays me. If a stranger to the village, known to none of us, needed us, then we would ask them to pay for some or all of their treatment.'

'And this Lord Croft of yours? He gets away scot-free?'

'Sir, this is his home!' He continued, more calmly, 'Naturally, I visit him every time I visit another patient here. If I am summoned specifically to treat him, then the estate pays my bill. It also settles the accounts of the specialists I consult.'

'So is he getting worse? How long has he got?'

Page shook his head gently but firmly. 'You will understand that I cannot answer those questions. No medical practitioner may divulge information about his patient. That is entirely confidential.'

Baker narrowed his eyes. 'So you don't tell these trustees of yours? Anything?' A hit. A palpable hit.

'Only inasmuch as his lordship's health affects the running of the estate. A sudden improvement, a sudden deterioration – yes, I would report on those.'

'But I am his heir, Doctor. Don't you think I am entitled to know at least what they know?'

Coughing, Wilson raised a minatory finger. 'You will understand, Mr Baker, that some heirs might wish to make use of details of their predecessor's health – adverse use. There would be legal processes to go through before Doctor Page might divulge them.'

'What's to stop me simply walking up there and talking to the guy?'

A couple of burly guards, of course – but Page produced a more tactful response. 'There are protocols, sir.'

Mrs Baker spoke for the first time. 'You mean to say that my husband is forbidden to visit with his close relative?'

Wilson's lips tightened. 'Close by sanguinity or close because the two men have established a deep and lasting relationship? To the best of my knowledge, his lordship has never heard any American accent, let alone heard your husband's.'

'But how will he get to know him if—'

'Mrs Baker!' her husband rapped out.

'I'm sorry.' The pretty doll subsided, eyes filling with tears, I thought.

Had Thatcher been eavesdropping? 'Ladies and gentlemen, dinner is served.'

Mrs Baker half rose, then sank down again. 'Mr Baker, I have one of my headaches coming on. The travel, Mrs Rowsley, I fear. Please – excuse me.'

Baker was on his feet in a second. 'We'll have you lying down in a trice.' He scooped her into his arms.

Page was on his feet. 'May I help her, sir?'

'No, sir. She'll be fine.'

'Are you sure? I—'

'She said it was just a sick headache. That's all it is.' And he bore her from the room without another word.

Thatcher turned to me. 'I will despatch Miss – I mean *Mademoiselle* – Dubois to her immediately.'

'If you please – and I will pop up and see how she does,' Harriet said. 'And to see if Mr Baker wants to have his dinner served up there.'

Still standing, Page spread his hands. 'I wish I—'

Wilson got up and laid a firm hand on his arm, 'My dear man, you did your best. And I am sure that woman of hers will summon you if she needs you.'

TWENTY

I t was a long time since I had tapped on a bedchamber door and had to wait for a reply. What had I done? Tapped, waited – waited for a count of thirty – and tapped again.

Perhaps my second attempt was too loud. The door was flung open, and a furious Mr Baker glared. 'What the hell is the meaning of this?'

'I beg your pardon, Mr Baker,' I said, but with no note of subservience. 'I came to tell you that Mrs Baker's dresser is on her way and to ask you if you wished me to send one of the nurses to come to attend her. And to remind you of Doctor Page's offer.'

He seemed to recollect himself. 'Her servant can help her into bed. I see no need for a nurse. Or Page.'

'And you, Mr Baker – would you like to have your dinner served up here, or would you prefer to join us later?' Which would mean, of course, that Bea's wonderful food would no longer be at its best.

'I guess I'll be down as soon as that woman of hers deigns to show up.'

'Ah – here she is.'

'But what's that?' He pointed at the tray she was carrying.

'If you please, sir,' she replied, bobbing a curtsy, 'it's a glass of warm milk and a few biscuits – to help her settle, I thought.'

With something between a snort and a sigh, he admitted her. And shut the door in my face. Unable to restrain myself, I dropped in my own ironic curtsy at the woodwork.

Three ladies and four gentlemen would never have made for an easy seating plan, but Dick and I had dealt with similar or even more unequal numbers when the archaeologists and historians had stayed here. It seemed right that Mrs Baker should sit by Montgomery, but who should be at her other hand? Ellis as an honoured guest or Matthew as the host? Ellis, perhaps, so that he did not sit next to Bea. Heavens, it had been much easier in the summer with just two ladies, one of whom sat at the foot and the other at the head of the table. At last, we decided that Montgomery would sit at the head, with Mrs Baker beside him on his right, with Ellis beside her and me his other side. Opposite me would be Mr Baker, Bea and Matthew. In terms of the strictest etiquette, it was far from ideal, and I feared yet another of Mr Baker's black marks against us. The only way round it, however, would have been to invite Hannah or Nurse Webb to make up the numbers, and though he might have relished the latter's genealogy, her straight talking might not have suited, any more than Hannah's beauty would have outweighed her lowly birth.

Now, of course, all that juggling was in vain.

Only Dick and young Tim – apparently, none the worse for his dreadful experience – would be in attendance. Bea had been able to reduce the number of dishes on the table, too, many of which she had been able to prepare in advance for her staff to cook. She had relied on her favourites – a carrot soup, lightly flavoured with coriander, for instance, and a chicken with tarragon cream. A pheasant pie.

A feast. A feast that would have been steadily going cold, but for the chafing dishes Bea had chosen to serve the food in. No, there was no sign of Mr Baker. Perhaps his wife had taken a turn for the worse? Perhaps he was lost in the maze of dimly lit corridors, his candle having gone out?

Exchanging a glance with Matthew, I spoke to Dick. Yes, he would despatch young Tim to go in search of him.

We waited. Dick had already taken away Mrs Baker's place setting; should he remove Mr Baker's too?

I shook my head. Surely that was him now.

It was.

And he did credit to the food, all washed down with Bea's exquisite cordials. He had a seemingly gargantuan appetite.

The conversation was almost exclusively about what I imagined was the safe subject of food, Ellis introducing his hobby horse that apples should be on everyone's menu at least once a day.

So far, so good.

'And what will my cousin be dining on?' Mr Baker shot at Ellis. 'He must have more than apples in his diet.'

Cousin? It was surely a very generous term given that Mr Baker's part of the family was many times removed from his lordship's. Montgomery's eyebrow quivered each time Mr Baker claimed such close kinship.

'Indeed he does. The Family wing—'

'The hospital, in plain English.'

'Forgive me, Baker,' Ellis continued, 'it has been known as the Family wing for as long as I can remember, and almost certainly well before that. It was the part of the House her late ladyship liked best, was it not, Harriet?'

'It was indeed. Certainly, her bedchamber and sitting room were always there, and are now used by guests who are taken ill here. When his lordship came into his title, he took over his father's rooms, and that is naturally where we look after him now. To answer your question, there is a separate kitchen for the wing.'

'So you are doubling the number of servants involved.'

'It is largely because most of our patients need – obviously – an invalid diet quite different from the sort of fare we are now enjoying,' Ellis replied.

'And also,' Bea added, 'because the distance from the kitchen to the wing would mean the patients' food was cold by the time it reached them. And although the cooks and their kitchen maids are in separate places, there are no more than there would be if we cooked everything downstairs.'

He waved a dismissive hand. 'That's the other patients. I asked about my cousin.'

That word again. Surely at any moment Montgomery would remonstrate.

'My apologies,' Ellis said, jumping in quickly. 'In fact, his lordship is allowed many of the dishes that he has always enjoyed.'

'Such as?'

Bea smiled. 'He is particularly partial to kedgeree for breakfast, and loves the carrot soup you have just been served. Curry, too. And once, in Derbyshire, he discovered Bakewell pudding, and that is served at least once a week. I prepare it; it is cooked in the Family wing.'

'Carrots? Curry? And does this strange regime include alcohol?'

'I must answer your question in two parts, Baker. His regime, as you put it, is as normal as we can make it. Almost all the ingredients come from the home farm and the estate vegetable gardens – as do those we have consumed this evening. Secondly, experience shows that some forms of alcohol increase his slight tendency to melancholia, though at Christmas and on his birthday he is permitted a glass of champagne, which many distinguished physicians believe has quasi-medicinal properties. Everything he is served is in accordance with the guidance of the very senior medical men whom the trustees appointed.'

'Who chose them? You? And these *trustees*?'

At any moment, good, patient Ellis might justifiably react to our guest's suddenly hectoring tone. But his first response was a smile. 'Rest assured we took the best advice in the country. One of my distant cousins is Her Majesty's physician. He suggested physicians from Chester and Manchester who specialize in the field.'

'You have a mighty convenient cousin, Doctor. You can pick his brain but as sure as hell I wouldn't be able to.'

'On the contrary, Baker; I will provide you with his address if you wish.' His smile remained, but had changed slightly. 'Please remember that every physician, from the greatest in the land to mere foot soldiers like me, takes the Hippocratic Oath. I may not believe in the Greek gods, but I certainly believe that I must keep the promise I made when I became a member of this honourable profession. I strive to do no harm; I do not share medical information about my patients; I give them no harmful medicine; I make sure they are fed well. Indeed, I sincerely hope that his lordship will be offered some of these wonderful preserved apricots. A triumph, Bea.' He raised his glass to her. There was no mistaking the love in his eyes, and in hers, as she responded to his compliment with a modest nod.

At last, Matthew suggested that the gentlemen adjourn to the billiards room so that Mr Baker might smoke if he wished.

'Actually, Rowsley, I do wish to smoke. And I wish to smoke right here.' He jabbed the table with his index finger. 'After dinner. As gentlemen do. At least the gentlemen of my acquaintance, while their ladies withdraw. Hence, I believe, the term *withdrawing room*. You came up with some cock and bull story the other night about fire. We can use an ashtray, for God's sake.'

Montgomery spread his hands. 'My dear Mr Baker, it is his lordship's legacy and – presumably – your inheritance that the trustees voted to preserve. Yes, the decision was made after a wonderful building in this very county was destroyed in the spring. But it should carry double its weight after the inferno at Temperleigh Hall last week. All the priceless hangings, all the great paintings – gone!' He snapped his fingers. 'Now, you beat me hollow last time we played; pray allow me the chance of revenge.'

Would Ellis join them? It seemed not. He needed to check on his patients up in the Family wing, he said. But perhaps he would see them after their game.

Or perhaps, from the exchange of glances between him and Bea, he would not.

'Shall we have tea?' I asked her after we had *withdrawn*.

'Or *coffee*,' she suggested, with a wicked twinkle. 'Come down to my room for a change; you may be in for a treat.'

And a surprise. The servants' hall was full of singers with Tim, his voice vacillating between a sweet treble and a deep rumble, joining in with vigour. He seemed to have put aside all the terrors of the icehouse. Bea smiled at me – yes, we must raise our voices too.

At last, those on early duty excused themselves and headed off with their chambersticks. Any moment now, surely, Ellis would come down: he and Bea must be given their moments of privacy.

I caught Hannah's eye as I bade everyone goodnight. 'You have done so well,' I said truthfully. 'Now, do you remember I mentioned making life over the winter more bearable? Billiards is one idea, and warm sitting rooms. But what about opening up the music room? It's not been used in years, and would need a very thorough clean and certainly a visit from the piano tuner. Shall we look at it on Monday and see what you think?'

TWENTY-ONE

'Reopen the music room, Harriet? Heavens, it's never been used all the time I've been here,' I pointed out. 'Why? And why now?'

'Keep still or I can't undo your studs. For one thing, like all the other state rooms it contains valuable pictures and furniture, not least the piano and harp, if they may be described as furniture. It needs to be aired just as the others do. It may well be that Mrs Baker, as a lady, plays the piano and even the harp – but I suspect that that would need more than the attentions of the usual piano tuner. Are there such things as harp-stringers?'

'My cousin always used to string her own as and when a string broke. Maybe Mrs Baker would – assuming we have spare strings?'

Arms akimbo, she glared at me in the mirror. 'Where would I look? Assuming I knew what to look for, of course. I do recognize a piano when I see one at least. And I rather think I recognized singing when I heard it tonight! Oh, Matthew, the pleasure on those faces as they joined in together. We must encourage them. We must. And perhaps one of them can play – no, not well, but enough to accompany the others?'

I turned to face her. 'Oh, Harriet, can you imagine Baker's reaction to the idea? He'd love it as much as he would love welcoming the footmen into the billiard room.' We laughed together. More seriously, I added, 'You know how two people may look through a rainy window, and both see what's the other side – but because of the raindrops they see quite different versions of it? I feel the same with him. As if we see the same object but my view of it makes no sense to him and vice versa. But you – you seem to ask the right questions and not take umbrage at his responses. Is that because you like him or because you have years of experience being tactful to unpleasant people?'

She considered. 'It must be hard for him. Imagine coming into a situation where everyone knows his or her place, and you make an awful mistake thinking the first person you meet is the man you really want to meet. And some of his questions make me want to cringe as much as you and Mr Newcombe do quite visibly, but yes, I suppose my years of keeping an impassive face may have helped me not to react. Do I like him?' She shook her head. 'I thought at first he was quite charming. He was polite, ready to be pleased. But now everything he says seems a threat to the House and even to his lordship. And I can't get the gypsy's warning to our colleagues out of my head. Many – even Dick and Luke – are genuinely frightened for their future.'

'Hence the choir, the billiards, the common rooms. Hmm. On a different subject altogether, why do you think he and Page are so antipathetic to each other?'

'I really don't know. But it's hardly surprising that Ellis was offended by his tone.' She sighed. 'Mr Baker suspects, doesn't he, that we are all, at best, sponging off the estate or, at worst, on the make. I am glad Montgomery is here to act as some sort of umpire, though he is in a most invidious position, of course. Let us hope that tomorrow, when we are all less tired, and poor Mrs Baker is over her headache, everyone will be calmer. I wonder if they will come to church with us?'

It seemed that Mrs Baker was still unwell, but not sick enough to require the services of Page or even a nurse. Baker himself, however, wished to join morning worship – but only in a Baptist chapel. Amazed that we did not have one in the village, he rejected out of hand the notion of Anglican or Methodist services.

It would set a notably poor example to the younger staff if Harriet and I failed to occupy our usual pew, but I had a strange reluctance to leave him on his own in the House – one nothing to do with the simple bad manners of leaving a guest to his own devices.

Fortunately, Wilson discovered a touch of neuralgia which precluded him from venturing out in what he feared was a cold wind. Perhaps he was discussing a simple remedy for the condition when I saw him in conversation with Luke.

We set out with a good party of servants, the Methodists parting from the Anglicans at the village crossroads – it always seemed to me a vaguely symbolic moment. Then we fell into step with

Elias Pritchard and his family, coming to a halt together just inside the church porch.

'I'm so glad I've seen you. I actually wrote this in case I didn't.' He flourished a letter which he pressed into Harriet's hand. 'I've been transferred to Wellington, with immediate effect.' But there was little delight in his voice, just puzzlement.

'We leave first thing tomorrow,' Aggie added with asperity. 'Imagine it! Thank goodness we don't have much to take,' she added dryly.

Harriet put her hand on Aggie's arm. 'Shall I send down some baskets and some dustsheets? Anything else? Are you sure? And how will you get there? Marty Baines's cart?'

She nodded. 'He's a good man, ma'am.'

'Is this the promotion that's long overdue?' I asked Pritchard himself, shaking his hand vigorously.

'Not quite. The sergeant there is nearing retirement, and they say I shall step into his shoes – boots, I suppose I should say – when he leaves. But I'd have liked – well, we'd all have liked – longer to get used to the idea. And say goodbye to our friends here.'

Harriet smiled, taking the couple's hands for a moment. 'We will miss you all, you know. Everyone in the village will.'

'Especially the cricket team,' I put in.

'But fancy going to live in the town where they had the Shropshire Olympian Games in the summer,' Harriet added. 'You run fast, you throw a long way – I see you winning a medal next year! And the children will have more opportunities there than they do here.'

He responded with his shy smile. Then his face became serious, and he dropped his voice. 'The funny thing is they said I had to hand over my work notebook and my occurrence book. Straightaway. And—'

'Who are "they", Elias?' Harriet asked.

'An inspector from Shrewsbury, Mrs Rowsley. And a Scotland Yard officer. Another inspector!' He looked around and dropped his voice. 'Why should these senior officers have come all the way to our house? It felt . . . felt as if I had done something wrong. But if I had, why should I be promised this promotion?'

'Papa, Papa! The bells! It's time to go in,' squeaked his daughter, jumping up and down.

It was indeed. We took our places in the church.

I found it hard to concentrate on the service – even the prayers. Part of my mind kept slipping back to the House and the Bakers. Did the man genuinely believe Page might fail in his duty? At least he had listened to Harriet's plea not to move Mrs Baker till she was better. What would he do in our absence? Surely he would not try to gatecrash the Family wing again. Out of the blue, I had a sudden and very unchristian vision of him prowling round, like a hunter after game, ready to purloin choice pieces from the collection. Why should I think that? He had shown no more than a polite interest in his future domain. All the same, I was uneasy. I must content myself with the knowledge that wherever he was, with the exception of his bedchamber, a trusty footman would be within earshot and Wilson might actually be with him. And he had no need to steal anything! It would all be his sooner or later anyway.

'Amen.'

And this strange business of Pritchard's promotion. Why should his move to Wellington be so speedy, if promotion was yet some while away? Why the senior officer, why the man from Scotland Yard? Would this be the man who threatened Harriet yesterday? My mental meanderings had just reached the head's protracted stay and then precipitous disappearance when the clerk finished the New Testament reading.

'Amen.'

And now for the rector's sermon. He would expect intelligent criticism, or preferably discerning praise, as he shook hands with us at the end of the service, so it was time to concentrate.

'This is a bad business, Rowsley, a very bad business,' Newcombe declared, as we left the church together. 'Young Pritchard is an ideal village Peeler. Yes, of course he deserves promotion – and definitely a better house! – but to remove him like that!' He snapped his fingers. 'There's something afoot here; you mark my words. Something I don't like the smell of. Ah, I'm sorry – my wife is summoning me. Her family,' he sighed, rolling his eyes.

Mr Pounceman, the rector, said much the same about Pritchard as we shook hands in the porch. 'And I hear from our good doctor that you have trouble at the House too?'

'Indeed,' Harriet said. 'One of our guests is unwell.'

'So Doctor Page tells me – we met as he was on his way to see a patient of his.'

'Sadly, Mrs Baker's husband does not – cannot – for some reason, see eye to eye with Doctor Page.' She smiled suddenly. 'You will see for yourself soon: Mr Wilson wishes to convene a trustees' meeting.'

He laughed. 'It may be that he will not see eye to eye with me either, then, Mrs Rowsley – ah, am I right?'

'He would prefer you to be a Baptist minister, I suspect.'

He shook his head sadly. 'Of course – but only one from his neck of the woods. There has been a sad schism over there. Not all Baptists think alike, you see, any more than all we Anglicans do.' He gave a dry laugh. 'I happen to know that the excellent Baptist minister at Wem is as strongly abolitionist as one might wish. Now, I have promised to come to read to Samuel and pray with him one day this week – who knows, I may just meet this gentleman.'

Harriet shook her head. 'Please don't prejudge him. He's in a difficult position, is he not?'

He peered over the spectacles he had recently started to wear. 'And you are not, dear lady? Likely, when he comes to power, to lose your home and all you have striven for, for so long? You have weathered so many storms – let us hope you weather this.'

'Amen,' I said, aloud this time.

A very pale Mrs Baker was able to join us for luncheon which, as always on the Sabbath, was a cold meal largely prepared the previous day. It did not seem much to her taste, but she listened with a mixture of interest and disbelief to Harriet's explanation that most large establishments we knew preferred staff to go to church or see their families rather than toil in the kitchen or elsewhere. Dinner would be a simple affair too, one that the chief kitchen maid could cook. Next week a different kitchen maid would be in charge.

'Apart from anything else,' I added, eager to head off any criticism from Mr Baker, 'it means that the owners and their guests can recover from the usual excesses of Saturday evening – a fine dinner and often entertainment, perhaps a ball lasting well into the small hours.'

'You have balls?' Mrs Baker asked, round-eyed.

'Not now, of course,' Harriet said. 'Entertaining stopped when her ladyship died. Oh, Mrs Baker, you should have seen the place then. She loved to have guests filling the place, and even if she had not organized an official ball, often she would invite a few families to supper, with an informal dance for the young people. It was hard work for us – very – but guests would bring their own maids and valets, and there would be little flirtations going on while the masters and mistresses were twirling round. Yes, we could hear the music downstairs, and many a time a couple or two would move the great table in the servants' hall and imitate the steps they had seen.'

'Ideas rather above their station,' Baker observed.

Perhaps Harriet did not hear; more likely, she chose to ignore him. 'Christmas was wonderful here – though I have worked at establishments which treated their staff very unkindly. They gave – as presents, remember! – cloth to the maids with which they had to make up their own uniform, and white gloves for the footmen. Here Lord and Lady Croft made sure we all enjoyed putting up the decorations and, just as if we were part of their family, gave us all individual gifts. I still treasure the books they chose for me . . . And then, when Christmas was over and all the guests had left, they threw a party just for us, with musicians and food and champagne.'

'Pardon me? Champagne for servants?' Mrs Baker repeated. 'I do declare, Mr Baker!'

Ignoring our guests' appalled stare, Harriet giggled. 'Most of us hated the taste, truth to tell. But we loved the dancing – yes, her ladyship brought in a dancing master every year to help the young lady guests, and then, when he had finished, he would teach those of us whose work was over for the day. Oh, we had such times! Matthew, how did you and your family celebrate? You understand, Mrs Baker, that my papa-in-law is a clergyman, so Christmas for him was a period of hard work. It still is, of course, the more so since he's now a dean in a great cathedral, especially one undergoing much restoration.'

I smiled at her, loving to see her face so bright with reminiscence. 'Yes, ours was dominated by worship, of course. My mother's role is much as Harriet's is now – not organizing great balls but ensuring that the poor in the parish have as much as possible to make their lives easier.'

'Isn't that the work of the lady of the manor?'

'Thorncroft, as you can see, is rather more than a manor, and Lady Croft always saw it as her duty to share the load,' Harriet said. 'In fact, Mrs Baker, I have promised to run a little errand to the village this afternoon – would you care to join me in the trap? I promise you that Robin is the most docile of horses and possibly a gentle trip on such a mild afternoon would do you good.'

'On the Sabbath?' Baker almost squeaked. 'You work on the Sabbath?'

'It is an errand of mercy,' she said crisply. 'Another time, perhaps, Mrs Baker. Now, shall we take tea and coffee in the yellow drawing room?' She got to her feet, nodding at Luke. 'Could you ask Dan to persuade Robin to move in – say – twenty minutes? I want to get there and back while the light holds.'

TWENTY-TWO

I delivered to a weary-looking Aggie Pritchard the items I'd promised, adding, thanks to Bea's constant preparedness, a cold meat pie, a cake and a basket of fruit, including, of course, a ready supply of apples. Tucked away, they'd also find rag dolls: one for the baby and one for the still snuffly little girl. I had been tempted to add a couple of guineas, but had a sudden fear that someone might construe that as bribery if it were ever discovered. Would helping Aggie pack clothes – yes, a pitiful few – and her cherished china constitute corruption? I hoped not, especially as the baby was demanding to be fed, a job she alone could do.

Our sad farewells said, I was just cajoling Robin into action when Marty Baines strolled by. When he produced an apple, Robin was quite happy to let us talk. We had a pleasant gossip about the new village and the hopes for the school. Marty was one of those interviewing the candidates on Wednesday.

'You should be sitting alongside me,' he said.

'Indeed, I should love to be. But that might bring too much scandal to an already controversial business. Imagine, educating girls alongside the boys!' I said ironically.

He responded with a grin. 'Yes – you should hear my customers chunter on about it. They say it means change, and perhaps it will. And some people like that idea less than others.' He scratched his ear. 'You'll recall that family that adopted his lordship's by-blow—'

'I do indeed. The mother doesn't want anything at all to do with the Family – she made that clear.'

'Ah, a pretty forthright woman, that one. Afraid she'd lose the little nipper, I daresay.'

'Absolutely. But she wants schooling for all her children, not just the little girl she took in.'

'And bright as a button she's turned out to be, they say. What a shame she was the wrong side of the blanket – his lordship needs an heir, and that's as true as I'm standing here. And a homegrown ladyship, not an American lordship, would be welcome round here, as you can guess. But I can't imagine her mother permitting that, not in a month of Sundays.'

'Her real mother would have loved it, of course,' I mused.

'Ah, poor wench. Any road, things'll work themselves out, you mark my words. What d'you make of the new lord?'

I bit my lip.

'Oh, ah. That bad, eh? Needs to learn our ways, of course.' He looked about him, then jerked his head. Robin and I followed him out of possible earshot. 'These London policemen, Mrs R – a real nuisance they've been, asking strange questions, and trying to prove anyone saying anything is a liar. Anything at all. Asking respectable women if they've been touched up, like. You can imagine how well that goes down. And pestering us blokes about what we get up to after dark. "Respectable, God-fearing men, we are," I tell them. And then they say they never thought anything else, and they ask about sightings of ghosts, God bless us! I tell them the King's Head's haunted all right: if they stay over, they'll have the grey lady pull their blankets off their bed. And there's a woman they drowned as a witch – she'll holler blue murder if any of them try pissing in the duck pond – pardon my language, Mrs R.'

Pardon it? We roared with laughter together.

'You're actually saying something else, though, aren't you?' I looked him straight in the eye.

'Ah. Summat's up. And the least said to any of them the better.' He looked round again. 'I reckon it's not so much the bloke as done him in as they're after – he'll be safe and sound in Ireland by now; we all know that. It's something to do with who he topped, and why. So least said, soonest mended; that's my advice.' He touched the side of his nose. Then he grinned. 'I just happened to see young Dan the other day, when he came for the post. He'll have put the word around the servants by now.'

'You mean—'

'They'll want to blame someone, and I'd rather it wasn't any of us. *Any* of us,' he repeated firmly.

I put my hand on his arm. Selfishly, I thanked God again that we were away in Oxford when he was killed. And I had even kept Pritchard's telegraph asking us for help. 'We must all stick together, Marty.'

'And we will, my wench.' He put his hand on mine. 'We will.'

So much for Sunday being a day of rest.

Everyone I had left behind, with the exception of Jeremy, was assiduously reading in the yellow drawing room when I returned to the House. In a corridor, Jeremy was equally quiet and studious, but was seated in front of a Romney family portrait wielding his pencil with amazing results. He smiled, making room for me beside him.

'Just scared Mrs Baker out of her wits,' he said, with no particular sign of contrition.

'How?'

'Walking quietly, despite this.' He nodded at the single crutch he now used. 'Admiring over her shoulder the miniature she was holding. Nearly dropped. Didn't. Nicholas Hilliard.' He pulled a face – he managed to convey both anxiety for such a precious object and interest that she had removed it from the firmly fastened cabinet in which, with others such as an Isaac Oliver and a John Hoskins, it was kept.

'Dear me.' My response was meant to convey the same two ideas.

'And my stammer. Scares her.'

'Scares her? How ridiculous! But people are ridiculous – you may have noticed that we have a very young footman who needs support when he walks. Pregnant women in the village run from him lest their baby "catch" the same disorder.'

He nodded sadly. Then his face lit up. 'Ah! Very clever. Indeed. Billy.' He snapped his fingers as the name came to him.

'Billy it is. He even sings! Oh, Jeremy – such a treat last night. The house staff are forming a choir: you should hear them!'

'Have. Very good. Could be their pianist? Need to practise . . .' He rocked a hand. 'Very rusty. In private,' he added with a grin.

'Not in the yellow drawing room, then! As it happens, Jeremy, we're about to have the one in the music room tuned.'

'Music room?'

'Come and see.'

The plasterwork in the music room was the best in the House, with musicians and their instruments wherever the eye wandered. Jeremy gasped. To my chagrin, the room needed a very thorough clean: I could see dust on the frieze from where I stood, and my finger left a trail on a fine pietra dura table. He, of course, was more interested in the piano, pulling a face as he played – what were they called? – chords. When he played a run of notes up or down the keyboard, even I could hear some were wrong. As for the harp, forlorn in a corner, a peep under its baize cover made him shudder.

'Mr Baker thinks our colleagues' lives are too soft. Well, there is plenty to keep them busy here, isn't there?' I locked up behind us. 'Would you care to eat with us tonight? A very short, simple meal, of course. I'd welcome your eyes, Jeremy.'

He nodded, making his hands into claws and gurning horribly like a child being a monster. 'Can scare Mrs B again too.'

He returned to his sketching, I to the group of solemn readers in the drawing room.

Jeremy's presence at dinner clearly startled the Bakers. Mrs Baker actually shied away from him, like a pony attacked by a savage dog. Finally, she was reassured as he took his place beside me. He made little or no attempt to converse, but nodded or smiled appropriately.

And then it was time to withdraw – to do what? Sunday was one evening when Matthew and I could retire to our own sitting room. This meant privacy for us and less work for our colleagues, who could damp down all the fires and do whatever took their fancy. But it would be neither polite nor, in view of what Jeremy had said, politic to leave our guests to themselves. In fact, Jeremy almost saved the evening. He might have sat in silence as we took it in turns to read a psalm or uplifting sermon to each other, but his pencil was never still.

At last, he lifted his head and turned the paper – still endearingly held to its backing with pegs. We all gasped. He had produced a stunning portrait of Mrs Baker. With a flourish, he signed it and passed it to her with a profound bow. Behind her joyous smiles, she seemed moved almost to tears – and who could blame her?

'Sir, it is so beautiful! May I really keep it? May I? Oh, Mr Baker—'

'It is truly remarkable indeed, sir,' Mr Baker said. 'But I am so sad that you chose to do this work on the Sabbath.'

Jeremy dropped his head, but not, it turned out, in shame. His pencil worked again. In a fair imitation of a sampler's stitches, he wrote,

The Sabbath is made for man, not man for the Sabbath.

Leaving his handiwork on the sofa, he gathered his crutch and his pad and struggled to his feet. With a bow, possibly ironic, he left the room.

Fortunately, at this point Mrs Baker discovered that she was tired and craved our indulgence if she withdrew. She did not take the portrait with her.

Her husband did not follow her. We sat in an awkward silence that not even Montgomery chose to break.

At last, Matthew picked up the offending sketch, rolling it carefully. He too bowed and left the room.

Montgomery and I tried simultaneously to start an acceptable conversation. We stopped simultaneously too.

The clock struck ten.

We were reprieved.

But only until the following morning, of course.

Mrs Baker took her breakfast quietly in bed, but the rest of us endured another rather fragmented conversation. Montgomery was especially terse, which he often was at breakfast; today, however, he was especially preoccupied. Mr Baker used the term *cousin* at least twice too often. Matthew was almost silent; there was a difficult situation near Worcester, he said. I knew it concerned a tenant unable for several reasons to pay his rent; many landlords would have simply thrown him out, but Matthew always considered extenuating circumstances. I could recall no occasion when his mild approach had not been successful, with the tenant bringing his farm back in profit. Mr Baker, however, might see any clemency as wasting his inheritance, so I could understand why Matthew should not wish to mention it now.

Leaving Matthew to his problem and Mr Baker and Montgomery to their own devices, I accompanied Hannah to the music room.

'We servants couldn't use this room, ma'am – it's so . . . so grand!'

'It will certainly be grand when we've cleaned it. It can't wait for spring, either, can it? We'll need a team of footmen for the frieze, and so on – can you discuss that with Mr Thatcher?'

'If I might, ma'am – Mr Wilson has asked to have as many footmen on duty around the House as can be spared. As long as we have visitors, ma'am.'

I might have been hearing myself speak to her ladyship. There was no lack of respect, but a clear implication that things would not be as straightforward as one might like.

I nodded. 'Of course. And though Mrs Baker has her own dresser, all of you maids will have extra pressures. But as far as we can, I'd like to prioritize this room.' I smiled at a memory. 'Go and stand by the door. Just for a moment.' I did what his late lordship had done years before – I stood in the curve of the piano and recited quietly.

I was rewarded by her laugh and a clap of her hands. 'Ma'am, how did you do that?'

'The architect who designed the room did it. Wherever you stand in the room, you will hear the piano – or me standing beside it – perfectly. Let's try to make it usable by Christmas. Book the piano tuner again, because the sound made Jeremy flinch – and he'll want to practise out of earshot of anyone for a bit. Go on, try it.'

She did as I would have done, hitting the keys in turn with one finger. And like Jeremy, she grimaced. We both froze as the door opened; she because she was a young servant, I because I did not want another discussion with Mr Baker over how to treat servants.

But it was a friendly face that greeted us.

Jeremy's.

In seconds, he was seated on the stool, playing by heart – though some of the notes made him grimace. It was not just any tune, either – it was 'Barbara Allen', the folk tune Hannah had sung the other night.

'Music in this stool?' Jeremy shrugged. 'Take hours to sort all this – and look, more sheets, books there. All need sorting.'

'And dusting,' I added as if I thought it would be a grim task. 'Would you have time, Hannah?'

Of course she would! I even hummed a little tune to myself as I left them to their task.

I was making my way to Matthew's office when I encountered Mr Baker. He was staring at our Fra Angelico.

'Is that genuine?'

'Yes, according to the experts who examined it in the summer.'

'So why don't you put it where everyone can see it? Leaving it tucked away for no one but maids with dusters to see.'

'Because the experts instructed us to move it away from direct sunlight. We moved the Botticelli, too, which I really regret. I loved to see it as I went about my duties. But the experts made it clear that it was not here just for this generation. Like all the treasures in the House, it must be preserved for years to come. Centuries,' I added truthfully.

'No point in having something if you don't see it. Like having diamonds in a safe.'

'I can't disagree with you, Mr Baker. But in a sense no one person *owns* a masterpiece like this. That's why we ensure all the rooms are cleaned and aired, even if no one ever uses them.'

'By order of the trustees, no doubt,' he observed with heavy sarcasm. 'God, you people sure know how to live high on the hog at someone else's expense, don't you?' He turned his attention to some of the portraits, including one of his late lordship with his bride. At last he turned. 'Ah, Wilson, I've been looking all over for you!'

'Have you? I am sorry to have kept you waiting.'

'Shall we serve you coffee in the yellow drawing room?' I asked.

'That would be excellent,' Montgomery replied. 'But tea for me, if you please, Harriet. Thank you.'

What had he been up to? There was a tiny smile playing about his lips that had been all too absent for the last few days – the smile of a schoolboy who, without detection, has helped himself from a plate of cakes. Mr Baker? I did not like his expression at all.

TWENTY-THREE

By late on Monday, I knew I had no option but to travel down to Woakes's farm the next day. Fortunately, the trains connected well, and with luck I should be back before it got dark. I broke the news as we dressed for dinner.

Harriet smiled. 'It looks as if I shall have a quiet day, then. Montgomery has business in his office to deal with, and Mr Baker has decided he and his wife should travel with him and see the town.'

'Is she well enough?'

'Apparently. I presume that means she will come down for dinner tonight. Oh, Matthew, how strange this all is.'

Harriet cajoled Robin into taking us all to the halt in the estate grounds, waving off first the Shrewsbury party and then me. Much as I wanted to clasp her to me, as if taking a long leave, I had to content myself with a peck on her cheek as the station master approached. And then I was off to exercise the judgement of Solomon.

It was a troubling situation. I involved the farmer himself, his lawyer, even his vicar. If I delayed foreclosure, would it make any difference? It was clear that his wife, always the one with ideas and knowledge while he had brawn aplenty, was unwell. Would her health improve and thus the farm's profits? Or would it deteriorate and plunge the farm into further mire? In the end, I suggested a compromise: let his wife furnish me with some plans, some I could discuss with the trustees, since it was so exceptional a case, and I would make a decision after Christmas; they would not be homeless at such an important time of year. I rather thought Harriet would approve – and yes, I was looking forward to seeing her smile in the station lamp-light – I was arriving much later than I had hoped – as she and Robin waited for me at the station.

But there was no sign of her as the train slowed to a halt – and

here, my God, was Thatcher pushing me back into my compartment. 'Stay on the train, sir! You have to continue to Shrewsbury!'

'Harriet's ill?'

'No. In perfect health. I'll explain as we go!'

'But—'

'Luke and Mrs Arden are holding the fort, sir. You have to
listen to me.' He pressed a brandy flask into my hand as the porter
slammed the compartment door. He moved to sit opposite me.

'It's like this. Dear lord, I can hardly believe it, let alone say
it aloud! They've arrested Mrs Rowsley, sir. Yes, arrested. For
theft. The policemen that came to the House the other day –
Sergeant Swain and that Scotland Yard inspector. They barged
in on servants' dinner – yes, she was eating with us, as she
often does when you have to go off on your travels. They
manhandled her away – a lady like her! Wouldn't let her pack
or anything. I tried to stop them – but you know they told me
they'd charge me with assault or something the other day. Today
they said they'd charge me with being an accessory if I didn't
shut up. So I did. Thought I'd be more use to her out of gaol
than in it.'

'Gaol!'

'Yes, Shrewsbury Gaol. The Dana! I know, sir, I know.' He
took a deep breath. 'So I telegraphed Mr Wilson. Begged him
to meet her there. Get her out before nightfall. And – forgive
me, sir – I took this from your desk.' He passed me my address
book. 'So when we get there, you can telegraph people like Sir
Francis, sir – and that judge friend of hers. I've packed this for
you.' He patted a small valise I'd not even noticed. 'And one for
Mrs Rowsley. I've made provision for myself, in case you want
me to stay. Or I'll go back to the House if you prefer, sir.'

He looked near to tears. Certainly, his hands were shaking
as much as mine. I passed him the brandy. 'We're in this as
equals, Dick. Not *sir*, but Matthew. Please stay. I'd really
welcome your company.'

He swigged and choked, eventually managing an apologetic
grin. 'Thank you. She's been – like . . . not a mother . . . but . . .
a dear aunt to me, sir.'

'Matthew!'

He nodded. 'And they do this to her.'

'Did they say what they thought she had stolen?'

He shook his head. 'Can you imagine her taking *anything* that wasn't hers? You know she and I keep an inventory of everything in the House? In every single room that's open for use. And as we clean – you know she's started to open the music room? – we make a fresh inventory. We double-check each other. She gives, not takes, sir!' He dashed away the tears he could not control any more. Mine were flowing too.

Realizing the futility of all this emotion, we started to work on a plan. Wilson's office must be our first target, for we would probably not be allowed into the gaol ourselves. As her lawyer, he could demand to see her.

Shrewsbury! Would we be in time? Not unless Wilson kept his office open exceptionally late. No sign of a cab at the station – we ran.

Wilson's clerk, Hanson, was just locking up when we hurtled up the street.

The old man frowned. 'Telegraph, sir? Not yet – ah, here's the lad now!' But the lad refused to hand it over until we stood in the office itself. If only poor Hanson was quicker on his feet.

The clerk's face grew almost as troubled as our own. 'One night in the year, he goes home on time! Shall I accompany you to his residence, gentlemen? I fear—' He picked up his walking stick.

'Whitehall Street, is it not? Dick, this way!'

It was hardly surprising that the kind-faced housekeeper opening the front door to our thunderous knocking was taken aback by our breathless demands to speak to her employer. She immediately recognized me and showed us into her master's parlour. But find him she could not.

'He's gone out to dine, sir,' she said. 'And I don't know where – though he did say he did not expect to be late.'

'It's very urgent. Did he give you no hint – none at all?'

She gave a little snort of laughter. 'Only that he seemed – no, I'd say he didn't want to go. But he muttered, "Duty calls" – as if he'd rather duty hadn't, if you get my meaning, sir.'

'To see a client, then?'

The doorbell pealed a summons she couldn't ignore. I clutched Dick's arm – surely that was Hanson!

He bowed as he joined us. 'Forgive me – I had to lock up.

And you know my progress is slow. But I know he'd want to see the telegraph, even at this time of the evening. A sad business.' He shook his head.

'Did he mention to you, Mr Hanson, that he was dining out?'

Hanson shook his head with a sigh that suggested he would not have hurried so much if he'd known his master was not at home. But then he snapped his fingers. 'Perhaps – could he be dining with the client he spent much of the afternoon with?'

'Who?'

He bridled. 'I am not at liberty to tell you, sir – it is a confidential matter, you will understand, as is all Mr Wilson's business.'

'Indeed. But you might speculate aloud, perhaps, where he might dine with such a client?' I kept my voice calm and low, knowing that to succumb to my fury would not help. I could not simply scream and shake the information from him.

He bit his lip. 'It would be at an hotel, I should imagine. The Lion, perhaps, or the Bull. Or the Prince Rupert. We have so many establishments claiming to be hotels that are no better than coaching inns.'

'Mr Hanson, Mr Thatcher and I are in need of overnight accommodation ourselves. We can't leave Shrewsbury without my wife; she's locked in the Dana, for God's sake!' My voice broke at the thought of her spending the night there, not knowing I was desperate to help. I added in a more measured way, 'And to gain her liberty, we need your employer.'

The housekeeper said, quietly, 'Send word to me where you intend to stay; I will tell Mr Wilson the moment he arrives home. After all,' she added with a dry laugh, 'with the best will in the world, even he can't help till the morning, can he?'

Accepting the sense in her words, we trudged out into the night, rather more slowly than we had arrived since Hanson accompanied us. At last, as Harriet would have wanted, I flagged down a cab to take him home, paying generously.

'Which animal should we choose, Dick? The Bull or the Lion?' I asked.

'The Lion is just down there.' He pointed.

It proved to have two vacant rooms. I scribbled a note to Wilson – yes, a boy would take it straightaway. The rooms were clean and decent. And to my relief – I had forgotten that Dick might be as hungry as I discovered myself to be – the dining room was still open.

Dick gripped my arm as the waiter seated us. 'Sir – *Matthew*! – you didn't need to send that note. Mr Wilson is over there. With the Bakers!' He looked straight into my eyes. 'Please – I believe I might be better at dealing with this situation, if you care to trust me.' The pressure on my arm intensified.

At last, I realized that he might be right. Swallowing hard, I nodded. The young man, smart as any in the room – when had he found time before he left the House to don his best suit? – made his way unobtrusively across the room, to stand behind Wilson, just like a waiter. He bent to speak into his ear. Bent again to listen to the reply. Bowed. Returned.

I nodded to our waiter to fill both wine glasses as he resumed his seat.

'I asked him if we might trouble him for a few moments of his time when he had finished his meal.' To my amazement, he gave a snort of amusement. 'I don't think either Mr or Mrs Baker noticed my presence. And if they did, I would wager that neither recognized me.'

I found myself smiling. 'Harriet always said you were invisible when needs be, and obvious if called on. A perfect butler. Oh, Dick – we are here eating and drinking, and all the time she is languishing in . . . in a hellhole!'

'And we are going to get her out, remember.'

Normal conversation languished, but from the corner of his eye he could observe the Bakers' progress, so he kept up a sotto voce commentary. Yes, they were summoning a waiter. Yes, they were getting up to leave, Wilson with them. No, none of them showed any sign of coming this way. If Wilson dared ignore Dick's plea – all of me was clenched, from my jaw to my fingertips. Again, the young man put his hand on my arm. 'He may prefer them not to know you are here, sir.'

I nodded, forcing myself to breathe.

Our waiter cleared the table. I ordered brandy for both of us. A sudden smile from Dick. 'He is coming this way now. Would you prefer me to leave you?'

'I would rather you stayed,' I said firmly. 'Lest you have to stop me killing him.'

In fact, Dick was the one to recount the afternoon's events, signalling for another chair and even passing Wilson his own untouched brandy, which our old friend, suddenly grey-faced, gulped without, I think, noticing.

'Do we have precise details of the alleged theft?' he asked, his voice not quite his own.

Dick shook his head. 'Not that I heard. And I can't, sir, not for the life of me, think what Mrs Rowsley would want to steal, can you? Not unless,' he said less certainly, 'she was afraid Mr Baker might try to take it when he . . . when his lordship dies.'

Wilson's face regained a little colour. 'Let me assure you both – in absolute confidence, I need not say – that such an event is not in the immediate future, as far as I can see, at least. But then I did not foresee this – this outrage!' He raised a finger. 'Before I appear in court – yes, Mrs Rowsley must answer to a magistrate before . . . before any further action is taken against her.' He swallowed as he lost the thread of his sentence. 'Tomorrow there are papers I must retrieve from my office safe in order to show them to the magistrate. So I must be up betimes. Forgive me if I leave you now. I will see you in court tomorrow at nine.'

'One question first, Wilson, if you please!' I said more sharply than I had intended. Dick looked at me with concern. If he had put his finger to his lips, the message could not have been clearer.

Wilson smiled. 'I will answer it without your having the trouble of putting it. I dined with Mr and Mrs Baker tonight in my guise as a bumbling old idiot. I wanted to make them trust me, perhaps far enough to betray themselves. They would not be the first, as we know, to claim to be family. I still suspect that Mr Baker is indeed the heir, but I also believe he will not want to wait to take up his legacy inasmuch as it lies here in England. But much of the treasure is portable, is it not? It could cross the Atlantic.' He paused for us to absorb the implications. 'Now, knowledge is power, is it not? We must be ready to out-manoeuvre him. And dinner tonight has, I believe, helped us with that.'

TWENTY-FOUR

Yes, I survived the night in hell. But only thanks to the kindness of the other women. For many, it was not their first stay in such a place, and for many, alas, it would not be their last. There were rules, they explained, that they had devised themselves, to prove to themselves, I suspect, that though their morals might have been different from other people's, they still had morals of their own. There was prayer. There was motherly comfort for young girls already relying on prostitution for their living. There was quiet chat until their agreed time of silence – not that there ever was anything like silence, sobbing and the screams of nightmares replacing conversation.

But suddenly I was back in the workhouse. Hungry. Alone. My fate entirely in others' hands. And now back in the present. Dear God, the smells, the echoes, the distant clamour. Those, and the ignorance of what I was supposed to have done. Was it some act of revenge for the complaint I had made to the police about the head in the icehouse? Why else should a Scotland Yard detective have been with Swain (I would no longer dignify him with his official title)? There was a term for what they were doing. They were framing me. *Framing*.

Did I drift to sleep? If so, another scream woke me – was it my own? It could have been. Someone cursed me; another took my hand. Dear God, the sheer humiliation of being here.

I must think of something else. Someone else. Not Matthew. What if in his anger he attacked one of the officers? I prayed, with as much fervour as I had ever prayed, that he would be calm. But the very thought of him brought me close to tears. Not Francis, my dear brother, by choice, not blood. Not Gussie, my oldest friend. How would he cope with being friends with a gaolbird? He would have to forswear me. No. None of those. Dick, who had seen my ultimate humiliation. The son I had never had. What had his eyes promised as we gazed helplessly across the Room? Help. Action. And trust.

As had Bea's. Dear Bea. The perfect friend. She would run the House, she and Hannah. They would. They must.

No. I must not weep. Because my tears wouldn't be silent, but great sobbing howls.

I must think of something else. That kind woman, Lady Georgiana Verney, who had so impressed me with her devotion to her villagers. But that brought another urge to weep: would we ever renew our acquaintance? I must think of another, of any, strong woman. Who better than Miss Nightingale? But that made me think of our own Nurse Webb. And then I realized for whom I should be giving immediate thanks to the Almighty – for Mrs Elizabeth Fry. What must prison have been like before her dedication and toil? But what prayers could I form in this dark abyss? Heavens, Quakers did not need churches and set prayers to address the Almighty; they did not need to kneel. So, flat on my back, I spent the rest of the night calling on God for a miracle – not just for me, but for us all.

Before this morning, I would have laughed at the notion of dear, pedantic, finicky Montgomery Wilson as an angel, but here he was, taking my hand as I waited to be taken before the magistrate – for remand or freedom. He was so matter-of-fact about what would happen next that it almost seemed as if it were happening to someone else. But he told me not to look for Matthew on the public benches: 'In truth, dear Harriet, I believe that even after your ordeal, you are calmer than he is. You will soon be reunited; I give you my word.' He patted his file of papers. 'I have all we need here.'

'All?'

'Except one thing: precise knowledge of who made this vexatious allegation.'

I tried, before the bench, to concentrate. On everything. The location. The face, especially of the magistrate. The words. On dear Montgomery. But – yes, an intelligent woman like me – I was nonplussed. Confused. Distraught. All of those and more.

Then I heard the words, 'As you will see, Your Worship, in her will, Lady Croft left some items to Mrs Rowsley in perpetuity; she left others for her exclusive use in her lifetime, or until Lord Croft took a wife, to whom the jewellery would revert. I have myself seen the safe in which all the treasures are kept. It requires two members of staff to open it. I am sure the necklace in question will be found there – if anyone cares to look,' he added with a sudden waspishness. 'What is unequivocally Mrs Rowsley's is in a strong box quite separate from the items on loan, as I might put it. There is no confusion. And I submit, no case to answer.'

The gentleman read the papers, passing them from one hand to the other. He considered briefly. But although he looked me up and down, he did not set me free yet. Why not? Why not? Severely, he asked Swain why he had not established all the facts before they arrested me. He pressed him hard. Why had he acted on an unsubstantiated allegation? But he did not ask who had made it.

I would have had him ask two more questions. Why had Inspector Willis been present at my arrest? And why was he not here now?

At last, he dismissed the now scarlet-faced man, noting that his superiors should give him an official reprimand. He turned to me. Yes, that was a smile, that a nod. I was free to go. There was no stain on my character. Slowly but inexorably, his face disappeared, along with the rest of the court . . .

And then there were Matthew, Montgomery and Dick standing around me, concern on their faces. Dick? Why Dick? But I could not ask questions, and certainly not answer them, looking and smelling like this!

Matthew and Dick took an arm each, while Montgomery found a cab. It seemed we were going to his house, where I could bathe and change my prison-tainted clothes. Change my clothes? No, things were still not making sense . . .

In the care of his housekeeper, a woman a few years older than me, I bathed, and then dressed in the items I learned Dick had packed, just as he had packed Matthew's case and tried to summon Montgomery. I felt better. And could take an interest when the three men declared that they were taking me to lunch. For some reason, Montgomery declined the Lion – Matthew whispered that he would explain later. But the truth soon emerged, with Matthew and Dick making fun of each other over Dick's pretence to be a waiter, and Montgomery's going along with their antics. Soon, however, it was time for us to return to real life, and the subtle distinctions in our lives that set us in different ranks. Montgomery declared that he was needed in his office, but that he would return to us on an early train tomorrow. We three headed to the railway station – but not without stopping at a stationer's where we bought new drawing materials for Jeremy. As the train pulled out, the three of us were still happily on first-name terms. By the time it stopped at the estate halt, Dick was already reverting to using our titles, as he mentioned his desire to check the contents of certain rooms at the House against our inventories. He did not need to explain the reason for that.

Every last member of staff was on the steps to greet us as we returned to the House. As the great doors closed behind us, the formality ended. Bea rushed forward to hug me, and applause and cheers rang out.

Matthew or I needed to say something. I sensed he expected me to. Could I?

'Thank you, all of you. I'm not sure I'm free yet . . . Oh, of course I'm no longer under arrest, or I couldn't have come home to you all. But I'm not sure how much I'm allowed to say about all the goings-on. For the moment, at least. And – you know what? – I really would like to sit down and have a cup of tea. In our sitting room. But – unless our guests have returned – this evening I'd like us all to eat together in the servants' hall, and I'd like us all to share a glass of champagne.'

TWENTY-FIVE

'And what if the Bakers have returned?' Harriet asked, as we walked slowly up the main stairs, Luke having spirited away our overnight valises. 'I fear we should dine with them.'

'You are entitled once in a while to be unwell. And they need not know that I have not returned from yesterday's business.'

Before she could respond, Dick – soon to become Thatcher again, given the way he addressed us – ran up behind us. 'Sir, ma'am, Mr Baines and Mr Newcombe have just arrived. Shall I tell them you are indisposed? You have every right to be!'

Harriet clapped her hand over her mouth. 'Those interviews at the new school! We must hear their news, mustn't we? In any case, for us both to be unavailable sounds discourteous at the very least.'

'I've asked them to wait in the yellow drawing room, and I have ordered tea.'

Matthew looked at his watch. 'Can you apologize – explain we were unexpectedly called away and need to change after our journey? Twenty minutes, Harriet?'

'Ten, if we rush.' And she ran up the stairs ahead of me.

'You don't have to be so brave,' I said, as I caught up with her.

She turned to face me. 'I do, Matthew. And I need you to make me.'

To my amazement, and I think hers, Newcombe kissed both her hands as she entered the drawing room. 'The whole village is up in arms! To treat someone we value so highly in such a way! Clapping you if not in irons, then at least in handcuffs! Outrageous!'

What? I stared. But before I could speak, Marty Baines stepped forward, shaking her hand formally. But then took her right hand in both of his. 'Welcome back, my wench. Taking you like that on a public train, for goodness' sake! If any of us could have laid hands on them . . .'

There was an awkward, emotional silence. Harriet herself broke it, asking, as she sat down, 'Do you have good news? Whom did you appoint? The man or the woman?'

Why had no one told me she had been publicly humiliated like that? Why had she herself kept it from me? Her questions to the men told me: she did not want to even think about it, let alone have me fretting and foaming in rage.

'Miss Phillips. She has already worked in a village school and comes with the highest recommendations. The man lacked her experience, and had a very strong Welsh accent that defeated me a couple of times.'

She responded with a smile. 'I'm sure you made the right decision. Now, we must ensure that the school house is absolutely ready for her. It must be as cosy as possible, a house that shows how much we value her. Perhaps your wife and I might convene a working party to make curtains and so on, Mr Newcombe?'

Yes, whatever the situation, Harriet would do her duty.

Would her duty extend to welcoming Mr and Mrs Baker back to the House? And to dining formally with them? Perhaps they were extending their sojourn in Shrewsbury – even perhaps in Wilson's company. I still had doubts over his behaviour towards them, but told myself that in truth his ultimate loyalty lay not to us but to the Family and the House. Harriet needed a friend, someone unequivocally on her side. I had the germ of an idea.

Our visitors must have noticed Harriet's pallor and left as soon as it was polite. Newcombe, however, reminded us of our promise to dine with them very soon – this was, given Marty's responsibility for disseminating information throughout the village, invaluable. If the village Justice of the Peace supported Harriet, she must be innocent.

As to the Bakers, we had just sunk on to the sofa in our private sitting room when Dick tapped on the door. A telegraph. Harriet smiled: he should sit down and wait while she read it. The smile left her face. 'The Bakers will need to be collected from the station at half past six. Mr Wilson will be with them. Dear God, this should be an interesting evening.'

Dick and I exchanged a glance. He spoke first, a slow smile crossing his face. 'As your butler, might I remind you that you have a prior engagement? I don't need to inform the visitors where it is. You can use the back stairs, of course. Your visitors would be served in the breakfast room. I can't see that any useful purpose would be served by exhausting yourselves further tonight.'

I said quietly, 'I think the same might be said of you, Dick. You may have youth on your side, but I can't imagine how you dealt with yesterday and the wait outside the courtroom this morning. Surely you can take the evening off.'

He nodded slowly. 'I fear that I am so fatigued I might accidentally spill soup over Mr Baker . . . Yes, I suppose Luke and Tim can share the evening's duties, with other footmen assisting. And I know for a fact that young Billy would really like to serve the pre-dinner drinks. From his little trolley.'

'You will really allow yourself to eat downstairs with us? In that case, I will take your advice.'

I stepped out of the room with him. 'Well done. But could you do one more thing before you go? If I can write a brief message, can you despatch someone to the telegraph office before you take the evening off?'

'I'll wait here.'

It was the work of moments to dash off an appeal for help to an old friend whose address lodged firmly in my memory. I think Harriet was too tired to notice, but I said I was writing a private note of explanation to Wilson. As a swift afterthought, I did. Dan would make sure the telegraphs would go this evening.

As I handed them over, I struck my head. 'Jeremy! What of him?'

Our butler, his posture now as formal as ever, gave a dry, knowing smile. 'I think he might be joining us in the servants' hall.'

Servants' supper was always a simple meal, cooked alongside the dinner served to guests. But with Bea in charge, it was always going to be both tasty and nourishing. Many great houses insisted on a rule of silence during mealtimes, but here tradition was slipping away, and though conversation took place, it was always quiet, never raucous. As Dick served the champagne, I made the shortest of speeches, thanking him by his given name for all his efforts. He was duly cheered and applauded. By their faces, however, very few of the younger staff enjoyed their champagne.

'Never mind,' Bea declared cheerfully. 'All the more for the rest of us.'

And then it was time for Bea's wonderful roast beef – during which I believe Dick fell asleep.

Hannah deftly removed the plate on to which his head would have fallen, smiling at a silent but serene-looking Jeremy.

Bakewell pudding, a duplicate of which the Family-wing kitchen would no doubt serve to his lordship, and queen of puddings completed the meal and, for us, a warm and contented evening. Dick and I joked about pushing and pulling Harriet up the stairs, but in truth she fell asleep even as I undid her buttons. Would she sleep the night through? I feared a return of her nightmares. And the arrival of some of my own.

Mrs Baker did not join us for breakfast, but without mentioning her or any reason for her absence, Baker did. Wilson was his usual breakfast self, preferring, it always seemed, to prepare for the events of the day in silence. Jeremy preferred the lack of conversation, of course. I was happy to ponder a really difficult issue on my agenda for the day. Harriet claimed, perhaps truthfully, that she had a headache. Possibly taking his cue from the rest of us, Baker fell silent too, apart from curt requests to Luke or Tim. No one at all mentioned any plans for the day.

With the lift of an eyebrow, Harriet caught my eye: this could hardly continue. It was up to me to play the affable host. So I turned to Wilson, with an idle question about the weather. His eyebrows were, in their way, as expressive as Harriet's. His said he knew what I was doing but that he was reluctant to indulge me. However, he declared that he might take a walk before spending his day on some particularly important business.

'Say, how can you spend so much time here, when you have a business to run?' Baker asked, reasonably enough.

'Since so much of my work involves the Thorncroft estate, I have the use of a room here. There is, for example, a tricky case that Mr Rowsley is currently working on: he needs to consult me each time there is a new development.' As Baker opened his mouth in what might have been a perfectly reasonable question, Wilson added, 'Sadly, since the law may be involved, I am not at liberty to discuss any details.'

'But as heir, I need to know these things.' The man sounded almost plaintive. Then he added waspishly, 'I guess you discuss them with these trustees of yours.'

'When necessary, I do, at properly convened meetings, so that they may all share the responsibility for the decision. You will see us in action tomorrow afternoon, provided there are no completely confidential matters, when we might invite you to step outside.'

'So I have to break up this trust of yours. Right now. Get rid of all you trustees once and for all.'

'I fear you may not. Not while his lordship is alive.'

'And he will be at this meeting tomorrow?'

'I wish – we all wish with all our hearts – that he was well enough.'

'So we're back at square one: waiting for a medical expert who may or may not be one of you to say he's fine and dandy – or dead!'

Wilson looked ostentatiously at his watch. 'You may have an opportunity to raise these questions tomorrow. Meanwhile, if you will all excuse me?' He got to his feet. 'Rowsley, did that new material come through the post yesterday?'

New material? 'Yes,' I lied. 'We can go through it in, say, half an hour's time? After your walk?' I turned to our furious guest. 'What are your plans, Baker?'

'They are none of your goddammed business.'

'Forgive me, Mr Baker – they might be some of *my* business,' Harriet said. 'I need to talk to Mrs Arden about meals for today.'

'She's the cook. Let her just cook.'

'Does not Mrs Baker have a daily meeting with your cook?' she asked.

'How would I know? That's women's work.' He sounded genuinely puzzled. He dropped his napkin and also rose from the table. 'Seems I do recall I have a project to work on.'

It appeared to be a project that kept him away from the rest of the House, because it was left to Mrs Baker's dresser to summon medical help for her mistress, as Harriet reported to Wilson and me, closeted in my office.

'I am going up to see what I can do, and Tim is already on his way to the Family wing to consult Nurse Webb.'

'Not Page?'

She snorted.

'Ah. Exactly so. I'll come with you, if you will forgive me, Wilson?'

'Of course – I'm only here to substantiate my lie, after all.'

Nurse Webb dismissed my question with disdain. 'Hmph! She's simply suffering from women's trouble.' She patted her belly. 'I'm surprised no one thought to keep her in bed and apply a hot brick or a hot water bottle. All this fuss! What was her maid – my apologies, her *dresser* – thinking of? Would you have a word with her, Mrs Rowsley?'

Nodding, Harriet turned to me. 'I'll walk down with you in a second. I just need a quiet word with Tim.'

The lad, who had been deep in conversation with one of the guards, spun round. 'Ma'am!'

She drew him closer so I could overhear. 'How are you, after the ghost business?'

'Funny, ma'am, the policeman asked about that, ma'am, the other day. I said I might have been shit-scared – sorry, ma'am – at the time. But I knew that ghosts couldn't hurt living folk, and I'd forgotten all about it. He said to keep it that way. Which seemed odd, really.'

'Perhaps he has lads at home who are afraid of such things. But it was good advice. Now, off you go! And next time I catch you hanging around, chattering away, I might have to mention it to Mr Thatcher.' She smiled as he bolted, but, as she turned to me, her smile faded quickly.

I caught her as she staggered. 'I think . . . recent events . . . might have been too much for me. But I am sure a cup of tea will be all I need. And there is a matter I need to raise urgently with you, Matthew. If you will excuse us, Nurse Webb . . .'

And why should being arrested and incarcerated not have been too much? 'If you need us, we will be in our private rooms,' I said.

'Or if you need me,' Nurse Webb responded with a grim smile. 'And don't forget that dresser!'

TWENTY-SIX

All I knew was that I was in Matthew's arms and that I could not stop crying. It was as if the tears, the sobs, were wrenched out of me, much as my confession had been.

When had I sat down? When had he started to rock me as if I were a helpless baby? Now he was murmuring into my ear, the sort of things you say to a hurt child: 'It's all right. I'm here. It's all right. I love you. Quiet, now. There, that's better . . .'

At last, I could breathe again. But these great spasms kept shaking my whole body. 'I should have told you . . . This new will. I tried. But I was afraid.'

'Afraid of what, my love?'

'We've always been partners, haven't we? We've made decisions as partners. But . . . what if this – all this – was mine? How would we manage?'

His laugh felt genuine. 'Exactly as we do now. With love and trust. Whatever the law says, I would never claim it as mine. You know that. And so that the world does, I will ask Wilson to draw up a deed saying that I renounce any and all my rights to any part of it as mine.' As I shook my head, he turned me to face him. 'I might enjoy being married to a rich woman! My love, I did not fall in love with you because you were a workhouse brat, or because you were good at dusting, or because you taught me new tricks for when I bowl. I loved you for you. I still do. And the House is part of you. You are part of the House.'

'Which is why I need to find the will, you see. Oh, do I have to go to Oxford and beg Professor Marchbanks for help? Truly, I hope not – I want us to find it ourselves. But if Mr Baker . . . We have no idea what he might want to do with it. If he wanted to live here, how would he treat our colleagues? Our labourers? Our tenants? And if he decided to remain in America, what would he do with it then?' I bit my lip. 'Did I not see in the newspaper that rich gentlemen from the Southern states are raising private armies to fight the Union army? Selling the House, or even just some of the contents, could pay for a lot of soldiers. And their weapons.'

'And keep slaves where they are,' he agreed grimly. 'But he can't, surely he can't, take possession of anything until his lord-ship's death.'

I snorted. 'Look at the way he treats his wife! Do you trust him not to try?'

'I do not. And possibly only you may be able to save it. We both know that. Now, where do we start looking?'

I jumped. 'Dear me, I had forgotten about Jeremy! This is what I need to confess, above all. He knows. Before I told you, I told him. Because – no, I don't know why.'

'Because, if I know you, he was lonely and lame and wanted something useful to do.' I managed a smile. 'He has no one else until he can be reconciled with his family. And I – oh, my love, I have you. Of course, if we find the will, if it even exists, since what Mrs Marchbanks said might have been pure malice, then so much responsibility falls on us. So very much.' I shuddered: who would I leave it to? And then I almost laughed at myself for thinking that that was the greatest of my worries.

'If there were malice, I think it would be his. We don't have to see him face to face: we could simply write to him explaining the urgent situation and asking him for help, couldn't we? Ah! Your eyebrow!' He touched it gently. 'Not a good idea?'

'Only as a last resort. A very last resort! Would you want to crawl to him, even on paper? I wouldn't, the loathsome man. No, let us try to do this ourselves, if we can. Our hands are tied because no one can be in the library without me, but I don't think it's there anyway. He saw that I was too familiar with everything there. No, it could be tucked behind a picture, stuffed into the back of a wardrobe, anywhere. And in truth, I'm sure I don't want Mr Baker to know what we're doing. Either he'd mount his own search or – oh, I don't know. Dear me, I wonder where he is?'

'With Wilson, I hope, having some sense talked into him. Do you still trust Wilson, by the way?' He sounded very grim.

'As a friend, of course. But as a lawyer, he must do what the law says. And if Mr Baker has right on his side – no! Mr Baker must not . . . must not have his lordship put in a common asylum.

And he must not dismiss out of hand all the people who depend on the House and the estates. We have to fight for them. Oh, drat!' I turned my puffy eyes and tear-stained cheeks away as Matthew opened the door. Nurse Webb.

'Ah, a good cry does one the world of good, doesn't it? Now, just to let you know: I still think Mrs Baker is suffering from no more than women's troubles, as I said earlier. But she's come up to the Family wing in tears, so I've popped her into bed with the usual remedies. Why all this fuss about a London doctor, goodness knows!'

'Might I pop up later to see how she does? I promised to read to dear Samuel anyway.'

She smiled sadly. 'It's strange, isn't it: some people get tetchier and tetchier as they get older; he just seems to get sweeter and more grateful. As for Mrs Baker, mind, you know the official policy – no visitors.'

'I understand.'

Matthew opened the door for her. They had no great love for each other but, I was sure, a great deal of mutual respect. 'I'll pop down and see if Wilson is free.'

By the time he arrived, I had at least bathed my eyes and tidied my hair, resorting to pinching my cheeks to give them a bit of colour. I suspect I did not deceive Montgomery for one minute.

'Apparently,' he said, sipping the fresh tea Tim had brought, 'Mr Baker has taken it into his head to be driven to Shrewsbury. I'd have thought it common courtesy to mention it first. Perhaps, since he has so taken against good Ellis Page, he is looking for another doctor.'

Matthew asked, 'Wilson, what the devil is going on? You have had time to speak to him alone. Without breaking any confidences, do you have any idea of his plans?'

'Alas, I feel I am riding two horses: my loyalty to the Family and to you two, my good friends, and my duty to the future heir. We know he will want to disband the board of trustees and impose his own manager on the House and the estates. However, getting legal permission to do that would, I suspect, make Mr Dickens's Jarndyce versus Jarndyce case look like a mere bagatelle. I believe he will try to prove that all of you – me included, of course, though that seems to have escaped him – have been making unwarranted amounts of money from our positions. However, since enough of us are visibly independent and have been supervising those of you who are closely involved, I don't think that cock will fight, to resort to the vernacular. He will probably submit proposals to have his lordship removed to a public or even a private asylum, but since his lordship owns this property, that could be problematic. His big difficulty, Harriet, is that you are in total, unopposed charge of the library. He may shrug and say you may have the books, but he will have the room that houses them. And since by then you will be homeless, he may argue that the books should stay where they are.'

Matthew put down his cup. 'All this presupposes that Mr Baker wishes to live here. Harriet has another theory, one I suspect is nearer the truth – that he will sell everything here, lock, stock and barrel, to raise money for the war in America. You have seen for yourself how he appraises the masterpieces on view – not for any aesthetic quality, but for their monetary value.'

Looking at Matthew, I took a deep breath. 'Montgomery, there is something I want you as a person to know, but I am not sure if you as Mr Baker's lawyer should.'

'If it is something that he would be able to use against you, please say nothing.'

I shook my head. 'On the contrary, it is something that may invalidate at least some of his claims.' I told him what I had told Matthew.

'It is not a will with which I am familiar, I have to say,' he said slowly, as if warning me not to take too seriously the information that had become such a burden. 'I suppose the obvious thing is to ask Mrs Marchbanks or that overbearing husband of hers. But the obvious thing is rarely the most efficacious. Particularly if you think that the lady's utterance might have been her last. What do you propose?'

'I look for it; Matthew looks for it; Jeremy looks for it. The people I don't want involved yet are my colleagues. They were all warned by a gypsy of a terrible change, and I would hate to unsettle them further.' She bit her lip. 'May I tell you something else that worries me? No, it's not about the House. It's about the murder, which Swain investigated. He and that

Scotland Yard man. I am a factor in both the alleged theft and
the quite obvious murder. And I am not the only one involved.
Tim is, too.'

'The young footman?'

'Yes. It was he who discovered the head was still in the icehouse
– but he thought it was a ghost. And he was terrified. I said a
ghost with only a head wouldn't be any good at haunting – but
what if the London policeman that spoke to him the other day
is not happy with his responses then? What if he questions him
again about the head part of the haunting? And what if they find
that it was Jeremy whose sketches we sent far and wide: will he
be at risk? You were at hand to rescue me, Montgomery – but
you can't be everywhere.' The words poured out, incoherent and
nowhere near expressing my fears. 'Let me try again,' I said,
taking a deep breath.

'You fear that for some reason the police will silence this Tim
and young Jeremy as they tried to silence you?' Our old friend
frowned. 'What is the likelihood – of either? In the detectives'
position, I would wish to declare the case closed and hope
everyone forgot about it.'

'But what if they didn't? How can we protect the boys?'

'You'll recall it was Jeremy's drawings that were sent to
Scotland Yard and the Oxford constabularies,' Matthew put in.
'Duplicates or variants are probably in his room. If someone did
want to locate them, they wouldn't have far to look.'

'I will speak to him now and suggest he destroys them. And
also suggest a very fine line between not being wholly accurate
and downright lying. I will be there if and when they come
looking. As for young Tim, having persuaded him, Harriet, that
it was not an entire ghost he saw – please tell me that you never
said that it was a real head?'

'I was going to. Yes. Because he's seen corpses and not been
afraid of them. But then I thought better of it.'

'Thank goodness for that! I do not want him caught in the
act of perjury. Or you accused of the equally serious crime of
trying to influence witnesses and thus perverting the course of
justice. Given your connection with Lord Halesowen, my dear,
it would not do.' Suddenly, he looked me straight in the eye.
'I believe you recognized the man, Harriet. Please do not attempt

any sort of reply. Please try to convince yourself that you were mistaken. It's my belief that to have him identified might upset people – important people – which is why our good friend Pritchard was removed post-haste from his position and silenced with a promotion.'

'And why his notebook and occurrence book were taken away,' Matthew added.

'Quite so.' He ran his hands through his hair. 'I have a glimmer of why the police should seek to silence – a glimmer, no more. But I cannot for the life of me see how I might prove it – or even if I should attempt to. As for what Mr Baker is up to . . .'

'Perhaps if we discover why he went to Shrewsbury, we might find out.'

He smiled dourly. 'Novels are more your area of expertise than mine, Harriet, but I do recall that in a very famous work, one of the heroes went to London apparently to have his hair cut. Let us see if Mr Baker returns looking shorn, or if a piano mysteriously arrives . . .'

We chuckled together.

'Meanwhile, where do we start looking for the will?' Matthew asked.

Montgomery looked at me. 'I appreciate that you do not wish to cause panic amongst the staff, my dear, but I see no reason not to ask for their help. All you need to tell them is that the professor – whom none of them liked, as I recall – has played a trick on you and hidden a letter that was important to you. To *you*, I stress. You might or might not choose to say that its author was his late lordship: everyone knows of your mutual devotion. As a matter of fact, given the very slow deliberations of the Law, I do not feel your search is urgent for the outcome of any dispute – but I do see how important it is for you. To repeat Matthew's question: where shall we start?'

'Any half-public room,' I said. 'The drawing rooms, the corridors, the breakfast room, the dining rooms. Bedchambers – though you may imagine that I have been through those the Marchbankses occupied with a fine-tooth comb. We search drawers in ornamental tables, in side tables. We look behind pictures – though those are far less likely, since after the little trouble while they were here, all the cords have been replaced. Even inside large pots.

Yes, a trip to Oxford in sackcloth and ashes might be quicker and easier.'

When I spoke to her, Mademoiselle Dubois, whose French accent overlaid one much closer to home, was polite but firm. Yes, she had offered the usual homely remedies for monthly trouble. But when Madame insisted she was getting worse, not better, knowing that there were nurses in the building, she had done the obvious thing and summoned help. Since she had been in her employment such a short time, she had not liked to argue, she added, a mite defensively but with an immaculate curtsy.

I nodded. Being a servant was not easy.

Then I would undertake a labour of love – reading a psalm to Samuel.

First, Tom and Sidney, the former gamekeepers turned guards, then Nurse Webb greeted me. With a wry smile, she said, 'Someone's beaten you to it – young Mr Thatcher's just arrived. But if you think the delay grants you licence to talk to Mrs—Heavens, what's that?'

She darted off in the direction of furious shouts.

'That's Dick's voice.' Rules or not, I followed. To find Dick in Samuel's room, wrestling a pillow from the hands of Mrs Baker.

TWENTY-SEVEN

'**M**rs Baker was doing what, Tom?' I demanded.

'Caught in the act of smothering poor old Samuel – Mr Bowman, I should say – she was. Follow me!'

Follow him? Poor Tom, once so nippy on his feet, was left behind as I took the stairs two at a time.

Tom's fellow guard sprang to something like attention as I appeared. 'Can you just wait here for Nurse Webb, sir?' He indicated the area where Nurse Webb penned aspiring visitors. 'You know her rules, sir,' he added with a grimace.

'I do indeed. But when an old friend's life is threatened – ah! Harriet, what in God's name is going on?' I steered her to a chair. 'It can't be true, can it? A tiny little thing like Mrs Baker attacking an innocent old man?'

She spread her hands. 'Dick – he was going to read to Samuel – Dick swears that when he went into Samuel's room, Mrs Baker was about to press a pillow over his face. She swears, of course, that the pillow had fallen to the floor and that she had picked it up and was going to tuck it behind his head. She's fallen into hysterics and is being returned to her bed. Dick is simply reading to Samuel as if nothing had happened. Of course, it's quite possible that Samuel registered nothing at all of the goings-on.' Sighing, she covered her face briefly, looking up as Nurse Webb bustled over.

'What did that guest of yours think she was doing?' she demanded furiously, as if we were somehow at fault. 'A patient just deciding to pop in to see another patient, a complete stranger!'

'God knows!' Harriet responded. 'She may be a guest, but I am not privy to her thought processes. Do you think she was feigning those period pains? She must be a fine actress if she can convince someone like you!' she added, in a more conciliating tone.

'I'll fine-actress her!'

'Forgive me if I act as devil's advocate,' I said. 'Could she have heard him cry out and gone to help him?'

'He cries out and none of my nurses hears him? More to the point, can you imagine Samuel ever crying out? If that pillow slipped, being the patient old man he is, he'd have lain there quietly till someone popped their head round the door and saw the problem.' She paused for breath, her usually calm carapace cracking. 'Yet an hour before, she was doubled up in pain, sick enough to beg for laudanum.'

'Could the laudanum have confused her? As if she were sleep-walking?' Harriet asked.

'Not the amount I gave her. I wonder if I should report this to the police. Except we don't have a village constable now, do we? I wonder when we will.' She raised an index finger. 'I don't suppose Mr Wilson is in the House, is he? Do you think he might advise me?'

'The problem is,' Wilson said later, over our quiet and simple lunch, 'that whatever the situation, we have no witnesses. Which would you believe: a butler or an American lady? Both would hold to their stories, of course – but young Thatcher does not want Mr Bowman upset by any forceful questioning. In the eyes of the police, that might diminish his credibility. And one must wonder why on earth Mrs Baker might wish Mr Bowman any harm.'

Harriet said slowly, 'Unless – remember, he is in a very comfortable room on his own – she thought he was his lordship? No, no! Please forget I said that.'

'Why, pray? It is a reasonable speculation. But if Sergeant Swain is the only one we can repeat it to, I fear we might, as the saying goes, save our breath to cool our porridge. I will spend the afternoon putting in writing the allegations and comments' – he produced an astonishingly youthful mocking grin – 'just in case!'

Though she laughed at his gentle jibe, her face was soon serious. 'How would it be, Montgomery, if I spoke to Samuel, with you within earshot?'

'I'm sure that Nurse Webb would not permit that!' I retorted.

'She won't if I don't ask her.'

* * *

Her first plea had resulted in a straight and, I suppose, foreseeable negative. Samuel was asleep, as he always was at this time. But then Nurse Webb permitted herself to show a little compassion. 'I will give it some thought. And by chance Doctor Page will be here in a few minutes to look at a village lad who took it into his head to fall out of a tree and knock himself senseless. I will consult him then. Come back in half an hour or so.'

And so the three of us were dismissed. Off we went, to spend an intensive forty-five minutes – it would not do to provoke Nurse Webb with excessive punctuality – rifling through drawers in every side table in the public corridors. Suddenly, in the midst of all the frustration, there was a moment of sheer pleasure: as we worked away along the corridor leading to the music room, we heard the sound of two voices raised in song.

'Hannah believes that singing will aid poor Jeremy's stammer,' Harriet said with a smile. 'And she assures me that she can sing while she cleans. But please don't ask me to sing while I search. You two can, of course.'

I waited for her and Wilson outside the secure door to the Family wing, talking to Tom about his family, and in particular his cricketing grandson Joe, a very promising young spin bowler, who unsurprisingly had benefited from a few sessions with Harriet.

'I'm afraid I'll have to hang my boots up before he reaches his peak, though, Tom.'

'You're nowt but a lad yet, gaffer. Oh, I've seen you lose a yard or so's pace these last couple of seasons, but on your day you're still a match-winner. Thing is, gaffer, what you've lost in speed, you've gained in cunning. And you need to pass that on to the youngsters. Ah, Mrs Rowsley, ma'am, I was just telling the gaffer here the team can't spare him yet a while.'

However much I wanted to hear their news, I knew I must wait while she exchanged a few sentences with him, especially about Joe. Then she must speak equally kindly to the other man – Sidney, I now recalled. How on earth did she remember the name of the most minor employee? But at last, she managed to extricate herself with grace, and we walked down the first flight of stairs together.

We stopped in front of an ugly Flemish depiction of the Judgement of Solomon, not by accident, I guessed from the impishness in her eyes. 'I'm sorry, Matthew, but I don't think either of us could call that a success. Dear Samuel asked for one of the longer psalms and knows it too well for me to edit it as I read. He said it was a long time since anyone had last read to him – no, not even "that lad Thatcher". And promptly fell asleep again. But we tried. And learned that Nurse Webb has declined to give Mrs Baker more laudanum but has set a nurse outside her door. Shall we take a cup of tea before we adjourn to the state dining room?'

'I don't think I've ever been in there,' Wilson said.

'It's never used except on the most formal of occasions,' she replied, 'and has several enormous sideboards.'

Despite all the promising nooks and crannies, there was no will.

Baker returned via the grand front door at about six in the evening, but according to the footman on duty did not pause to admire the amazing entrance hall which still had the power to take my breath away.

'Just stomped off upstairs, he did, sir, according to young Tim,' Luke informed me straight-faced as I locked my office for the night. 'And not a word of a thank-you passed his lips.'

So I was braced for his less than gracious behaviour when he exploded into the drawing room where Jeremy was giving us an account of his hunt for the will.

'And what do you mean by this?' Baker flourished a sheet of paper. 'My wife in the Family wing? What is she doing there, in the name of all that's wonderful?'

Harriet spoke first. 'Good evening, Mr Baker. I fear your wife became unwell soon after you left. Accordingly, she is under Nurse Webb's care.'

Wilson added smoothly, 'Since you were not in the House and your wife was apparently in great pain, I took it on myself – as your proxy – to give permission for her to be treated there.'

'Did you indeed? And why did no one inform me of this the moment I arrived?'

'Perhaps, Mr Baker, because we did not want to cause servants' gossip by asking one of them to tell you,' Harriet said repressively.

'That is why I left that note in your bedchamber.' She paused, perhaps waiting for an apology. 'I will ring for one of them to escort you to the Family wing now, and Nurse Webb will tell you what treatment your wife is receiving and why.' Her smile would have frozen water. I had an idea that Nurse Webb's might too if he spoke to her as he had just spoken to us.

She rang. Thatcher appeared, again a model of polite impassivity as he bowed to let Baker precede him.

Jeremy rolled his eyes.

'I have never seen you so formal, my dear,' Wilson observed.

'You have never seen me face to face with a man who was so rude to us all, have you?'

Jeremy returned to his new sketch book.

Anxiety had replaced righteous fury on her face. Anxiety, and even despair. Should I confess that I had summoned help? Or let her wait till tomorrow to find out? I could not tell her now, in any case: here was Baker.

He strode straight to Wilson. 'Who the hell does that woman think she is?'

'Nurse Webb is the nurse in charge, is she not? Should that not be enough, they are the title and the name preferred by Lady – no, I must not reveal her true identity,' Wilson replied. 'She does not wish to embarrass her family by letting it be known that she prefers to work for her living. Suffice to say, her father is a duke. She herself was trained by one who is clearly at the peak of the nursing aristocracy, Miss Nightingale herself.'

Baker gaped. 'And no one thought to tell me?'

'It is not our secret to reveal,' I said. 'She was gracious enough to admit us into her confidence when she was appointed, but we never even think of her as anything other than Nurse Webb.'

'But she might join us at dinner. It would be a delight to dine with Lady—'

'With *Nurse Webb*, Mr Baker,' Harriet said firmly. 'Will Mrs Baker be well enough to join us for dinner?'

'Seems she is to stay in her *hospital* bed for the duration.'

'How unfortunate.' No, she had neither forgotten nor forgiven. It would be a very silent dinner.

TWENTY-EIGHT

'I believe you have some sort of delayed reaction to your terrible ordeal,' Ellis said kindly the next morning, binding the thumb I had sliced as I tried to gather the shards of a vase of neither value nor beauty, but the destruction of which had reduced me to an unstoppable flood of tears. 'There. And next time use a dustpan and brush, my dear.' Closing the door of the Room, where he had treated me, he continued, 'This Mrs Baker. What do you know of her?'

'What can one know of an illustration in a fashion magazine?'

He looked at me, raising an ironic eyebrow.

'Seriously, Ellis, I have never seen a more beautifully turned-out young woman, not in all my years in service. She is exquisite. But I wonder – and any woman might – at what cost it comes.'

'Cost?'

'You have met her husband! Can any woman be happy in such a situation?'

'I know of many women who would exchange much for her financial and social position,' he said carefully.

'So a nabob sweeps into the House – would you expect him equally to sweep Bea off her feet? Quite.' I laughed, leaning forward. 'My dear friend, you and Bea have loved each other since – in dear Marty Baines's words – Noah sailed his boat up the cut. Enjoy your happiness while you can. I don't expect either of you to be murdered or to be hauled off to gaol, but personal tragedies can and do happen, you know.'

It was as if someone lit a lamp behind his face. But he tapped his nose. 'Let me just say I have arranged a locum for the whole spring. No, you may not wish me happy yet. You must wait for Bea to know the moment is right. But you and Matthew will be the first to know. I hope,' he said more soberly, 'that Wilson is not still dangling after her?'

'Let him dangle in vain. He has an admirable housekeeper – she is a good, kind woman and would make a wonderful wife.'

Voice lowered, and the tears only just held at bay, I added, 'And she was . . . I couldn't have asked for more unfussy and imaginative kindness when I was let out in my gaol-soiled clothes.'

'What was the worst part of it all?' he asked, surprising me.

And I surprised myself by telling him. It was hard, so hard, but by the end of my tale I felt cleansed.

After a mostly silent luncheon, I was back searching for the will, this time in the bedchambers the archaeologists had used in the summer – naturally, I had stripped the Marchbankses' accommodation the moment Mrs Marchbanks had whispered her secret – when Matthew ran me to earth.

'My love, could you do me the most enormous favour? One of the parties in a dispute I'm dealing with has telegraphed to say that he's coming to see me today. Could you take the trap and meet him at the halt?'

I pulled an ungracious face. 'Oh, very well.' What on earth was he doing inviting a stranger into this chaos? But it was a fine bright day, and perhaps some fresh air would finish the good work that Ellis had begun.

I was so busy encouraging Robin to move that I hardly registered the fact that the dogcart followed us, ready to carry our guest's luggage. Indeed, I hardly registered anything of the drive I always loved. But at last, we arrived at the halt just as the train pulled in. A lad went to Robin's head. I got slowly down, reminding myself that this guest was not at fault.

And suddenly I was running as if I was a girl again!

'Francis!' He engulfed me in his arms. 'What are you doing here?'

'Just bringing a friend – here he is!'

And now James was pressing me to him, mopping my tears and laughing at me.

'Amazing what a telegraph will do,' James said, tucking my arm into his and escorting me to the trap.

The dogcart was already loaded and moved away. Robin looked at it in disbelief.

'Some people move heaven and earth: Harriet does better. She can make Robin move.'

'Come on: home!' Robin twitched an ear, responding with the urgency he usually showed when he was stable-bound. And he was soon rewarded by a carrot by Matthew, who, beaming from ear to ear, was waiting for us on the front steps. Dan, saluting Francis as a respected and generous old acquaintance, led Robin away.

Meanwhile, there were Hannah and Dick waiting at the top of the flight: Matthew had obviously warned them in advance.

'I have aired the blue saloon for the occasion,' Dick whispered, 'assuming you might want a little time with your old friends with no other guests at all present. Sir Francis has his usual apartment, Lord Halesowen the gold room. I will serve tea and coffee as soon as I have escorted them down.'

'Thank you.' We exchanged a smile – yes, Matthew had planned this carefully.

Hand in hand, Matthew and I made our way along the south corridor to her ladyship's favourite winter room. Aired? To be this warm, there must have been a fire in the grate overnight.

'You needed support. I telegraphed Palmer. He summoned James. But I wasn't the first to send an SOS. Wilson was. So as soon as you are ready, I will invite him along as well.'

'I thought – I feared . . . Oh, Matthew, to think I didn't trust him . . .'

'My love, I saw him dining with the Bakers – I didn't at that point trust him as far as I could have thrown him. Ah, here they are!'

And within seconds there was tea, green and Assam, and a selection of Bea's very best biscuits.

We had much news and chatted simply as old friends for several minutes. But at last, James raised a finger. 'Would you permit me to take notes, Harriet? Because I have questions to ask – and very much to say to you and to some of your friends and colleagues.'

'You sound very serious.'

'I am. First, you learned about the murder here in a telegraph from your village policeman? While you were staying with Francis?'

'From Elias Pritchard, yes. I have it upstairs.'

'Why?'

'I used it as a bookmark – and then, when a strange sergeant took over the case, replacing the officer we knew and trusted, I had a fancy to keep it.'

'Just in case,' Francis put in, winking at me.

'And you in no way interfered in their case?'

'Would discussing it with other villagers and the wife of our local JP be interfering? No? Then I did not. Not until one of our young footmen went to get ice from the icehouse in which the head had been stored. It should have been there for the shortest of times, pending the arrival of a police expert to draw or photograph it in the hope it might be identified. But it stayed and stayed there, even after Jeremy Turton had drawn it. You saw the results, Francis.'

'And passed them on to James,' he said. 'Because I suspected that I had seen him. No, I was not acquainted with him – but I somehow knew the face.'

'As did I,' James said. 'But as it happens, I was acquainted with him. My instinct was to post up here and talk to you. But I was presiding over a murder trial, for one thing, and also worried that such an action might compromise one – or both – of us. As would a letter. So I encouraged Francis to hide behind his illness. We agreed to stay mum until something else happened.'

'What happened here,' Matthew said, 'was that our JP was reprimanded for complaining about the lack of police activity.'

'In other words, our faith in the police was shaken,' I added. 'And then one of our young footmen, last Saturday, discovered the head – yes, it was still in the icehouse. He had hysterics, but was convinced he had seen a ghost. But as I told Montgomery, I did not disabuse him.'

'But you did, I gather, suggest quite strongly to the police that it was more than time it was removed.'

I nodded. 'Ghosts don't smell of decaying flesh. Imagine if the boy had talked. Can you imagine lads a bit older than he seeing it as a challenge? "I spent the night there and *I* wasn't scared?"'

'Or worse, using it as a football,' Matthew added grimly. 'Like they do sick animals.'

'Thanks to Montgomery,' I continued, 'I was not charged with criminal libel for saying that the head was still on the premises. No, I didn't go and check if it had been moved.'

'Then our village bobby was suddenly and inexplicably moved to a different area. And Harriet was arrested.' Matthew took my hand.

'Which is when Wilson contacted me,' Francis said. 'I know he was deeply worried that someone should risk trumping up a charge against you. At that point, he was bemused: could the police have done this themselves? And why? Would you agree that he should join us now? Because what I have to say should be said as little as possible. To no one except ourselves.'

'Of course. And I suggest that Jeremy Turton be invited too. He, after all, saw the head – and his sketches were sent to the local force, to Oxford and to Scotland Yard itself.' I rang for more tea and to ask Luke to exercise his utmost discretion in summoning them. Soon they joined us. Again, conversation became the exchange of news between like-minded friends. I cannot say that Jeremy was any less handicapped by his stammer, but no one in the room showed any impatience, and he was able to communicate when he wanted to.

At last, James asked, almost casually, if Jeremy had recognized the subject of the sketch he had sent Francis.

The young man screwed up his face like a child. '*Seen* him before. Didn't *know* him. Strange idea I saw him at the Ashmolean. Looking angry. Furious. Might have mentioned it to Matthew.' That sentence was a dreadful challenge.

Francis and James exchanged a glance.

James asked casually, 'Did you keep any of these sketches?'

Equally casually, Jeremy shook his head. 'Why? Job done.'

Did Montgomery give the tiniest sigh of relief?

Matthew jumped in. 'I confess that I did not see anyone at the reception who looked anything like him. As for anyone being angry, it seemed a very . . . genial . . . evening. With some surprising results!' He smiled at me and then at James, adding more seriously, 'Am I right to deduce you saw him there? And recognized him?'

'I was too busy being *genial*, Rowsley. Forgive me if I seem insufferably pompous, but might I ask you all to give me your word that you will never allude to what I have to say again. Even – and you will wonder if my wits have deserted me – in conversation with each other. Servants are trained to be invisible – but they do have ears. If a conversation is essential, let it be out in the open air. Can I trust you?'

It was impossible to deny that mix of authority and pleading. I believe we spoke as one.

'I'll make sure no footmen are within earshot,' Matthew said, getting up, but he was stopped in his tracks by a knock on the door. And another.

Dick, his face carved from wood, stepped in. 'Mr Baker, sir and ma'am.'

TWENTY-NINE

arriet rose to her feet. 'Good afternoon, Mr Baker. I trust Mrs Baker is no worse?'

Why did she not mention the incident in the Family wing?

'I'm not here about her. I'm here because one by one you've crept out, and now I find you all plotting together.' Did he look more distressed than angry? Suddenly, I saw him in a different light – a child not invited to a party that he desperately wanted to join.

'Forgive us: a matter arose in Oxford some time ago, and though it was of considerable importance to us, we feared you would find it ineffably tedious. Perhaps,' she looked around at us, 'we might adjourn this discussion for a few minutes while you meet Mr Baker and he joins us in a cup of tea.' She did not offer him coffee.

Wilson spoke. 'Lord Halesowen, may I present to you Mr Baker, his lordship's putative heir?' Oh, what a wicked little adjective! 'Sir Francis, Mr Baker.'

In turn, our friends stood, offering a bow, a grave smile and a hand. Mr Baker's response was polite, but certainly not warm. Yes, he was suspicious still.

'Would you care to sit by the fire, Mr Baker? Or would you find it too warm? Now, Lord Halesowen prefers green tea. Would you prefer that or the usual Assam?'

I had never seen this cruelly polite side of her before. But each smile to her old friends was a firm indication that she was part of this inner circle, servant or not. And it was something to which he possibly suspected he could never quite aspire, even when – or if, of course – he became Lord Croft. Soon, however, she was making every effort to include him in the conversation, as if she had suddenly remembered her own humiliations at the hands of aristocrats who should have known better.

To call it a conversation was to imply it was an enjoyable exchange. It was in fact excruciating, like billiards played with oval balls. Baker still clearly thought he had been excluded from something he had a right to hear; he kept staring at Jeremy, as if wondering how a man as young and ineffectual as he might be welcome. Eventually, he burst out with the question that had probably been troubling him all along. 'So this Oxford business. In anything to do with the estate or the trustees, as his cousin and his heir, I should be involved.'

Harriet said quietly, 'I promise you it concerns neither, Mr Baker. Neither Lord Halesowen nor Sir Francis is a trustee, and they are not here to talk about any aspect of his lordship's estate, any more than Mr Turton is. Like you, they are not even acquainted with his lordship.'

'As Mrs Rowsley says, we're here on quite another matter,' Palmer said. 'Something that arose when she and Rowsley were staying with me in Oxford. When they heard that you were here, although our business together was unfinished, they left as soon as they could.'

Halesowen added, 'As you must gather, Harriet and I are very old friends. How long is it, Harry? Thirty years now?' He laughed. 'That was very ungallant of me, my dear – forgive me.'

'Let me insist that we were both very young!'

'A lord – friends with a servant!'

'Close friends, Mr Baker,' Halesowen said. 'And for even longer than she and Palmer have known each other.'

'So exactly why are you here?'

'As my friends say, important private business.' There was a faint but perceptible stress on the second adjective. For a moment, James might have returned to his judge's bench. Would Baker be quelled?

It was Wilson who said, gently but firmly, 'I fear our work here may take some time, Mr Baker. I for one would not dare ask Mrs Arden to put back supper. So I suggest that we regroup in the yellow drawing room at the usual hour. Mr Thatcher or one of his team will apprise you and Mrs Baker of any delay.'

Baker flushed, as well he might, at being treated like an impertinent schoolboy.

Harriet was on her feet again. Laying her hand on Baker's

arm, she sent her best wishes to Mrs Baker, begging him to tell her if there was anything she could do.

Was she surprised when he rebuffed her? 'I gather that Nurse Webb is looking after her very well.' He oozed hauteur.

'She is such a good nurse, isn't she?' she pursued with a smile.

'That's what you told me.' As she removed her hand, perhaps unintentionally he brushed the place where it had lain.

I half expected him to rail against his treatment, but, straightening his shoulders, he strode off, earning at least a little respect.

'There will be no more interruptions, sir. I will set a man at either end of this corridor.' Thatcher permitted himself a grin. 'He may, of course, realize he can gain entry from the garden.'

I returned it. 'I will make sure the catch is fastened.'

'My dear, is there anything more you can remember about your arrest?' Halesowen asked taking both her hands and seating her beside him.

Harriet grimaced. 'I didn't know . . . Yes, I recall Inspector Willis looking from me to a portrait behind me and back again. Maybe he recognized some jewellery. Let me think.' She fingered the brooch at her throat. 'Yes, this is the one. One her ladyship wanted me to wear because she liked it enough to wear it in the Family portrait. A Philips.'

Wilson briefly interjected with a succinct explanation of her right to wear the jewel. 'The moment I showed the magistrate the paperwork, she was released – without a stain on her character.'

'It was an unpleasant few hours,' she admitted, adding with a smile, 'but it was good to see a knight on his white charger.'

Her attempt to dismiss her arrest and incarceration was waved aside.

'My dear, to send anyone to gaol is a serious undertaking, believe me. But to send a lady there – on the basis of an unsubstantiated allegation! I cannot understand—' James stopped. 'This adds credence to my theory. In short, I believe the person who was killed and mutilated – note, I do not use the word *victim* – was extremely prominent in public life. When the – ah – unusual details of his death reached the police, augmented by an extremely realistic portrait, I suspect there was a huge panic in the sphere in which he worked. The investigation had to be frustrated as long as it took the powers that be to find an alternative narrative. Yes, it is now known this person is dead, but the details have been suppressed in case all the rumours swirling about him for some time might be at last known as facts: he died because he sexually assaulted yet another young woman. Yet another,' he repeated. 'Only this time he chose one whose family were able to take an immediate and drastic revenge. An appropriate one, too,' he said dryly. 'I am sure the village talked of nothing else. Was that theory floated?'

'Indeed,' I said, sparing Harriet the need to say anything about the Twiss child. 'I believe our JP, Tertius Newcombe, a decent man and – yes – one of the trustees, actually went and bearded the leader of the gypsies who had rapidly decamped from his land. The gist of Pecker O'Malley's statement was that he would look into it, and try to find out what had happened. But Newcombe got the impression that the killer had long since skipped to Ireland. As for the victim – and I mean a child possibly involved, not the perpetrator of the sexual attack – I can imagine no country mother, no gypsy mother, ever admitting that her child had been raped.'

'No mother at all,' Harriet said, almost inaudibly.

'Harry?' James leaned forward, his face full of concern.

Her eyes filled. Glancing apologetically at Wilson, she said, 'I fear I should not say this, but I need to. I am sure I recognized the man in the sketches. I am sure I recognized the head left in the icehouse.' She pressed her hand to her lips. 'The head in the icehouse was this man's. I am saying this on behalf of his other victims.'

James was on his knees before her. 'My dear, say no more. Dear God, if I had known, I believe I would have killed and mutilated him myself. I had opportunities.'

'You?' She looked him in the eye, but it was clear she was struggling for control.

'When you are able, I want you to look at something.'

Our other old friend was on his feet. 'I am practically family here. I will find either dear Bea or your inestimable butler and request a restorative.'

Jeremy joined him. 'Corridors a warren. Guide you.'

At last, James returned to his chair. 'Harry, was this before or after our summer of cricket?'

'Before. The housekeeper at – at that place – helped me escape to a house she thought would be safer. Yes, my new housekeeper knew. And she – she wanted to heal me. Hence, she suggested the cricket, God bless her!'

'Amen.'

The silence was broken by a knock at the door: Palmer was back with a decanter and an ice bucket. He reached behind him and produced a tray of glasses. The door closed.

'Turton said that he was too new a friend to want to intrude. And there is a young lady in the servants' hall I think he has his eye on,' Palmer added with a grin. Sensing the tension, however, he subsided quickly, pouring a glass of wine that he pressed into Harriet's hand.

She managed a grateful smile. 'Would you excuse me if I do not talk about that house? That man? I had that golden summer with you, and then was ready to work properly for my living. The move here brought me into a family of fellow servants and, more important, into the life of his late lordship. He might not have taught me how to read and write – another servant did that, a housekeeper as I am now – or to play cricket, James, but he taught me almost everything I know. Matthew has taught me something else: that a man can love and marry someone who can't bear his children. You, Gussie, and Francis, and lately you, Montgomery, have taught me friendship. I am the most fortunate of women.' She raised her glass. 'Thank you. All of you.'

Palmer, sipping his wine, said, 'James, I thwarted your big revelation. Forgive me.'

'Never!'

A sudden shock ran through me. The two men spoke as tenderly to each other as Harriet and I. Did Harriet know? Of course she did.

But now James was reaching for his wallet, producing a cutting from a newspaper. 'There is no photograph, my dear, just words.'

She scanned them quickly. 'Yes . . . Harbury . . . *Died peacefully in his sleep*? Dear God!'

'Indeed. Poetic licence. Don't soil your eyes with the rest; it's like all obituaries – nauseatingly sycophantic. But it tells one big truth. The man who might have destroyed your life is dead.'

THIRTY

I suspect that all four men were expecting some huge and possibly embarrassing emotional reaction. Gussie had delivered his words as if he were making a huge revelation, not merely confirming something I had known ever since I saw the head. I must say something, however. 'So the world is a better place. Even if the truth can never come out.'

'I fear it would never have done. People look after their own, Harry. They look the other way when they should intervene. Some in power with secrets of their own mutter, "There but for the grace of God . . ." Inevitably, many would blame the victims for somehow tempting an otherwise pure man. It enrages me that I dare not tell the truth. But some people I know would find putting you and others you love in prison a mere bagatelle. You might not even survive. So – forgive me – I must remind us all of the vow we made.' He got up and refilled our glasses. 'To your future health and happiness, my friends.' As we sipped, he laughed. 'And now, I suppose, we must go and beard the pretender to the throne. I gather you do not know whether to fear him or feel sorry for him, Harry.'

'I suppose it's possible to do both.' I smiled. 'I will let Matthew and Montgomery tell you all about him, if you will excuse me – after all, it takes a woman much longer than a gentleman to prepare for dinner.'

And I had a lot to think about. First, however, I made my way to the Family wing, to enquire after both Samuel and Mrs Baker.

'She's gone, Mrs Rowsley. A few minutes after I sent her husband off with a flea in his ear. And since I never thought she should be here in the first place, I couldn't argue.'

I would take a risk. 'Did you see any bruises when you examined her?'

She shot me a look. 'You don't have to hit someone to impose your will on them. A good solid bank balance often has the same effect. As for Mr Bowman, he is playing draughts with another estate pensioner. And as you will have noticed, the usual men are on duty and will let no one past my desk. I suspect they might have helped Mr Baker decide to leave.'

I smiled. 'And would deter him from making a second visit, I trust. Now, I daren't disturb Samuel if he's busy. But if he should say anything about earlier—'

'Mr Wilson will be the first to know. Or this new guest of yours – I gather he's a judge.'

I nodded. Yes, the House grapevine had been as efficient as ever.

It dawned on me that it was not just Inspector Willis and Sergeant Swain who might have noticed that I was wearing jewels once worn by her ladyship. When I had shown Mr Baker round, I must have stood beside two or three portraits of her wearing her beloved sapphires – my favourites for her sake. Wearing something had caused me immense trouble, and perhaps it would be tactful not to wear them tonight, if Mr Baker had been involved. Or even, come to think of it, if he had not. But I did not want to be tactful. I had endured that night in gaol. So I would wear exactly what I wanted. The sapphires were ideal with my dress. I would wear them. And the matching bracelet, though I conceded that it was excessive for a private dinner.

The jewels lay invitingly in their strongbox. Yes. It was the work of moments to clasp them round my neck and wrist.

'Very nice, if I may say so,' Dick said, whose key I had needed to work in tandem with mine to open the safe. 'And a nice response to those nasty allegations. Pardon me – that's your key; you have mine.'

'So I have. Dick, what do we do if Mrs Baker comes down to dinner? We know *he* will, of course.'

He did what dear Samuel used to do – silently mimed a spit in the dust. 'As for her, if she says nothing, I shall say nothing. There is, after all, this much chance I was mistaken.' His fingers were perhaps a twentieth of an inch apart. 'But I really don't think I was.' He rubbed his face. 'Then I ask myself, why should she do it? Smother an old man like Samuel who never hurt a fly?'

'I wish I knew. I promise I will try to find out.'

'And I promise not to spill soup over her!'

'Did I ever doubt you?' Then, as we both did so easily, I stepped back into a more formal mode. 'Now, would you be kind enough to invite Lord Halesowen, Sir Francis and Mr Wilson to our private sitting room before we convene for sherry before dinner?'

'Mr Turton too?'

'I think not. I saw him heading to the music room with Hannah as I came down.'

'Smelling of April and May, aren't they?'

'They are indeed. And I want to discuss the Samuel business with the gentlemen – and yes, they will want to talk to you, I'm sure. So be prepared for a long stay!'

I was not surprised that Dick formally announced each in turn, and even less surprised that Luke and Tim produced champagne.

Montgomery said, 'Mr Thatcher, I wonder if I might trouble you to tell our friends here exactly what occurred earlier? Pray sit down. Luke, might I trouble you for an additional flute? Thank you.'

Dick's account was succinct.

'Thank you.' Montgomery continued, 'Harriet tried to question your old friend in my presence, but I fear his memory . . .' He shook his head sadly.

'Does this Baker know about his wife's alleged actions?' James asked. 'I beg your pardon, Mr Thatcher – I am not doubting you, but that is the usual adjective in a situation like this.'

'I didn't feel it was appropriate to ask him this afternoon,' Montgomery replied, 'so I do not know. The poor man was intimidated enough, was he not?'

'If he does know, if he even condoned it or encouraged it, perhaps our silence will have worried him a little,' James said. 'It would be good to know that a second attempt could not succeed.'

'Mrs Baker has apparently left the Family wing,' I said. 'But guards are there round the clock, and though Nurse Webb obviously can't be, she will certainly warn the night staff to follow their usual practice and admit no one. So unless Mrs Baker were taken ill again and her husband had to help her up the stairs . . .'

'I believe, my lord,' Dick said, hesitantly at first, then growing in confidence, 'that Mrs Baker wasn't ever in the common ward. A very nice room – one of the former guest bedchambers.' He added with a smile, 'Not quite as nice as Samuel's, though. We moved some of his favourite pictures there when he found it hard to read, and a couple of comfortable chairs. No one would think a mere retired butler would be there.' He let that sink in. 'It's not just us staff who visit him, my lord – the rector comes too, and I seem to recall you, Sir Francis, telling him all about the excavations.'

'Yes – because he could see our activities from his room, and we didn't want him to worry that we were doing something wrong. Bless him, I am sure he took in some of what I said – he asked some sharp questions but then quietly fell asleep.' He narrowed his eyes. 'I think, Mr Thatcher, you might be hinting that someone who did not know Lord Croft's circumstances might have made a big assumption. A very big assumption. So – to quote you, Harriet, *just in case* – should Lord Croft's rooms specifically be guarded? I know he has to be kept in, but what if there were a need to keep someone out?'

Matthew spoke first. 'Dick – between friends – do you *really* think that it is possible that Mrs Baker might have mistaken Samuel for his lordship?'

'I couldn't possibly say, sir.' No, now he was back doing his job, he was happier with the usual formality.

'But it would be incredibly convenient for the Bakers should his lordship die,' James observed quietly. 'Do they know how old he is? How young, I ought to say?'

Montgomery shook his head: 'I am sure that I have never mentioned it. It is such a given in our lives that he is less than thirty . . . Harriet? Matthew?'

I shook my head. 'Ellis Page certainly would give nothing away. His refusal to do so has set him at odds with Mr Baker. But a glance at the *Peerage* would have given all the information he needed.'

'Is there a copy in the library?' James asked.

'There is – but I am the only one with a key, remember. And I made sure I left my keyring with Dick when . . . when I was arrested.' Matthew took my hand.

'Excellent. Tell me,' he continued, turning to Montgomery, 'how does this "putative heir" view his legacy? Will he and his wife live here when he comes into it?'

'He doesn't like our weather, of course, or the state of our roads. And while I deduce he and his wife are leading lights in their community, he would be starting from scratch here,' Montgomery said. 'All of which might encourage him to do something less desirable – to sell up, lock, stock and barrel. I know this is what Harriet fears. Oh, he might keep some of the pictures for his American estate. But I fear he has neither the ability nor the commitment to the future we would hope for in an heir. Certainly, he thinks that we trustees are wasting a great deal of money – as in fact I suspect many outsiders would. You might yourself! But I would argue that we are preserving the House and its glorious contents for the future – and saving the current heir from a terrible fate, of course.'

'He certainly does not care for any aspect of our philanthropy,' Matthew said. 'The new model village, the fact that villagers are treated alongside his lordship . . .'

James shook his head. '*Noblesse oblige?* No? Though I suppose one might, as devil's advocate, argue that any local philanthropy involves a degree of self-interest – keeping the local workers well and happy, so that they work harder for you. And maintaining the fabric and contents of your palace means you can always sell some of the family silver in time of need. Tell me, Harriet, what part of his possible plans worries you most?'

'Incarcerating his lordship in a public asylum. Not so much for his sake, because he – his behaviour always gave his parents a great deal of grief. I saw them both in tears, on more than one occasion. But for *their* sake. It was her late ladyship who wanted the present arrangement. As for us? If he set about dismissing us and all our colleagues, Matthew would find another post easily, but most of them know nothing except this House and its ways.'

Dick nodded. My heart swelled with pride as he spoke up. 'Mr Bowman – Samuel, my lord – might end up in the work-house. People working here now – and I mean the outdoor workers too – might have to leave the place they've known all their lives and go into factories, my lord, and you know what those are like. Imagine – moving to Coalbrookdale or Manchester

or Birmingham! Here they will have new sanitary houses, not
like the slums there. My cousins . . . they lasted less than nine
months before the typhoid took them.' He fought for control.
'As for me, thanks to Samuel and Mrs Rowsley, I can be a
butler anywhere.'

'And then there is the library,' I added. 'The precious heart of
the House.'

'I wondered when you would mention that.' James smiled.
'May I see it, Harriet?'

'Whenever you want.'

'Forgive me pursuing this – have the Bakers ever seen it? No?
Would it offend you terribly, Harry, if we took our pre-dinner
refreshment there? Mr Thatcher could tell the other guests of a
slight change of plan and enquire if Mrs Baker might be well
enough to join us.'

What on earth was he up to? He responded to my startled
glance with a slow smile. The one he had always given when he
was up to some mischief.

But this time I was a grown-up. 'You're wearing your Gussie-
up-to-no-good face. Be as naughty as you like, but not in the library.
There is too much of value to the whole nation in there to risk a
prank going wrong.' Heavens, what was I doing? Rebuking a judge!

He was on his feet, taking my hands. 'Harry, bless you, you
haven't changed. Gentlemen, if it hadn't been for her, I would
probably have been on the other side of the court in which it is
now my privilege to sit. Or transported. Or even hanged. You are
right, my dear, and I was wrong. But there might be another part
of the House – heavens, there are enough rooms! – where I might
be a little naughty?'

It was not James who chose to be naughty, but Francis, who was
downright mischievous.

Mrs Baker had miraculously recovered enough to join us for
drinks before dinner. She clearly had gone to a great deal of trouble
for the evening. Her dress, her complete ensemble, put mine in the
shade, her diamonds clearly trumping the sapphires. In any company,
she would have drawn admiring eyes. But the poor lady seemed
terribly ill at ease, fluttering and simpering and fretting her exquisite fan; at any moment, she might break one of its delicate ribs.

Soon Francis was reminiscing to the whole company about our after-dinner play readings, and begging us all to tackle a Shakespeare comedy this evening. '*Measure for Measure*? No, too serious. *Love's Labour's Lost*? *Much Ado about Nothing*?'

All of which involved foolish constables, of course.

'Like Mr Bumble, our friend clearly believes that the law is an ass,' James said. 'Shame on you, Palmer. I shall have you charged with contempt of court.' He smiled apologetically at the Bakers. 'Perhaps you have not read Mr Dickens's *Oliver Twist*? Absolutely worth reading. You must have a copy, Rowsley?'

'You must ask Harriet. She is the one in charge of the library, after all.'

'In charge?' Mrs Baker repeated, with big round eyes.

'Indeed yes,' Montgomery said.

'You mean dusting and such?'

'Rather more than that,' James said. 'Perhaps tomorrow morning you might have time to show off its glories, Harriet?'

'I would be honoured.' I glanced at James. He might have promised not to be naughty tonight, but I was suspicious, none-theless. Why did he want us all in my precious space? What was he planning? Why had he and Francis dragged literature into the conversation?

Mr Baker pulled a face: 'I'm sure she's very busy, running errands. We'll look round on our own.'

Dusting and such? *Running errands*! I was ready to snarl. Montgomery flashed a glance at me. I was to keep quiet.

'Oh, Mr Baker, do we really want to spend a morning just looking at shelves of dreary old books?' Mrs Baker asked.

There was a shocked silence. I had better end it.

'If you tell me what time would be convenient,' I said crisply, 'I will ensure that all the *dusting*, all the *errand*s, have been done so that I can admit you. James, would you care to join us? Francis knows it very well, but would still be more than welcome.' We exchanged a smile. Yes, I knew he was up to something.

And I suspected him all the more when, just as I expected the announcement that dinner was served, into the room slipped Bea and Ellis.

THIRTY-ONE

I could cheerfully have murdered Palmer for introducing Bea and Page into the mix. And yet perhaps it wasn't the cheerful malice I suspected it was; they had always got on extremely well, and he could hardly have imagined the animus between Page and Baker. I braced myself for further sparring tonight.

Meanwhile, Harriet had taken both Halesowen and Palmer to one side. Could she be giving them a telling-off? Or, more politely, imploring them to calm a potentially unpleasant situation?

Perhaps it was Dick, very much Mr Thatcher this evening, who had organized the place cards – Mrs Baker was at one end of the table, Page at the other. Harriet took the head of the table, with Halesowen at her right hand and Baker at her left, with Palmer at the foot, squiring Mrs Baker. As usual, rules for not conversing across the table had gone, along with the Family epergnes that had prevented such a solecism. Halesowen led the conversation, asking Baker about his travels, much as we had once done. But I sensed he was guiding the younger man with what could only be called leading questions – about purchases, items he meant to ship back to America, where they were to be displayed and so on. From what I could occasionally hear, Palmer was asking Mrs Baker much the same questions. At last, there was a foray into the weather, and the whole tedious evening plodded on as we adjourned to the drawing room.

What next? Amateur dramatics? More banal conversation? Whatever mischief the cunning mind of a distinguished lawyer was planning? It seemed not. Although the evening was still young, he surprised me by openly yawning, apologizing penitently but claiming that his exhaustion was caused by a hard day's travel on top of a trial that had taken longer than expected.

'A trial?' Baker repeated, an odd edge to his voice.

'Don't worry, Baker – I wasn't in the dock. I have the honour to serve in our friend Wilson's profession, have I not?'

The two lawyers exchanged a smile. Neither gave any hint that one was not just a Queen's Counsel but a judge.

Harriet turned concerned eyes to Mrs Baker, saying she hoped that she would be well enough to join a tour of the House the following day. 'More than the library, I promise you. Far more. Although James and I have been friends for some thirty years, he has never been here before. There is a great deal to see, is there not, Francis?'

'A very great deal. Will you be joining us, Wilson? Or will you be spending the morning preparing for the trustees' meeting as Rowsley assures me he will?'

'You too, Page?' Baker piped up. 'Or does caring for the village waifs and strays trump paperwork?'

'Both are my priorities,' Page said, getting to his feet. 'If you will all excuse me, I must go home now and lock myself in my study. Forgive me, Harriet.'

'Of course. We know how busy you are.'

Kissing Bea's hand, he bowed and left.

The Bakers had a swift muttered conversation. Mrs Baker delicately raised a hand to her mouth. 'Guess Nurse Webb was right. I'm afraid I am—' She groped for a word, looking apologetically, anxiously, at her husband.

'I fear my dear wife is indisposed still,' the loving husband declared. 'Will you excuse me if I return her to whatever you choose to call the hospital?' Tenderly, he helped her to her feet. And off they went.

I left the room too. Sprinting after Page and shouting to Luke to take two or three footmen up to the Family wing – just in case.

Page shook his head when I asked for his help. 'You know how her husband would react if I so much as offered an opinion of her health.'

'I do. But this is not so much to treat her as make sure no other patients are injured. I'll explain as we walk.'

Whatever I expected to see as we took the last flight of stairs at the run, it was not Nurse Webb in an unexpectedly frivolous dressing gown, with a cascade of hair falling to her waist. Still formidable, she was gathering it into a knot, pins passed by her

night-time deputy, as we caught our breath. Our presence was
unnecessary. The night guards had persuaded Baker to sit on one
of the waiting-area chairs.

'That is quite enough!' Nurse Webb declared. 'Doctor Page,
there has been something of a disturbance here. Would you oblige
me by checking that none of the patients has been upset?'

It was a strange order to give to a doctor, but with an ironic
glance at me, he complied. I stayed where I was.

'And you, Mr Rowsley – it has long been my opinion that a
husband's job when his wife is ill is to drink a dram of medicinal
whisky. So I would be grateful if you would escort him downstairs – enough, Mr Baker – and pour him one. A double, if you
please. Good evening to you both. Oh, and tell Mrs Rowsley that
Mr Bowman is receiving the intensive care we discussed.'

I presumed that this was code for a guard on his door.

I led the way to the main staircase, saying nothing but
gesturing Baker to lead the way. To precede a man so thunder-
ously angry might have been to invite an accidental push down
the entire flight.

Arriving unscathed in the yellow drawing room, I found Jeremy
laughing uproariously. He – and all the others – stopped immediately and donned serious faces as Baker entered. Halesowen
chose to interpret his fury as extreme anxiety and stepped forward,
all concern and solicitude, asking about the patient. He responded
to Baker's snarl – 'A man should be allowed to be at his wife's
bedside, for God's sake!' – as if it were a lament, taking his
elbow gently and sitting him beside him. 'How is she? Did the
nurse give any indication of what might be ailing her?'

'Did she hell! Woman's troubles, that was all. And then you,'
he said, glaring at me, 'produce that damned Page of yours!'

When I murmured Nurse Webb's advice, Halesowen nodded.
'My dear sir, I understand that you would never drink for pleasure
or relaxation, but in this instance, I am sure the Almighty would
forgive you for imbibing. I am sure Luke could find the very
smoothest single malt in Croft's cellar. Yes?'

Luke bowed and disappeared.

No one spoke. Was the advice meant kindly? Or was Halesowen
having a Gussie moment? Harriet was notably quiet and declined

firmly when Luke proved to have brought enough tumblers for all of us to taste the ambrosia. Luke solemnly poured Baker a good finger. As he presented it, on a salver, Baker rose and dashed it to the floor. 'You are doing the devil's work. A man who has signed the pledge does not break his word.'

In one movement, Luke bowed, bent to retrieve the glass, still intact, and dropped the napkin from his arm on to the liquid.

James got up to offer Baker his hand. 'Forgive me. I was wrong. We all make mistakes, do we not? And I venture to suggest that if Page is the only doctor in the area, you may not have the luxury of choice, unless you insist on moving Mrs Baker to Shrewsbury.'

Baker stared at the hand. And turned on his heel and left the room.

To our amazement, both Bakers came down to breakfast the following morning. It was he, however, who responded to our gentle questions about her health, assuring us that she had completely recovered and was keen to join the tour Harriet had promised.

'But she will rest up until Mrs Rowsley has finished her errands,' Baker concluded, with a noticeable emphasis on the last word.

Harriet produced another arctic smile. 'How sensible. One of them will be to welcome a piano tuner to the House – do you play, Mrs Baker? No? The harp, perhaps? What a shame. Another, of course, will be to notify Mrs Arden that you will – presumably – be joining us for luncheon.'

'For sure. We need to get our strength up for the meeting this afternoon. I guess it'll be pretty long.'

Wilson smiled, reminding me not for the first time of a tortoise. 'There is a fairly extensive agenda, but most of it will not trouble you.' Was he being deliberately ambiguous? 'Unless, of course, they agree to co-opt you.'

'And not Mrs Baker?'

Wilson shook his head. 'I fear that that is not a foregone conclusion. You see—'

'This is outrageous: you have a *cook* and a *housekeeper*, for God's sake – but not the future Lady Croft?'

Harriet was on her feet. 'What time would you like to start our tour, Mr Baker? In forty-five minutes, perhaps? We might meet in the entrance hall, if that is convenient?' she added with a smile, as if anticipating the explosion of anger we all expected. She looked around, much as my most feared master at school would stare at each pupil in turn to ensure obedience. 'Excellent. Should any of you be unavoidably detained, then a footman on duty will guide you so that you can join the rest of the party.' A smile and a mere dip of a curtsy and she was gone.

So, with a profound bow, was Halesowen. I would have given much, as I made my excuses and dragged Wilson with me on a feeble excuse, to have known what they were up to.

THIRTY-TWO

'What exactly do you hope to achieve during this tour, which promises to be excruciating?' I asked James, as we walked together up to the Family wing – a part of the House, like the servants' hall and accommodation, the tour would not be covering.

'Come, Harry, you know I want to see what his game is. *See*, not ask. To my immense frustration, I can't be at this meeting this afternoon, can I, and a spot of gun-spiking might be in order.'

'I tried that last night, wearing those wonderful sapphires. You see,' I added, 'I wonder if Willis acted alone when he arrested me. Yes, he registered the cameo brooch, I'm sure of that. But what if he had a supplementary prompt from Mr Baker when he disappeared to Shrewsbury for the day?'

'In common parlance, he snitched on you?'

'In part, I wouldn't blame him. He sees us as some cabal conspiring to rob him of his rightful inheritance. And, in his position, I might be suspicious too. There is something very – exclusive – about the friendship that has evolved between us all, and your and Francis's arrival, miraculous though it was from my point of view, can only have helped confirm his fears. Anyway, let me introduce you to dear Samuel, who is not strictly speaking a patient, so you can see for yourself how he is housed, and deduce how his lordship is cared for.'

Nurse Webb greeted us graciously, possibly even recognizing James from her days as a debutante. 'I am doing my medicine rounds at the moment, your lordship. But afterwards I would welcome a word with you both.'

We found Samuel playing patience in front of a comfortable fire. As soon as he saw me, he got to his feet, holding his hands out. Had he been my father, my uncle, I could have embraced him. As it was, I settled for taking his hands and kissing his cheek.

'Lord Halesowen, may I present my dear colleague and mentor, Mr Samuel Bowman?'

Samuel quavered to attention. He bowed almost as low as in his younger days. 'Welcome to Thorncroft, my lord. A privilege to see you here, may I say.'

'Here, Mr Bowman, I am James.' He took the age-spotted hand between both of his. 'Or Gussie, as dear Harry may have called me when she told you about our younger days.' He eased Samuel back in his seat, moving one of the armchairs round so he could talk to him face to face. 'You have been here many years – do you recall a visit from my aunt, who married into . . .'

'Have that good old man despatched to a workhouse? Never!' James said. 'This is his home – all those memories! And he is very well cared for, is he not? Nurse Webb, you are doing wonderful work here.'

She beamed. 'It occurs to me, my lord, that you might care to see his lordship. No, not face to face – that might disturb him, as he is never so good on a grey windy day like this. We have a peephole through which we can check on his well-being. This way, if you please. Mrs Rowsley – I think one person might be enough.'

I did not argue; even on a good day, he was a sad enough sight. While they walked down the corridor, Nurse Webb unlocking and relocking doors, I spent a few happy minutes in the male and female wards talking to the estate workers and villagers whom I knew. And then I was invited to join them in Nurse Webb's sanctum.

'"What a noble mind is here o'erthrown", Harry.' James was clearly moved. 'But how well he is kept amused.'

'"Noble?" I'm afraid he had a very bad reputation,' Nurse Webb said. 'You would know that better than I, Mrs Rowsley.'

'Indeed: he was wild and rude and disrespectful and spendthrift. If he had been able to come into his inheritance, I doubt if anything would be left of it now. But young men are often like that, and I think he genuinely loved the maid who carried his baby. The girl drowned herself, James. Before Matthew and I ran her to earth, a narrow-boat skipper and his wife had taken the baby and made her part of their family. We . . . let us say, we eased any financial burdens the family might have, now or in the future. She is well provided for, very clever, apparently, but her adoptive mother – no! her *mother*! – wants her to live happily as she is, not to be dragged into ways which would be completely alien to her. Personally, I think we should respect her wishes – but the trustees will do their level best to raise her in society as far as she wants to go, certainly in her education and any future career. And I could not be the one to tell her that her father died young in a common asylum!' I pulled myself together. 'Forgive me: you wanted to speak to us, Nurse Webb.'

'I did. I do. I want to say that if you hope to keep everyone safe here, you need those two visitors out of the House. Mrs Baker went on the prowl again last night – claims she often sleepwalks. Hmph. And if you thwart her, Mrs Rowsley, I think you might put yourself in danger. No, I can offer no evidence – none at all.' She smiled grimly at James. 'I am a rational woman, as you know, Mrs Rowsley. But in this case, my thumbs are twitching. Please be very careful.'

'A rogue police inspector and a rogue guest or two,' James mused, as we walked slowly down the stairs. He paused by a Turner landscape. 'What a shame this isn't a Constable!' he added with a Gussie grin. 'But what do we do about Nurse Webb's warning?'

'What could such a tiny woman do?'

'I would like to search her room. I should imagine the admirable Mr Thatcher has a master key? Well, if he passes me a telegraph in front of everyone, I can make my excuses and leave the rest of the guests in your hands – surely she would not risk any action in front of Wilson. Though a quick push down the stairs . . .'

'If you want to search her room, you will have to deal with her dresser. No lowly maid for her.'

'Even superior dressers can be venal. Or kept out of the way. A plumbing problem? A problem with a window catch?'

'Gussie, you are as devious now as you were when you were a boy, claiming you were not out leg before wicket.'

His plot with Dick went well, and I was soon left with Jeremy, Montgomery and the two guests. I took them slowly through all the state rooms, including some of the bedchambers, and the main corridors. The chapel. Finally, the library. Wherever we were, footmen, today in the dress uniforms they so rarely wore, were in attendance – smart, polite, raising blinds and lowering them as we left, opening and shutting doors. They were there to assist Mrs Baker on the stairs. One gathered up her reticule when she dropped it. He caught my eye very deliberately: why should Dick have recruited a gamekeeper to the ranks of footmen?

By the time we arrived at the library, I had worked out a little plan. 'You must forgive me, everyone, if I remind you of the rules that his late lordship imposed on me. On all of us. No one is allowed to be alone in here without me. If – and this has happened in the past – anyone is suddenly taken unwell, the other guests must summon help. I must remain at my post, as it were. There are other awkward rules. None of the maids dusting in here—'

'I thought that was your job,' Mr Baker interjected.

'None of the maids dusting in here is permitted to wear an apron with pockets,' I continued, extemporizing freely. 'And – my profound apologies, Mrs Baker – no lady is permitted to bring in her reticule. There is nothing I can do to change this, as Mr Wilson can testify.'

He knew as well as I did that I was lying, but he nodded sagely, adding, 'And we gentlemen have to turn out our pockets as we leave. Even Lord Halesowen would have to submit. Ah! Here he is!'

Whatever he planned to say, Mr Baker stopped. Then he addressed himself to James. 'Is this true, my lord, that we are to be searched as we leave this room?'

'I have never been admitted to it, so I do not know the laws. Wilson, you know more about this will than any of us? I should imagine the rules are pretty clear. And I for one would certainly obey them. Anticipate them, indeed.' He stripped off his coat, leaving it on a chair. The other men did likewise. 'Mr Thatcher and his team will guard them – or will they be on duty inside?'

Dick managed to produce a silver salver for Mrs Baker's reticule.

We went inside. James, very much Gussie again, headed for the very far end of the room, firing endless questions at me and, when he ran out of those, drawing everyone's attention to details of the plasterwork.

Then came the moment I had been dreading. Mr Baker, clearly bored by all the architectural detail, demanded to see the treasures the room was supposedly holding. No, I could not show them the Book of Hours, the one I valued most. My gorge rose at the very idea. I reached down large and much less important volumes – *just in case.* They were still precious enough to require me to don gloves. Sadly, there were none in the room to offer anyone else. I handled; they looked.

James asked about dates and printers; Mr Baker asked about values.

'You will recall that the trustees asked an expert from Oxford University to help assess and catalogue everything in here. Sadly, his wife became very unwell, and they had to abandon the project.'

'There was also a question about their honesty,' Montgomery added. 'We will be more careful next time – and there must be a next time, for your sake as much as anything else, Mr Baker. But the truth is, be the books worth hundreds, indeed thousands of pounds, nothing can happen to any of them without the consent of the trustees and the person into whose impeccable care they were left – Mrs Rowsley.'

'And – in the case of her death?' James asked.

'That is dealt with in my will,' I lied, knowing that I must make it the very moment I could. 'And no one, of course, is at liberty to reveal the contents of that.' And would find it very hard, since it was not yet committed to paper. 'I did not want dear Mr Wilson to feel in any way compromised, so I asked a contact of James's to act.' Another lie – *just in case* anyone might try to persuade him to reveal the contents. I replaced the tome on its shelf.

Mrs Baker had drifted away from us. Towards the table on which his late lordship's netsuke always lay. It lay beautifully in the hand – so well I had thrown it once with almost lethal accuracy. If she was planning to handle it, everyone would know.

'I see Mrs Baker has found one of my favourite inhabitants – in fact, the only mouse I could ever be fond of. It's from Japan, a netsuke . . .'

James hung back, as if to speak to me as the gentlemen, now ready to return to the drawing room, donned their coats and Mrs Baker retrieved her reticule.

'What a tour de force, my dear. Dear me, I wish I might be a fly on the wall this afternoon.'

'Unless you're a trustee, James.' I added, barely whispering, 'Ask Dick Thatcher about the servery just off the dining room—'

But Mr Baker took his arm. 'This meeting – am I right: you're a judge and you're not allowed in?'

'My dear Baker, if I punish people for violating the law, it is all the more incumbent on me to observe it, is it not?' James responded, his most charming smile taking the sting out of his implied rebuke. 'This corridor never fails to amaze me. That Breughel – do you prefer the father or the son?'

THIRTY-THREE

All the trustees and guests had been invited to luncheon, today a cold collation in the red dining room. It had not found the Bakers at their best, though Halesowen and Palmer kept the conversation afloat. At last, we trustees adjourned to the wonders of the state dining room and its grand table for the business of the day. Bea slipped in just before the proceedings started with Pounceman leading us in prayer. Newcombe's secretary, drafted in for the afternoon, recorded Samuel Bowman's apologies for absence: Thatcher had insisted that taking his place as a trustee was too presumptuous. Wilson raised the issue of whether the Bakers might be admitted as observers. 'We might, of course, consider co-opting Mr Baker if he chooses to remain in this country,' he added.

Page said nothing, but the expression on his face spoke volumes.

'I'm sorry, Ellis, I know you won't agree, but I do think inviting him in now might be useful,' Bea said. 'He is convinced that we are robbing the estate, all of us; sitting through an hour of us going through the accounts might shut him up once and for all.'

'And Mrs Baker?' Harriet asked.

I nodded. 'Better than having her roaming round unchecked.'

'Carried nem. con.' Wilson rang. 'Ah, Mr Thatcher, would you be kind enough to invite Mr and Mrs Baker to join us? Thank you.'

To their credit, they sat mum throughout all the figures – the expenditure on the model village, legal costs for dealings with tenants' disputes, income from tenants and the home farm, repairs to the roof, the cost of the Family wing, possible restoration of the chapel . . .

'As you – as *most* of you know, I would not see this as a high priority,' Pounceman said. 'The cost, as we can see, would be disproportionate to the number of likely worshippers. I think it is praiseworthy that so many from the House here at all levels come together with the villagers every Sunday. It sets a good example. If there is money to spare,' he added, with a smile, 'let it be given for the relief of the poor. As it happens, I would like to put on record my appreciation of the way that Mrs Arden and Mrs Rowsley support our families in time of sickness and other distress.'

What Baker muttered to his wife I could not hear – but it did not seem that our rector impressed him.

Next came the wine bill. 'What, Rowsley, have you turned teetotal, sir?' Newcombe asked with a guffaw. 'That's only a quarter of my bills!'

'Maybe because Rowsley is drinking the Family cellars dry, not his own!' Baker exclaimed, to an audible gasp.

I had better not speak. Not yet.

'My dear sir, we have the records here of the contents of the cellars,' Newcombe said, jabbing a finger. 'And – yes, this account correlates with the previous ones. The presence of the archaeologists this summer explains the need to purchase more, of course. You cannot expect the Rowsleys to fund the academics' far from abstemious stay, any more than you would expect Mr Baines to give the labourers on the site free beer. I propose we waste no more time on this topic.'

Mrs Baker piped up next – the expenditure on bedlinen and soap, of all things.

'Look, ma'am,' Marty said as slowly as if he were speaking to a child, 'if you have guests, you need sheets, and if you have sheets, you need to wash them. Stands to reason, ma'am,' he added, thickening his accent a little.

On and on it went.

'We have heard a great deal, Mr Baker, of what you think is wrong.' No, this was not Wilson or Newcombe speaking; it was Marty Baines again. 'Do you think that we might hear what you would do with all this? The House, the estate – everything?'

'None of your goddam business!'

The publican shook his head. 'It is if you want us to co-opt you on to this board. And being on the board is the only way you can influence it, isn't it?' He sat back, tucking his thumbs into the armholes of his waistcoat.

Pounceman, once his sworn enemy, nodded sagely.

'I'm the heir! I can do what I goddam like!' Baker erupted to his feet. 'For a start, I'll get these shysters clapped in gaol. For fraud. For theft.' He pointed his index finger at us as if it were a gun.

'Mr Baker, please answer Mr Baines,' Wilson said.

'I *am* answering the liquor-selling bastard. What right does a publican have making decisions about my future?'

'The powers the law invests in him by reason of his position as a trustee. Mr Baker – I explained the other evening how things stood. I thought you were in no doubt as to the situation.'

'The situation is that my future and the future of my country are being stymied by this woman – this gaolbird! All this stuff about preserving the property – bunkum! You know what, I shall take it all to Virginia, every last stick, and make decent use of it, selling it and saving my country. *My* country! Do you understand? Yes, it'll fetch a good price, pay a lot of soldiers, buy a lot of guns. Even fund a proper hospital for the troops. It'll be put to good use – in other words, not keeping alive some wreck of a man who could die next week anyway. Yes, some stuff can go to museums. We have those aplenty back home.' He glared round the table, daring us to object. Now he pointed to Page. 'All that stuff that quack spouted, saying his damned lordship was being treated by top people, kept safe, taking a sail on the goddam lake! He can barely open his eyes. You're a liar, Page. But not as bad as her.' He jabbed straight at Harriet. '"His late lordship this, his late lordship that,"' he said in an approximation of an English accent. 'You were his whore! Pretending to revere him! All this hogwash about the library – dammit, we'll see what the University of Virginia has to say about it. And a thief to boot. See that fancy brooch? How did she come by that? And the sapphires she was flaunting last night. Eh? A thieving bitch. I'll have her strung up!'

I was on my feet, but found myself pressed firmly back into my seat. By Halesowen. Behind him, Jeremy and Hannah peered through the open door. What – but Halesowen was speaking.

'Ladies and gentlemen, I apologize for gate-crashing this meeting – but not, I have to admit, for interrupting those action-able comments. Mr Baker, I would prefer you to sit down. And you, Mrs Baker.'

'You can prefer what you damn well like – you're not a trustee, so why are you here?'

'Please sit. Everyone in the room needs to hear what I have to say. And that includes you especially, as heir. I am waiting, Mr Baker. Thank you.' He turned to the door, gesturing to the two youngsters to enter. 'My young friends here have been helping preserve the House and its contents, working long hours in the music room to restore it to its former glory. They planned a concert in your honour.' He bowed towards the Bakers.

All this was news to me. I glanced at Harriet. The horror on her face was gradually being replaced by another emotion. Was it – disbelief?

'The piano has been tuned, the harp restrung. And the piano stool searched for appropriate music. They found plenty, they tell me. And they also found this.'

With a deep curtsy, Hannah passed him a document, which he held up.

'You can see the instruction written here: "To be opened only in the presence of a lawyer." It had in fact already been opened, as they were quick to tell me, when they brought it to me. Accepting their word, I duly opened it again in front of them. It turns out to be the last will and testament of—'

'Dear God, it's the missing will!' Harriet gasped.

He smiled. 'Indeed. First, Wilson, it carries his late lordship's apology to you – for asking another lawyer to draw it up and have it witnessed. He says he knows you would have argued against it for the sake of primogeniture, but the behaviour of his son made him regretfully come to the conclusion that he would destroy or fritter away everything. So this was drawn up in London, on what I suspect was his last visit. There is a note to you, Harriet: he deliberately hid this in the library to prove to doubters that you were entitled to the bequest he is making – no one but you would have found it.' He looked at her very seriously. 'So how did it arrive in the music room, if you please?'

She stood up, as straight as if she were in court. 'I can only surmise that it was removed by the two corrupt individuals who were supposed to be cataloguing the library and its contents.' She explained briefly the story of their time here. 'Mrs Marchbanks became seriously ill. Her last words to me – maybe her last ever – were that her husband had found a will leaving—' She stopped abruptly. 'Had found a will which, in his malice, Professor Marchbanks had hidden somewhere I would never find it. He knew I am not musical. I wish I were. So never in my lifetime would I have looked where my kind friends looked.' Tears ran silently down her face. 'Might I ask you to read it all?'

'Stop right there!' Both the Bakers were on their feet. 'Throw it in the fire. Now. Do as I say. Right now.' He produced a gun; so did she. 'Do it.'

There was a terrible silence. Harriet said, 'Hannah and Jeremy are completely innocent, Mr Baker.'

'In that case, I'll shoot you if he doesn't do as I say.'

Halesowen said quietly, 'Please drop your weapons, both of you. Mrs Baker, I would hate to see a bullet hole in the ceiling. You might even shoot yourself. It's a pretty little toy, I know, but it could be lethal. Just put it down.' Pounceman, who was seated next to her, simply reached across and removed it from her bemused grasp. 'And you, Mr Baker. I'm sure you're a fine marksman. But so is Mr Grice over there.' He pointed to the gamekeeper turned footman emerging from the little servery. There was no mistaking the direction of his rifle. In any case, Baker had been distracted long enough for Marty to punch the back of his neck. For a moment, face down on the table, he flailed. But Marty pulled both his arms up and held them in the grip he had perfected on drunkards. It took Grice a moment to tie the wrists tightly with rope he pulled from his pocket and yank him to his feet.

Bea meanwhile dealt with Mrs Baker, darting up behind her, grabbing her hair and jerking her head back until Grice could complete the task.

Grice leaned forward with a satisfied grin. 'Nice work, Rector. Thank you.' Taking both weapons, he moved to a side table on which he broke them open. 'You weren't in no danger, ma'am and sir. No bullets, see. Took them out this morning when you was all in the library. And helped his lordship here go through their belongings to collect these.' He laid a collection of bullets beside the weapons. One rolled harmlessly down to the floor. After all the drama, it seemed to be pure bathos – someone even gave a nervous giggle, quickly suppressed. 'Come on in, lads!' he called. 'We've cleared out a cellar, like his lordship said, ma'am, and we can take them down now.'

Harriet raised a still shaking hand. 'Not a cellar, please. A secure room, yes, but not a cellar. One of our colleagues will find one.'

'But ma'am!'

She looked Baker in the eye. 'That night in prison – and I believe you colluded in putting me there – was so bad I would not wish it on anyone, not even you, who were ready to kill me. Now, James, if that will contains what Mrs Marchbanks told me it contained, I would definitely like the Bakers to hear it. Every last word. Would – perhaps you should all sit down now. Yes, Hannah and Jeremy too, if you care to.'

'. . . In short, then, his late lordship left the House, the contents and the entire estate to his beloved servant and friend, Harriet Faulkner, to do with it whatever she saw fit. Should she marry, the property will still remain hers and hers alone. Congratulations, Harry.' At last, to a round of applause, James folded the will and laid it on the table. He gave a little laugh. 'In fact, Mr Baker, even if that had been burned, there would have been three witnesses here, and possibly more in Oxford if Professor and Mrs Marchbanks are still alive, to testify as to its contents. Lord Croft you might be one day, but you will have the title only. And I fear Mrs Baker might have tried to smother the wrong man.'

She gave a little scream. Baker snarled at her.

'Mr Bowman,' James continued, with an ironic inclination of the head, 'known to those who love him as Samuel, used to be the butler here. He is rightly looked after in his old age in a comfortable room. We pray that he won't die next week: perhaps the odds of his survival will improve if no one alleges he has dropped a pillow. As for Lord Croft, he is well protected from any intruders who might benefit from his death.' Another pause as he looked at the Bakers. 'Ill he undoubtedly is, very ill, but Doctor Page has shown me written testimony from the physicians who oversee his treatment that he may enjoy more years yet. In any case, there must have been some doubt, had you smothered or shot anyone, that you would have inherited the title – it would have been hard, you see, had you died on the gibbet. Thanks to Grice, you are spared that – but . . .' He stroked his chin. 'I suppose . . . yes, there's the 1824 Vagrancy Act. It was really meant, as I'm sure you all know, to stop former soldiers using for nefarious reasons the weapons they had brought back from the Napoleonic wars. If a person is carrying a gun or pistol with intent to commit a felonious act, they can in fact be arrested. Of course, you'd have to find a handy policeman and then prove that the owners of the firearms weren't just carrying them for protection,' he added with another ironic smile.

'So that bitch gets the lot. Lock, stock and goddam barrel. She swans round while I struggle to feed my troops. While we run out of ammunition. While wounded men die for want of care. And you – another of her damned friends – stand there with a smile on your face and preside over this . . . this travesty of justice.' He took a breath. 'Look, even Mrs Baker is going to have to learn to shoot. For her own protection. We will be fighting for our survival while you sit around in comfort. Shame on you. Shame on you all. Shame.'

Tim slipped into the room, speaking to James.

He smiled. 'Excellent. Now, Grice having shown me the bullets this morning, I took it on myself to contact the chief constable to solicit help at the highest level – help and advice as to how the law should proceed against people who are, after all, American citizens. Would you excuse me if I go and confer with him?'

Harriet clapped a hand to her mouth. 'Mrs Baker's dresser. Mademoiselle Dubois. You might wish to speak to her first. And – assuming she is innocent – offer her a night's stay here until she can return to . . . France?' To laughter, she added, 'I'm sure Mr and Mrs Baker will wish to pay all they owe her and cover her expenses.'

At a nod from Halesowen, the gamekeepers stepped forward and led the Bakers away. Kissing Harriet's hand, James followed.

Into the ensuing silence, Harriet took a deep breath. What would she say? Perhaps she did not know herself. At last, with a wry smile, she observed, 'I fancy we all need a cup of tea before we continue our meeting. And I would like to invite Sir Francis too.' She rang. Then she stepped towards Hannah and Jeremy, putting her arms round them and kissing both on the cheek. 'Thank you from the bottom of my heart. Oh, how inadequate even that is! Would you care to go and spread the good news? Or prefer to stay with us and observe the meeting?'

It was hardly a choice. Hand in hand, they bowed and bolted.

'My dear Harriet, there is only one thing to do in the meeting now,' Wilson protested. 'We vote to abolish ourselves.'

'You can vote to continue, if you would. My friends—' For the first time, her voice cracked. And then she had to pause while, in Palmer's wake, Billy entered, pushing his little tea trolley and helping Luke serve us. 'My friends, when Mrs Marchbanks told me about the will's existence, I did not know what to think. What to *feel*. I was more than happy to continue with the status quo. But then, when I saw what harm a disaffected heir could do, I wished more than anything to find it. I had to protect my friends and colleagues, scared out of their wits by a gypsy's warning. And I had to protect all the values and traditions of service that are so dear to me and to Matthew.' Just as she had in the Ashmolean, she gathered our attention with a smile. 'So I would propose another motion: that since the House is so much involved with the parish and with the village as a whole – two villages, soon – the board of trustees, perhaps under another name, continues to run matters as they have done so conscientiously and kindly. Some changes, perhaps, cannot be countenanced. Some will arise naturally.' She flicked a smile at Bea and Page. 'It would be an . . . an honour as well as a relief to know you are here to advise Matthew and me. Not least, because we have no children, we will have to decide what do to with everything when I die.' She took my hand. 'Now, the first item on my new agenda would be a request to you that you draw up the terms of reference for a new board of trustees.' She looked around.

So did Wilson. 'Carried nem. con.,' he told Newcombe's secretary.

'Thank you. Second, that we co-opt our dear friend Francis as an expert on the history and archaeology that must be shared with the world.'

Another nem. con.

'Next,' she laughed, 'can we organize a celebration for all of us? *All*. The sort her late ladyship used to throw at Christmas for us servants. A grand one.'

I nodded. 'We have our dinner parties and our champagne. They have our cleaning up to do. I propose that we invite caterers – the sort who provide everything for the great London society parties – to come and put on a party that they will all remember. I would like to include the outdoor staff too – would you agree to that?'

A third nem. con.

It was time to adjourn the meeting.

THIRTY-FOUR

We adjourned to the drawing room together for Dick and Luke to serve champagne. The first toast was obviously to Hannah and to Jeremy, who had reappeared, to thank them for their determination.

Raising his glass, Francis said something in Latin. The gentlemen, educated in such things, laughed. The rest of us didn't understand. Hannah giggled and blushed with delight when Jeremy whispered a translation in her ear.

Marty grinned. In his broadest accent, he said, 'You'll have to learn to talk proper if you're a-joining us, mate. You come down my end, and I'll give you a lesson for free.'

'You're on, my friend.' Francis shook his mocker's hand. 'They say you brew a good mild?'

'They say right. Come and try it,' Marty added, 'to celebrate, like.' They shook hands again.

Would our faces crack with all the smiles, our ribs break with laughter?

At last, Bea introduced a note of reality. 'The police and James are taking their time, aren't they? I just hope those two don't have to spend another night under this roof.'

'I'll wager Halesowen will make damned sure they won't,' Mr Newcombe said. 'Now, Page – did I deduce . . . you and Mrs Arden?'

Men and their tact! Of all the days for them to make such an important announcement, this must be the worst.

Bea was the first to laugh as she looked at Ellis, holding out her hand. He took it, drew her closer and kissed her lips.

'You'll have to marry her after that!' Marty said. 'How about right here and now, Rector?'

'In my experience, brides usually prefer to wear a pretty dress.' He smiled. 'The moment the dress is ready, I shall be honoured to perform the ceremony.'

Francis chipped in: 'In the past, they used to hold ceremonies known as hand-clasping. Surely you can do that now, Pounceman. Or is it a bit too heathen for these days?'

The old Pounceman would have huffed and puffed. The changed one joined in the general laughter. 'Please excuse my lack of old Norse, or whatever it should be. But it is a pleasure to be able to put this hand into this one.' He closed his eyes in prayer and made the sign of the cross as he blessed them.

'One minute!' Jeremy managed, wielding his pencil. 'One more! There!' He walked up to Bea, kissing her cheek. Clearly, he had spent a lot of time in the servants' hall. And then he passed her a piece of paper.

She held it up. He had captured the instant with the three of them in a just few strokes.

At this point, James came in, taking in the situation at a glance and offering his congratulations. The handshakes, the kissing of her hand, went on longer than necessary. Yes, he was Gussie, impishly delaying when he knew we all wanted serious news, now accepting a glass of champagne and toasting them.

And me.

'You're out-Gussie-ing Gussie!' I told him, wagging a finger at him. 'Just like a boy of thirteen again.'

'And you're as sensible as you always were. Very well, ladies and gentlemen, the situation is complex. Come,' he added as we all groaned, 'you know it is. You have two American citizens who came here by invitation. The guns they threatened us with were already empty. They swear that they genuinely, if quite erroneously, believed that they owned all the items they had packed, ready to take home.' He paused for effect. 'Yes, Mademoiselle Dubois, alternatively known as Miss Ethel Wood, from Hounslow, told us that when she packed at lunchtime – they planned to leave this evening, apparently – she found a number of small and expensive-looking items.'

'How come you missed them when you looked for the ammunition?' Marty asked.

'Because, as a gentleman, I did not search Mrs Baker's petticoats, into which they were sewn. Thank God she didn't go to such lengths with the bullets.'

'And these small and expensive-looking items?' he pursued.

'That might be an understatement; "priceless" might be a better word. A couple of miniatures – one a Hilliard, the other an Isaac Oliver. Some snuffboxes. Other items of silver. Many of gold. But as I said, the Bakers insist that, at the time, they actually belonged to them.'

Marty had listened, arms akimbo. Now he raised one, pointing to the window. 'Look, a pig flying across the grounds! Honestly, judge, if you believe that, you'll believe anything,' he said, turning back to James.

Montgomery stared. 'They lie. I made it clear to them time and again that nothing, nothing whatsoever, was theirs until his lordship died.'

'I know whose word I would take, Wilson.' James put his hand on the older man's shoulder. 'Once the will was read, they knew that they had made a mistake and that they would have returned them, of course,' he added, his voice as expressionless as his face.

'Oh, the police and I share your view. Now, theft is one thing, conspiracy another. It seems very likely that Baker did complain to Sergeant Swain about you, Harry – and that with the encouragement of a certain Scotland Yard officer, now safely back in London, thank goodness – he seized on the chance to have you removed from the scene. He had reckoned without Thatcher's acting on his initiative, of course, and on Wilson's reacting to the SOS.'

Marty frowned. 'There might be another issue to consider. That there head.'

'Indeed. I ask you all never to raise it again, albeit inadvertently.'

Marty frowned even more deeply.

'In a few moments, I promise you the explanation you and several others here deserve. I ask you to trust me and say nothing – to anyone – about it. Can you do that?' Since my dear friend was now as stern as he must be in court, looking at each in turn, it was hardly surprising that no one argued. 'Thank you. Just five minutes of your time before you go about your daily lives.'

'As to the Bakers, since they didn't actually manage to commit the crimes they had begun, it would be so convenient for them simply to be popped on the very next ship home,' Francis said, voicing all our thoughts, I was sure.

'After he has signed a document agreeing to renounce all claim on the title, of course,' Mr Newcombe added.

'My friends, those are my views too. And after he has written an excellent reference for Miss Wood and her friend Mademoiselle Dubois.'

We laughed. We drank to it. Then I said, 'If you are happy to speak now, James? Then we can all adjourn.'

He nodded. 'It won't take long. But remember there are some things we can only surmise, not state as facts.'

Mr Newcombe caught his eye. 'I have had another conversation with Pecker O'Malley. Yes, the murderer is now in Ireland – having killed the man who was trying to rape his daughter. You will recall those small stab wounds? His daughter inflicted those as she tried to fend off her assailant. Her father dealt with his body in what seemed an appropriate way. The genitalia found their way on to a fire, for some arcane reason; the head – well, to make a statement, I deduce. He took the wallet for obvious reasons, but trying to fence the gold items might have attracted too much attention.'

Marty nodded. 'Raping a wench: well, he got what he deserved. And the police wanted to pin the blame on someone, so that's why that upstart from London was trying to make out we were all going round raping innocent women . . .'

'Probably. But I truly do not advise pursuing him. Corrupt policemen might have corrupt friends.'

Mr Newcombe was scratching his head. 'But why should the man – I can hardly describe him as a gentleman – want to come all the way up here?'

I froze.

James said smoothly, 'It seems he had a long-standing dispute with someone and decided to solve it once and for all. But please, for everyone's sake, do not speculate. This should be a joyous day for our dear Harriet – let us not spoil it any longer. Now, I must ask you all to make the promise I have extracted from the people who heard all this earlier.'

It was over, the solemn oaths given.

I was so tired now that I was afraid I might weep. 'My friends, will you indulge me? There is something I think we should do. Some of us know our staff very well. Some less so. But I would like us all to go backstairs and thank them. And wash up the glasses afterwards.'

*   *   *

Bea hooked her hand under my arm as we walked down the corridor. 'You're as pale as if that . . . that bastard had shot you, you know. There, I used a word I never use, didn't I?'

'I can't say I'm surprised. I've used it a lot in my head. But he's not our problem, now. Oh, Bea, I'm so happy for you. I could have wrung Mr Newcombe's neck, mind you.'

'Actually, it all worked out for the best, didn't it? I didn't want to leave you in the lurch, Harriet.'

I laughed. 'I think I might just understand, don't you? This wretched sense of duty! How are we ever going to become ladies of leisure, Bea?'

'When you've been my matron of honour. That's when. It took all of a minute for Sir Francis to tell me he's giving me his arm going down the aisle. And I know Ellis wants Matthew as his best man. And Dick – I want him to be a sort of master of cere-monies at the wedding breakfast.'

'Which will be here. Would you want the chapel opened for the wedding?'

'Dear me, no! Lord knows I've worshipped down the lane for enough years. In any case, I want to wave at all the villagers! Now, I just want to make sure the kettle's on. For those who don't like champagne. Yes, Dick's got a lot on ice – from the Newcombes' icehouse, before you ask.' She bustled off.

In a moment, Dick was beside me. 'Mrs Rowsley – I am so glad for you. So glad.'

'Lend me your arm for a moment, will you? My legs have gone quite wobbly. Thank you. And please agree to become a trustee. I know you may not want to work here for ever, but I'll be glad of your counsel as long as you wish to. Especially as we'll need to recruit another housekeeper. I had hoped Hannah . . . But I think she might want a different future.'

'With Mr Turton? Hmm. But however will he support her? It's clear he won't be a clergyman, but he's got to find something he does want to do and make money at it before they could ever marry.' He dropped his voice. 'Have you heard her sing? That voice of hers!'

'That voice helped find the will, didn't it?'

He laughed. 'I know that tone of yours. You're plotting some-thing, aren't you?'

'Well, do you see her as a born domestic servant?'

'To be honest, not entirely. She's very good at her work, don't get me wrong. But her attitude to other people – it'd give poor Samuel a heart attack.'

I nodded. 'Ah! In we go.'

'You first.' He even gave me a little push.

The servants' hall had been built to accommodate far more staff than worked in the House these days, and the servants of guests too. Even so, it seemed full now, with stable hands and outdoor staff crowding in, all cheering as I went in. One of the gardeners had found some late-blooming flowers, enough to make a little bouquet he blushingly thrust into my hands.

I had to speak. 'My fellow workers – my friends! That gypsy's talk of great change – well, there is great change, and yet there isn't. I promise you this. You, the House and everything you know are safe.'

I didn't cry till Dan brought Robin to the door to congratulate me. And then I buried my face in his stubborn old neck and sobbed my heart out. This was my home. My home. And no one could take it from me.

EPILOGUE

While the death of Prince Albert a few weeks later changed the face of the Queen's England, we were too far removed from society to be deeply affected, and life continued much as usual.

The first and biggest change to the House was Bea's marriage to Ellis. Mr Pounceman officiated, of course, in front of the biggest congregation the church had seen in years. As she had planned, Matthew was best man, Francis giving her away. I would have fought anyone else wanting to be her matron of honour. Naturally, we held the wedding breakfast in the House. It was a gloriously happy day. They moved to Ellis's pretty house in the village, but spent much of their time with us, Bea insisting on cooking whenever we had important guests. Like us, they remained childless; like us, they never repined.

The younger lovebirds had a different fate. Two unseen and unloved paintings in the attics fetched enough money at auction to send Hannah to a music teacher in Birmingham, where Jeremy, funded by the sale of a particularly ugly sculpture, moved to study art. Their relationship did not flourish, however: she soon found work in a London theatre, a move that I suspect shocked her suitor. During the art school holidays, he joined Francis's team, eventually working for him full-time and joining him on investigations in Italy and Egypt: Matthew and I met them both there on some of our many holidays. He also pursued his music, singing in the House choir whenever he came to stay with us, which was often. Perhaps his stammer improved. Certainly, the choir did: it was getting regular invitations to sing at local festivals – and some further afield. To my terror and then my joy, they invited me to join in at their rehearsals. Yes, suddenly I could sing!

Sadly, there was no improvement in the health of either Samuel or his lordship. Our dear friend, gentle and God-fearing, simply went to sleep one night and did not wake again. It was probably exactly the unobtrusive death he would have chosen. He might have been embarrassed by his funeral, however, every inch of the cortege route lined with present and former servants and, it seemed, every last villager.

His lordship continued in the Family wing, but in time there have been more bad days than good. Dear Montgomery continues to search for an heir to the title, at least. I still hoped that his lordship's love child would take some role in the House one day – might Matthew and I even adopt her? – but her mother, though happy to accept our help in the education of all her children, still would not countenance one being singled out.

Our calm was briefly shaken by a letter from America. It was, to our amazement, from the former Mrs Baker to announce her marriage to a New York businessman. They met when, gentlemanlike, he came to tell her of the death of her husband in a battle won by the Yankee forces. Mr Baker died a hero, apparently.

Matthew, stepping back from his role as land agent, took on not one but two assistants, one to do most of the paperwork his job involved, the other to engage in the practical running of the large estate. The older one moved his family into the house that had been ours – it was a sad wrench for us, especially for Matthew, but Thorncroft House was now our home, after all. The younger assistant moved to a house in the new village. The new cook, not up to Bea's standard, of course, but adapting well to the patchy demands for her skills, had a widowed sister-in-law, who took over Hannah's role and proved she was a woman after my own heart.

Marrying after a whirlwind romance with the village school headmistress, Dick became the delighted father of three dear children. Their presence brought much joy to all of us; as they grew older, it was such fun to teach them all the cricketing skills James and I had once learned. Dick remained as butler, but his role gradually evolved as the nature of the House changed. Letting Luke take over most of his traditional duties, he became in effect our chief curator. His wife, too, took on a role when their children went to school: she developed an amazing talent, learned from visiting experts, for repairing the aging fabrics.

We had guests much of the time – most working at conserving the treasures within. There was a stream of students of art who worked on our masterpieces before and after they were lent out – and with them came young artists needing a base. One by one, our unused rooms became studios and exhibition rooms. Jeremy's work was always on show.

We welcomed others too. A team of retired police officers guarded the library inside and out when I could not be there. More books found a new life being admired in great libraries and museums. And we brought on a generation of new scholars too, including Billy, clearly destined for great things as he headed off to Manchester and the university there. We set up classrooms in the now underused stables, employing both men and women to teach children who had left the village primary school at eleven.

Mr Pounceman, ever growing in kindness and understanding, reluctantly accepted a post at the cathedral where Matthew's father once served. The new rector has boundless energy and will one day be as well loved as his predecessor.

James and Francis spend a great deal of time with us. Perhaps one or two people might have muttered that their friendship is too close, but while Matthew and I both know what the other of us suspects, neither of us ever voices the notion even to each other. I think in all these years of happy marriage, it is the only secret we have ever had.

ACKNOWLEDGEMENTS

This is my fiftieth novel, and actually marks the sixtieth anniversary of my first being published as a short story writer. So many thanks are due.

I would never have started writing had it not been for a grumpy English teacher, who had too much marking to do and told us to write a short story in class time for the Critical Quarterly competition – not that any of us would stand a chance, of course. Piqued, I saw that as a challenge. And won. So thank you, sir, I suppose.

And then I learned that people can be good to aspiring writers. The first and most momentous was the late Murray Pollinger, who told me that at the age of eighteen I needed an agent. Sadly he had to wait many years to see my first novel published – which I owe to the immense patience of an employee of his who has seen me through my entire career. Thank you, Murray, and thank you, dear kind Sara Menguc, never wavering in your support and trust.

Many women have been vital to my writing: a BBC producer who took an entirely unknown writer's work for the *Morning Story* slot; editors of women's magazines and crime magazines; all the unsung heroines who edit and copy-edit and proof-read and organize publicity. Thank you.

There are heroes too. Martin Edwards especially has been generous in selecting my short stories for various anthologies. Thank you.

Endless people have been amazingly helpful when I've been researching, from police officers to professional cricketers, from members of the clergy to National Trust guides. Thank you all for your patience.

Every writer needs tolerant family members and friends: I am blessed with mine. Fortunately my husband, a far more famous writer than me, knows the problems well. And every writer needs readers. I hope my life's work has given you the pleasure it has given me.